Unwritten RULES

ELIAH GREENWOOD

ISBN: 978-1-9994390-0-2 (Paperback)
ISBN: 978-1-9994390-1-9 (eBook)

Editing by One Love Editing

First printing edition 2018.

Reality Survivor Publishing

www.eliahgreenwood.com

For my father, my number one fan and the person who always believed in me even when I didn't believe in myself.

PROLOGUE

The Way It All Began

Unwritten Rules. Rules that are not written anywhere or indicated in any way. Rules that you are supposed to know naturally. People will automatically assume you are aware of them, which leads to another term I personally like to use to define unwritten rules—pain in the ass.

Don't sit next to a stranger if there are other seats left in between, smile back to whoever smiled at you, don't cry in public, and don't date your friends' exes. Pretty easy, right?

Wrong.

I spent my entire life thinking I had it all figured out. Until I met him. The unwritten rule of Riverside High.

It wasn't like anything I'd ever seen before. This unwritten rule wasn't a what. It was a *who*, and it came in the form of a blue-eyed Greek god with a bad temper and rock-hard abs.

He was feared. People quivered at the sound of his name. His footsteps echoed in the terror-filled hallways, leaving racing hearts and sweaty palms behind. Rumors and violence followed him like a shadow. He had rules. Rules that no one dared to break. Or at least, no one but *me*.

Everything could've been different. Every wrong could've been right. If only someone had told me…

Welcome to Riverside High, Winter. Oh, and by the way: *Never look Haze Adams in the eyes.*

ONE

Everything Could Go Wrong

Dear Universe, why do you hate me?

A question we've all asked ourselves at least once. Why did I get out of bed this morning? What did I do to deserve this? Is it because of the time I threw sand at that annoying little boy in kindergarten? Or maybe it was the time I tossed something in the trash, missed, and didn't bother to pick it up? It's pretty hard to tell, especially when I'm the living proof that Karma has a sense of humor.

Nevertheless, my eighteen years of life have been a series of unfortunate events and sick twists that led me here. To this moment. To asking *why me?* Payback for all the times I refused to eat my veggies, I guess.

"Are you excited for your first day?" Kassidy asks.

"Excited for it to be over." I sigh, nervously fidgeting with the strings of my hoodie. This is it. The day I've been obsessing about. My first day as a senior in Riverside High School. As I come to the realization that we'll be there soon, I can't help but wish the car ride lasted a lot longer. *Twelve hours longer.*

Moving to a new country and transferring schools right in the middle of my senior year wasn't exactly on my bucket list, to say the least. Being the new girl is about as much fun as waiting for a text back after a love confession, thinking you've been at work for two hours but realizing it's only been ten minutes and knocking your big toe on the table you swear wasn't there before.

In other words, I am *not* having any fun right now.

"Oh, come on. Don't be so dramatic." Kassidy lets out a mocking laugh. "You'll fit right in. Everything's going to be okay."

If someone had told me a couple of months ago that I would end up here, watching the palm trees parade past the windows of my cousin's red car, I never would've believed it. My mother does not trust me to be home alone for a few months while she's away with my stepfather on his work trip. The crumpled note placed next to a plane ticket on the kitchen counter made that clear. She gave me a choice: either move to Florida to live with my aunt Maria and my cousins, or move in with our neighbor Ms. Davies, a retiree whose biggest regret is not having children. As kind as Ms. Davies is, she's also the queen of "Oh, you're not hungry anymore? Here are two more pieces of cake."

Needless to say, I chose option number one.

My stepsiblings, Jaden, fourteen and moody, and Maika, five and so cute it hurts, were spared the temporary move, allowed to stay with my stepfather's parents until I return from hell.

And so here I am, hours away from Toronto and on my way

to a whole new life. The only problem is, *new* isn't exactly my thing.

"Anything I need to know? Any mean girl I should stay away from?" I try and get my mind off the anxiety eating me alive.

"Bianca Reed and her minions," Kass automatically replies. "Definitely don't give them a reason to hate you."

I nod. "Noted."

My heartbeat increases considerably when I spot the building I now get to call school in the distance. Bigger than any high school I've ever seen back home, it's just as intimidating as I thought it would be. My cousin pulls up into the school's parking lot, and suddenly, hitting my head against the window until I pass out seems like an option to consider.

Seek discomfort, they say. This isn't even discomfort anymore. We're *way* past that point.

"Ready?" Kassidy smiles, turning off the engine.

"Absolutely not."

"It's going to be fine. You're not alone. Kendrick and I are here, remember?" she tries to reassure me. I do feel better knowing that I have family to turn to if I need help.

Throwing my bag over my shoulder, I get out of the vehicle and slowly make my way to the entrance. My eyes jump to a faded sign where Riverside High School is written in bold letters. Next to it, a red graffiti tag—that they obviously failed to completely wash away—of the word "get" along with an arrow pointing at the word "high."

Get high.

Typical.

I push the front doors open and walk into the overcrowded hallways. I glance at the students. I can't even imagine how hard it's going to be to make friends. We're seniors. Everybody already knows everybody.

Trying to make friends is going to be like trying not to cry while watching *The Notebook*—an impossible task.

As we make our way through the commotion with difficulty, I am surprised and a bit disappointed when I don't see students that stink of clichés. No jocks, no cheerleaders, not even a couple of nerds. They seem like regular teenagers. Extraordinary ordinary. I assume the American high school movies I've watched in my life are to blame for my ridiculous expectations.

Kassidy scoffs. "See? It's just like any other school."

When I notice signs and directions are hung up on almost every wall, I sigh in relief, the fear of getting lost slowly fading away. What was I so afraid of?

"We're here." She stops in her path and points at a locker with the number 308 on it. I will never be grateful enough that she arranged for us to be partners. I carelessly stack my books inside of it and look up. I immediately know something's wrong when the happiness drains from my cousin's face in a matter of seconds.

She isn't happy anymore.

She's scared.

What in the world is she looking at? I turn around, my eyes stopping on the students who were laughing seconds before. One thing is clear: they're not laughing anymore. The entire room has gone quiet. Too quiet. The kind of quiet you can't possibly find in a packed high school hallway. Their eyes seem to be glued to the floor. No one dares to look up. Then, the million questions racing through my mind find an answer.

There he is.

Down the hall. A very tall, broad-shouldered, and undeniably attractive guy. Walking with ease, he holds his head up high as a lock of his brown hair falls in front of his eyes. Tanned skin, tattoos, blue eyes.

Never mind, I found a cliché.

Everything about him screams trouble and "I just escaped from a bad teenage movie, someone take me back."

Sure, he looks good. Fine, he looks more than good, but not "my simple entrance was enough to shut everyone up" kind of good. Then, like he can feel the weight of my eyes on his shoulders, he looks up.

Our eyes meet.

I expect him to ignore it and carry on with his "I'm the terror of the school" job, but he does exactly the opposite. He frowns and maintains the eye contact like he's waiting for me to look away.

I don't.

"Tell me she didn't," I hear a girl mutter in the distance.

Wait, what? Whispers surround me, creating a wave of murmurs from all the way down the hall to where I am.

"What did you do?" Kass exclaims, horrified.

"You tell me," I let out, unable to even begin to understand the scene I'm witnessing. I look around the room, helpless. Absolutely everyone is staring at me, the look on their faces similar to the one you'd have if you'd just witnessed a crime.

"You got a problem?"

My heart skips a beat.

Creepy but strangely attractive dude is standing right in front of me, his cold eyes piercing through my soul. His eyes... they're very blue. Pale and clear. Almost unreal. His intimidating presence is a lot harder to ignore now that barely a couple of steps separate us.

"Excuse her. She's new. She doesn't know." I'm astonished when Kassidy intervenes, apparently begging him to have mercy on my life. What in the world is going on? What do I not know?

He stays silent for a little while, carefully analyzing me without bothering to be subtle.

"What's your name?" His voice is deep and husky. I'm sure his demanding tone usually gets him everything he asks for, but truth be told, right now, all I feel like giving him is a slap. He looks me up and down. I can't tell what he's thinking.

"She won't do it again," Kassidy falters.

"Did I ask you?" he says. It's official. I hate his guts.

His eyes find their way back to me. "What's your name?"

"Winter," I answer, confused as to why it matters so much.

"I am so sorry," Kassidy begs yet again.

What the hell is this?

"Are you deaf? I said I'm not talking to you." The way he raises his voice is what sets me off. That's it. I've had enough.

"Who the hell do you think you are, jackass?" The words leave my lips before I can stop them.

The whispers stop abruptly as he raises his eyebrows in disbelief. Someone's clearly not used to people talking back.

"What did you just say to me?" He steps closer, tilting his head to the right as he thoroughly examines my face.

"Winter, don't." My cousin reaches for my arm. I glance at her. Her eyes say *don't you dare*. Mine say *watch me*.

"You heard me." I remove my arm from her grasp, gathering up what's left of my courage.

From there, everything happens so fast I can barely keep up. He fills the distance between us, causing me to step back so quickly my body hits my locker, the noise of the rattling metal ricocheting down the silent hallway. I instinctively close my eyes, anticipating a hit of some sort.

But it never comes.

"What are you doing? I'm not going to hit you." A hint of mockery can be heard in his tone.

I look back at him in shock. A small smirk tugs at the corner of his lips, the distance between us so small I can smell his cologne. He smells disturbingly good. *Of course he does.*

He leans forward as my heart thumps against my rib cage. Then, without a word, he pushes a strand of my hair behind my ear.

"I'm going to let this go because you're new, love. But watch your mouth from now on."

He looks into my eyes one last time before pulling away.

Chills spread throughout my entire body.

I can't speak. Hell, I can't *breathe.*

I watch him disappear down the hall, his words playing in my mind like a broken record. The students understand that the show is over and start dissipating. Kass still hasn't moved a muscle, biting her lower lip roughly, an obvious sign that she feels guilty.

"What just happened?" is all I can say.

"I am so sorry. I completely forgot to tell you about him."

I can't bring myself to listen. The students acted like it was normal. Like they were used to it.

Just a regular day at Riverside High.

"Winter, y-you don't understand. That's Haze Adams."

I frown. "I'm sorry. Your tone implies that I'm supposed to

care?"

"Not looking at him is like breathing. It's a habit—I don't have to think twice about it. No one really knows what—" She pauses and glances around as if she fears someone might be listening. "What stuff Haze is into, but it's better not to know. You do not want to be Haze Adams's enemy. He has rules. Don't talk back, don't get in his way, and whatever you do, never look him in the eyes."

I scoff. "Why? Is he Medusa?"

She sighs and rolls her eyes. "That's just the way it is. No one dares to question it."

I mentally curse, wondering why she couldn't just hit me with a quick "Welcome to Riverside High, Winter. Oh, and by the way, never look Haze Adams in the eyes."

"It's like provoking him. I just assumed you knew, even though it's completely normal that you didn't. I'm such an idiot," she says, undeniable sincerity in her eyes.

"You don't even know what he does, but you assume he's dangerous? He's a high school bully, not God." I shake my head in disapproval.

"That's where you're wrong. Rumor has it Haze is part of something bigger than you could possibly imagine. A street gang of some sort. His family is the most powerful and wealthiest in town, and his father is a big sponsor of the school. Don't be surprised that Haze's behavior never gets questioned. You do not want to get in trouble with him, trust me."

Eye roll.

"What are you saying? What am I supposed to do?" I ask, staring at the now almost empty hall where this crazy guy used to stand.

"Keep a low profile. Don't break any of his rules ever again, and do everything you can to make him forget about you."

I nod, unable to make sense of this madness. The bell rings, reminding us that the nightmare technically hasn't begun yet.

"You're right. Avoiding him can't be that hard, can it?" I laugh faintly, trying to convince myself. Here's one more thing to add to this long list I like to call "Proof the Universe is pulling a joke on me." Getting the tyrant of my school to hate me on my first day? *Check.*

"What could go wrong?" As Kass and I walk to class, I can't help but wince at my own lies. Seriously, Winter? What could go wrong?

Everything.

Everything could go wrong.

TWO
The Deal

"Give it back! Now," I yell at the overly annoying six foot four of bad jokes I have the misfortune of calling my cousin. Here I am, running after Kendrick as fast as the lack of exercise in my daily life allows me to.

"You have so many beautiful pictures in there, Winter." He cracks a laugh, scrolling through the pictures on my phone.

A week has passed. After the rather traumatizing experience with Mr. Don't-Look-Me-in-the-Eyes, life went back to its regular course and I became exactly what I was meant to be— the invisible new girl. Although the whispers in the hall followed me for a couple of days, I quickly went back to what I'm good at, which is merging with the walls. I haven't seen him again. That's all that matters.

I had a lot of things planned for my first weekend in Florida. Chasing my arrogant cousin around the house while he scrolls through all of my most embarrassing pictures certainly was not one of these things.

"Kendrick, stop!" I beg, panting. This will definitely be my cardio for the week.

Fine, my cardio for the month.

"Kids, no running," the familiar voice of my aunt warns in the distance. Kendrick doesn't stop, purposefully ignoring his mother.

"Oh Lord. What is that?" He bursts out laughing, then rushes into the kitchen where the delicious smell of my aunt's famous lasagna awaits us.

He stops in his tracks, raising his arm up so high it's impossible for me to reach my phone. "You do realize wearing a foundation ten shades darker than your actual skin tone doesn't fool us into thinking you have a tan?"

I wince.

Well, I sure wish fourteen-year-old me had known that.

"Kendrick Kingston, give me my phone back before I rip your eyes out," I threaten, failing to sound even remotely credible.

"Give her the phone, brother," Kassidy chuckles as she passes through the kitchen with nothing but a towel tightly wrapped around her body.

Dripping from the shower she just stepped out of, her blonde hair carelessly falls all the way to her lower back. She is a natural beauty. Ocean-blue eyes, tanned skin, blonde hair. While Kendrick breaks hearts, Kass desperately tries to keep hers intact. Needless to say, they got the good genes. Kass looks like the female version of her brother. I bet these two can't even count how many times people asked them if they were twins.

The fact that Maria had a thing for the letter K when it came to naming her children doesn't exactly help.

"Kassidy, you're dripping on the floor. What did I tell you about getting out of the shower?" Maria says.

I can't help but smile at the complete madness that is my family. No matter how crazy they drive me, I think—no, scratch that, I *know* that I could never live without them. The simple fact that my aunt Maria welcomed me into her home while my mother and my stepfather are on a work trip says it all. She's a nurse and a divorced woman taking care of two kids, and still she took me in without hesitation. Sometimes I think she's more of a mother to me than my own mother ever was.

I think back to one of the rare conversations I've had with someone besides my family since moving to Florida. Being the girl who "looked Haze Adams in the eyes" didn't owe me a very good first impression to say the least—whatever that means.

"Why didn't you just stay with your biological father while your mother is gone?" a girl in class asked.

"Can you live with someone you never met?" I answered.

"I'd like to annoy you longer, but I've got friends coming over." Kendrick hands me my phone, a stupid mocking grin still plastered on his face.

"He has friends? Since when?" I tease him, my eyes jumping to Maria, who, to my great surprise, doesn't follow me in my teasing Kendrick session like she usually does. Instead, she looks away, a stern expression on her face.

"Shut up. I have lots of friends."

I've almost never seen Kendrick in school ever since it started. We don't share classes, and our lockers are in completely different sections. I'm pretty grateful that he's not around to annoy me during the day. I already get enough of him at home. Maybe having a school that's way too big for the number of students has its perks after all.

"Did you pay people to hang out with him again? I thought we said we weren't doing it anymore." I try a joke, only to get the same reaction from my aunt. She doesn't reply, distinct discouragement in her eyes.

"Don't mind her. She hates my friends." He shrugs.

"Why?" I lean against the kitchen table, crossing my arms against my chest.

"She thinks they're bad influences."

"Consider me intrigued."

"There's nothing to say, really. She believes the stupid rumors going around town." I can tell Maria is biting her tongue in an effort to not talk back.

"When do I get to meet your so-called friends?"

He laughs.

"Oh, you might already know them. They're the popular kids. You know, the people you never talk to?" Kendrick says, looking at his phone. "I have to go. Annoy you later."

I consider asking Maria about Kendrick's mysterious friends but decide against it. Now is not the time. One thing is certain: if my aunt who likes literally everyone doesn't like them, she must have a good reason.

I tell Maria I'm going for a walk, and she answers to be safe, her mind wandering to an unknown place filled with secrets I wish I could unravel.

Today is such a beautiful day. I'm not going to waste it by staying inside. Plus, I do want to explore the city I'll be calling home for the next couple of months. I look up the great places I could go today and find a park not far from Maria's house. The walk to the park is a good twenty minutes, but I enjoy every second of it. With my earplugs deep in my ears and my worries drowned out by my favorite songs, I shove my hands into my pocket and let myself enjoy the heat of the sun on my face. What else could I ask for? I can't help but smile thinking about my hometown where the snow is not even close to melting yet. I won't miss it, that's for sure.

When I finally get there, I notice three guys sitting on the skate ramp, their gazes wandering around as if they're looking for something. Then, my attention shifts to a lonely skateboard left on the ground a couple of steps away from them. Hidden behind a bush, it's impossible to see from where they're sitting. I assume it belongs to them. A part of me considers carrying on with my peaceful walk, but then I decide to make this tiny effort to help these strangers out.

I mean, I could definitely use some good karma.

I begin to walk toward them, the skateboard in my left hand and all the courage I can find in the other. Before I know it, I'm standing in front of the high skate ramp, looking up at them. Three guys—one with dark hair, one with dirty-blond hair, and the other with light brown hair. Recognition washes over me. I think I've seen them around at school. Only then do they notice me.

"Do you guys see what I see?" The blond guy hits his friends with his elbow.

"Wait, I think I see her, too. Is she real?" The dark-haired one and, in my opinion, the cutest of the three pretends to rub his eyes as if he expects me to disappear. His eyes are pretty red. The obvious scent of weed reaches my nostrils, and that's when I realize I got it all wrong.

"Is there really a girl with a skateboard in front of me? I told you they exist," the blond says to his friends more than to me. I look down at his hand to see a joint and understand immediately. This is why they were looking around. They weren't looking out for something. They were looking out for *someone*.

"Stereotypical much?" I laugh.

At first, I'm a bit surprised to hear the words come out of my mouth, but then I remember that I'm the girl who talks back to the ultimate bad boy of her school without blinking.

Nothing new here.

They seem taken aback for a brief instant.

"Sorry. Harsh. I found it over there and thought it belonged to you. My mistake." I offer them a timid smile, drop the skateboard on the ground, and turn away, ready to get back to my peaceful walk around the city. Or what's left of it anyway.

"You're not from around here, are you?"

I stop in my tracks and turn around, looking up at the dark-haired stranger whose blue eyes probably seduce a lot of girls.

"That obvious, huh?"

He offers me a charming smile in return. "The cute accent kind of gave you away, I admit."

"I guess I should work on that." I look away when I feel my cheeks heat up. *Oh my God, seriously, Winter? A guy hits on you once and you're living in tomato land. Get a grip.*

"I'm Blake. These two buffoons are Will and Alex. What's your name?" He eyes me up and down. I'm assuming my pale skin is one of the main reasons why everybody seems to know I'm not from Florida. Might as well write "Canadian girl" on a Post-it and stick it to my forehead.

"Winter."

"Where are you from, Winter?" Blake's eyes refuse to leave me.

"Canada." I'm not surprised when the guys suppress a laugh. If they tell me a joke about my name I've never heard before, I'll throw a penny at it.

"You mean to tell me that you're from Canada, a country that's buried in snow practically all year long, and your name is Winter. Your parents hated you or something?" Will, the blond one, says.

Blake gives him a reprimanding look—one that obviously means *don't be rude, dumbass*—and I'm tempted to tell him how many times I've heard this. Probably as many times as people have wanted to punch him in the face for being obnoxious.

"Something like that." I find myself laughing at the irony. If they knew my mother, they'd be laughing, too.

"What brings you to Florida?" Blake asks.

"I'm visiting family. What about you guys? You're from around here?" I try to imagine what it's like to live in Florida all year long, without snow, ice, and storms. It must be so different.

I come to learn that they were all born and raised here except for Blake, who comes from a small unknown town called Colton Gate. He remains very secretive about the details of how and why he moved to Florida, but I don't think much of it, assuming that he's not comfortable with telling his life story to someone he just met.

The basic small talk quickly turns into a surprisingly long and interesting conversation. We discuss the most random things I can possibly imagine, and before I know it, I'm sitting next to these complete strangers on the skate ramp, laughing so hard my stomach hurts. Their immaturity and snarky comments remind me of Kendrick's.

I throw my head back, laughing at Will's impersonations of celebrities, and I'm forced to admit it's been a while since I've had so much fun. Then, for a brief moment, for just a second, I dare to believe that maybe... just maybe, a great new life is possible for me.

AS THE HOURS PASS, THE SUN begins to set, offering the most beautiful view I have ever seen.

"Damn it. Is it 8:30 already?" Blake looks up from his phone.

"Man, we are so dead," Will laughs. I have no idea what they're talking about. But it seems pretty obvious that they forgot about something. Or is it someone?

"Yep. He's going to kill us," Alex agrees. "Well, it was a pleasure meeting you, Winter. But we really have to go. Looks like this is goodbye."

"Well, it doesn't have to be." Blake sends a flirty smile my way before suggesting that we exchange numbers.

I hesitate for a second but then I tell myself I could use knowing someone in Florida. I nod and reach for his phone to register my number into his contacts. Just as I finish typing my number, I'm stopped by an incoming call. I almost drop the phone. *No freaking way.*

"Seriously? Again?" Will says. "That's like the fourth time in a row. He is pissed."

I can tell my face must've changed from the confused looks the guys are giving me. My mind racing, I quickly put all the pieces together. No. That's impossible. What are the chances? My lips part as I stare at the name written on the screen.

Kendrick Kingston is calling…

THE WALK BACK TO MARIA'S HOUSE turns out to be a lot of questions and confusion. As soon as I drop the "Kendrick's my cousin" bomb on them, a million scenarios start spinning in their heads. They seem hesitant. They know how bad Maria hates them and are probably worried she's pinned me up against them.

We also found out that, just like I suspected, Will, Alex, and Blake go to my school. I don't share any classes with them either and their lockers are in a completely different section, which explains why I rarely see them. An unshakable thought haunts me as we walk. What is it about them that inspires such hatred in Maria, the most loving person I know?

Yes, they were smoking and that makes them a bad influence. But to say that Maria *hates* them because they do stupid things teenagers do every now and then seems far-fetched to me.

"Home, sweet home." I smile, unlocking the front door to a very quiet house. Kassidy is probably up in her room watching

America's Next Top Model on repeat, and Maria will be working a night shift at the hospital for two days in a row. As soon as we walk inside, we hear Kendrick's heavy footsteps in the distance. I recognize the sound of his feet thumping against the wooden floor right away and crinkle my nose at how he drags his feet and always has. I used to call him "elephant" when we were kids.

"Where the hell have you been?" he blurts out, too focused on complaining to notice me standing behind Blake.

"Oh, you know. Here and there. Laughing, skating, talking with your cousin." Will grins.

"Wait, what?" Kendrick exclaims. Will motions to me. Only then does my cousin become aware of my presence.

"Winter, the someone they met is you?" He comes to the realization that I am to blame for his ruined plans.

"Surprise." I laugh lightly, putting my hands up.

"Why didn't you tell us your cousin was so hot?" Will smirks. To say I am shocked would be a lie. It's become pretty obvious to me that tact and William Martins are not friends. He makes his way to the fridge, which he shamelessly opens to grab whatever food he can find.

"Because she's not. Look at her," Kendrick hooks his arm around my neck to tousle my hair. I push him away with all my strength but still barely escape his grasp.

"Sure. She's hideous with her big b—"

Kendrick cuts Will off. "Hey. Watch your mouth, dick."

A small smile tugs at the corner of my lips. Good old protective Kendrick.

Will puts his hands up. "I was going to say big brown eyes."

"How about a big black eye?" Kendrick warns.

Blake scoffs and looks up at the clock on the wall. "We really have to get going."

"Oh, you guys are going somewhere?"

A hint of discomfort can be seen on my cousin's face.

"Yeah. A party." He rubs the back of his neck.

I immediately know he's lying.

How? Simple. He rubbed his neck. Multiple flashbacks hit me as I remember the way he lied to his parents when we were kids. I think about the time he ate all the Popsicles and said someone came into the house and stole them. Or the time he accidentally hit his sister with a basketball and said the wind knocked her out. Maria and I developed a very specific technique to know if Kendrick is lying. Guess what comes shortly after every single lie? The neck rubbing.

"Can I come? Maybe I can make some friends." I say the first excuse that comes to my mind. "Since I'm new and all."

He rubs his neck again, "I'm sorry. It's a private event. You have to be invited. Plus, there are already too many people going."

"Okay. No problem. Have fun." I force a smile and watch them walk out of the house. They hop into Kendrick's car. What

24

could be so important he has to hide it from me? I mentally battle myself, desperately trying to fight off this need to know.

Winter, don't, my voice of reason whispers.

Winter, do, my curiosity replies.

It doesn't take long for my body to go against my mind. Looks like making bad choices is a trend in my life at the moment.

Next thing I know, I've grabbed Kassidy's keys—that she constantly leaves lying around the house and loses—and gotten into her car to follow Kendrick and his friends. I leave Maria's driveway in a roar and find myself wondering where the hell they're going. Thirty minutes later, they still haven't stopped. I glance around to see I'm in a part of town you definitely don't want to visit alone at night. Old houses with boarded windows, abandoned buildings, and dark little streets surround me.

What the hell are you doing, Winter? You should be in bed right now, watching movies and complaining about your nonexistent love life. Go back!

I try to keep what I assume to be an appropriate distance between us so they don't suspect I'm stalking them.

Yes, stalking. I'm not going to try to deny it.

Then, after what seems to be an eternity, they finally stop, turning into a dark intersection that sends chills down my spine. They get out of the car and quickly enter an isolated brick alley. I should turn around. I should go back home. But instead, I find myself parking Kassidy's car a block away and waiting a couple of minutes before following them.

Easy Ways to Get Killed written by Winter Kingston.

With each step, my heart thumps harder against my rib cage. God only knows how I manage not to faint when something I can't see brushes my leg in the darkness of the alley. I stop dead in my tracks when I hear voices in the distance. I follow them until they grow louder, refusing to breathe, afraid even just one noise will be the death of me. Hiding behind a brick wall, I can see them—Will, Kendrick, Alex, and Blake. Lit up by a faded yellow light hanging above their heads, they are looking straight ahead of them at someone I can't see.

"This isn't over, Adams." I recognize my cousin's voice.

My mind immediately goes on overdrive when I hear the last name Kendrick spit out in a menacing manner. Adams.

Him? Here?

"On the contrary. It's just the beginning," a deep and husky voice answers. A hint of arrogance lingers in his tone, and my blood turns cold. No doubt—this is Haze Adams.

"The fight will be memorable," Will barks.

"I expect nothing less," Haze says.

The memories of my first day in school come rushing back as I hear Kassidy's voice: *"Rumor has it Haze is part of something bigger than you could possibly imagine. A street gang of some sort..."*

The pieces of the puzzle assemble themselves as I come to the dreadful conclusion that the rumors are true.

Haze is part of a gang. And obviously, his gang is an enemy to my cousin's. This is real. This is happening. That's when every ounce of reason I have comes kicking in and I realize I have to get out of here. Fast. I have seen way more than enough to be scared for two lifetimes.

I jolt around, ready to run away, and literally stop breathing when I come face-to-face with something. Oh no, someone. A guy the size of a building.

"Going somewhere?"

Heart failure.

I can't see the man's face when he tightly wraps his gigantic hand around my arm and drags me out in the open away from my hiding spot. I wince in pain, every nerve in my body telling me that my only chances at survival are to use the element of surprise and escape when he doesn't expect it.

I freeze, my eyes traveling from Kendrick and his friends to Haze Adams and a couple of other guys I assume to be members of his gang or whatever the hell they call themselves. Including the very nice man that's holding my arm, there are three guys to be exact. When he sees me, Haze's blue eyes light up in recognition.

"You again." He seems surprised.

"Winter? What the hell are you doing here?" My cousin tries to hide his anger and fails. If Haze Adams doesn't kill me tonight, Kendrick will.

"Come on, the neck rubbing? You can't seriously expect me to fall for that."

"You know her?" Haze raises his eyebrows, apparently finding this moment very amusing.

Kendrick sighs. "She's my cousin."

"Is she now?" Haze says. "Bring her over."

He motions to the gigantic man holding me against my will. Donkey Kong obeys. Of course the gorilla-sized guy couldn't be on Kendrick's side.

"Haze, please, don't hurt her." Kendrick raises his voice. "God, she's just… so freaking stubborn."

"Believe me, I know." Haze smirks, obviously referring to our charming meeting in the hall. "She looked me in the eyes and called me a… what was it?" He pauses, looking up as if he's trying to remember. "A jackass."

Kendrick gasps. "Tell me you didn't."

Here we go again.

"Oh, for God's sake. Yes, I did. I looked him in the eyes." I can't stop myself. "What's the big deal? Do they throw lasers?"

Then, against all expectations, Haze tries to suppress a laugh, biting his lower lip roughly to keep a straight face.

"Now what? Are you going to hurt her?"

"Hurt her?" Haze scoffs, taking in every single bit of my features. "Of course not. She entertains me."

What am I? A freaking amusement park?

"Well, it sucks to be you, then, because I'm not going to let you anywhere near her." Kendrick takes a step forward, his eyes darkening by the second.

Haze doesn't answer, examining me like he's never seen a girl before. I can't possibly tell what he's thinking.

"I'll make a deal with you." His words sound more like an order than a proposition. "You want the next fight to be memorable. Let's make sure it is," he says. "If you win the fight, I'll stay away from her. But if you lose…" He pauses for what seems to be an eternity. "The girl is mine for a month."

Time stops.

"What? No, you can't do that," I blurt.

"Let's make something clear, gorgeous." He steps closer until his face is so close to mine my breath gets lodged in my throat. Kendrick clenches his fists.

Bringing me back to the day we met, the proximity between us sends shivers down my spine. Then he finally speaks.

"You have no idea what I can do."

"And if I refuse?" Kendrick dares.

Haze brings his attention back to my very angry cousin.

"Can you imagine if word got out that you have someone to protect? Kendrick, the powerful fighter of the East Side, weakened by love? How awful would that be? I mean, we wouldn't want anything to happen to her, would we?" He glances at the other fighters behind him. They nod in agreement.

My cousin doesn't say a word, his eyes shifting back and forth between Haze and me. The hesitant look on his face says it all. He is actually considering this. He can't be serious.

"Then, what? You let her go? She's free. Just like that? I don't buy it," Kendrick says with scorn lacing his tone.

"Trust me. When I'm done with her…" A cocky smile takes residency on Haze's face as he observes me intently. "She won't want to come back."

This can't be happening.

Kendrick frowns. "How do I know you'll keep your word?"

"The same way I know you'll keep yours." Haze pauses. "We both fight for what we want—and you know I always get what I want."

"And what exactly do you want?" Kendrick glares at Haze with killer eyes. The same killer eyes he gave me when I stole his pudding when we were five. He is *not* playing.

Haze smirks and walks toward me until he is barely a couple of steps away from me. I find myself trembling in fear.

"Her."

My heart drops.

"I'm going to ask you one last time. Do we have a deal?"

Kendrick doesn't say a word, his thoughts probably going a thousand miles an hour.

"Kendrick. Don't," I beg.

Haze scoffs. "He doesn't really have a choice, you see?"

I quiver, my breathing unsteady. It feels like the ground is about to collapse under my feet. I look at him, shaking my head in disapproval. Then he says it. The one word I wish I could forget. The word that's going to change everything.

"Deal."

THREE

Run Away

"Are you mad?" I ask Kendrick as soon as we enter the kitchen. He hasn't said a single word to me since we left the alley. He insisted on driving me for "safety reasons" and asked Will to drive Kassidy's car back. The house is completely silent. I know for a fact Maria is working a night shift again while Kass is probably sleeping like a baby.

"Mad? Why would I be mad? You just became a target to my enemies. No big deal."

"Are you seriously blaming me right now? How the heck was I supposed to know about any of this? I had no idea you were going to some creepy meeting with Haze Adams."

"Yes. I am blaming you for this, Winter. None of this would've happened if you had just stayed home. What were you thinking?"

"Maria was right. They are bad influences," I spit.

"Don't you get it? I'm the leader. Me. Not Will, Blake, or Alex. They're not bad influences, I am," he yells.

"Fine. Congratulations. You're a troubled kid. I still can't believe you did that to me. Why in the world did you agree to this deal?"

He grows irritated. "Do you really think I would've said yes if I had a choice? That's Haze Adams we're talking about. You don't know him like I do. That sneaky bastard."

"What is that supposed to mean?"

"You heard him. If word gets out..." He pauses midsentence. "Let's just say if anyone finds out about you, terrible things could happen. In the street fighter world, love is weakness." He covers his face with his hand, sighing. My blood turns cold.

"What about Kass and Maria? If that's true, don't you have to protect them, too?"

"No. Because unlike *someone*, they never followed me. Nobody knows about them. Or at least, for now."

"How did you even get yourself in that situation in the first place, Kendrick? What happened to you? How the hell did you become a street fighter?"

He doesn't answer, staring blankly ahead of him. He reaches for a chair and sits down at the kitchen table, then motions for me to do the same. I obey, uncertain. The tension in the atmosphere is so thick it's hard to breathe.

He doesn't speak for a while, obviously wondering if he should tell me everything. Then, after a long and unbearable pause, he breaks the silence.

"It started two years ago."

I immediately know what time he's referring to. We thought

we'd lost him back then. Two years ago, something changed in Kendrick. Something broke. When he eventually made it through and turned back into the goofy guy he used to be, we thought it was a miracle. We didn't know it at the time, but the reason for Kendrick's previous breakdown was the discovery of his father's affair. Nick manipulated—practically blackmailed—Kendrick into keeping it a secret from Maria for years, said it would tear the family apart. Recently, Kendrick flinched and spilled. I shouldn't be aware of this. Maria went through hell and back to keep it from everyone—even Kass. She knows it would destroy her daughter. I only know from overhearing my mother on the phone with Maria.

"I was so angry at my father. There was this rage inside of me all the damn time. I was ditching school, failing classes. I didn't care about anything anymore. My mom was so desperate to help me, but I refused to let her in. I had anger management issues. I just... I hated him so much." He looks down, the topic clearly stirring up old and buried feelings.

"Then I met Blake, Will, and Alex. Blake was new in town and clearly had a lot of anger of his own. Will was angry about his mother using again, and he'd been kicked out of his house by his dick of a stepfather. Alex, on the contrary, literally had everything. A great family, a bright future, money. But he still felt empty. Like he needed more. We all bonded over our misery. Then, Blake told us he'd found a way to release his anger, and he thought maybe it could help us, too. That's when he took me to my first fight."

"Your first fight?"

"Illegal street fights. Top secret and really hard to find unless you have someone on the inside. They constantly change location. Blake knew a guy. It had been going on everywhere across town under the authorities' noses for a couple of years already. Anyone could fight. As long as they were aware of the risks."

"Risks?" I ask.

"Dying, breaking every bone in your body—you know, the usual," he jokes, but I can't bring myself to laugh. "There are rules, of course. But you have to be willing to surrender. If you don't, your opponent has the right to finish you off. Not exactly rainbows and unicorns, is it?"

I squirm.

"We started training intensely. We could make money and fight to release our rage. We thought we were in heaven."

"Were you?" I nervously fidget with the fabric of my shirt.

"No. We couldn't have been more wrong. They don't call them illegal street fights for nothing, Winter. It's not just fights. People gather from everywhere across the country to see the show. It's drug dealers browsing the crowds before the fight to get people hooked. Fighters owing money and having to kill their opponents to pay their debts. It's criminals betting huge amounts on the fights and refusing to pay when they lose. All sort of shady things. It got out of hand so fast. Let's just say things went south, and by the time we understood what we'd gotten ourselves into, it was too late."

"Why didn't you just leave?" I look up at him and become aware that asking him why he stayed is like asking a woman in an abusive relationship why she didn't just leave. It's not that easy. It never is.

"You don't understand. These fights aren't something you can just leave behind when you feel like it, Winter. You can get in. *But you can't get out.*"

The fear takes over a lot quicker than I thought possible. I think back to Maria and how she knew better than to ask questions. She knows her son's doing way more than casually smoking weed in a park with his friends. Why did I have to see for myself? Why couldn't I trust her instinct?

"Street fighter groups quickly formed. We call ourselves gangs, although we're not what you see in the movies. It didn't take long for us to know we needed alliances to make it through. We needed backup, people that we could trust. That's how the East Side was born. Each gangs are from different parts of town, so we picked our names according to where we come from. We managed to stay under the radar for a while until recently—" He pauses. "—when we started winning all of our fights. Back then, we were just a bunch of teenagers who wanted to make money.

Now, we have more enemies than we can count."

I don't say a word, eager to hear the rest of the story.

"Haze is the ultimate fighter, and his brother is next in line. I know he's young, but trust me, no one wants to mess with him. No one's ever won more fights than him. That's why he leads the West Side."

My racing thoughts stop on the word "brother." Damn it, you mean to tell me there's more than just one Adams?

"I mean, until me."

"You beat him?"

"No. Or at least, not physically. I beat his record. When I did, people started to question Haze's title as the most powerful fighter. Needless to say, he didn't like that. He challenged me to a one-on-one fight to regain his status. And well, here we are." He sighs. "You know what they say. If you go looking for trouble, you might just find it."

"When's the fight?" I try to hide how terrified I am.

"About a month from now."

I am positive he can see the panic in my eyes in that moment. All this time, the reason for Kendrick's miraculous recovery was his involvement in illegal activities. He seemed to have found a new purpose back then. Now I know he fell into a trap without meaning to. Kind of like what I did.

Except I didn't get caught in the crossfire.

I literally jumped in it.

"Don't worry. It's going to be okay," he tries to comfort me. "I'll win the fight. No one's going to know about you. I promise."

I get up, "Don't make promises you can't keep."

"You'll have to stick with us at school. It'll stop him from getting to you. Understood?"

I nod and exit the room, heading toward the staircase. Kendrick's words are deeply anchored within me. He says hanging with the East Side will stop Haze from getting to me.

I wish his words made me feel better. A part of me desperately wants to believe him. But the other knows that it would be foolish of me. If Haze wants to talk to me, he'll find a way. After all, he said it himself. Haze Adams always gets what he wants.

I WALK TOWARD MY FOURTH CLASS of the day and sigh in anticipation. English class is already making me suffer, and I haven't even stepped inside the classroom yet. It's been around a week since my life got turned upside down. To think that barely a couple of days ago, my only worries were getting lost in my gigantic new school and not making friends. I have been hanging out with Kendrick, Alex, Will, and Blake since school started, afraid I'll run into Haze at every corner.

Just like I expected, he hasn't been in class. I know that I share English and science class with him from the way the teachers say his name during the attendance only to end up not writing down that he's absent. Kassidy was right. He disappears whenever he feels like it, and no one dares to ask why.

Must be nice.

His absence has reassured Kendrick and made him think that maybe he forgot about me. I sure hope so.

As I make my way through the crowded halls, I let my mind wander to my friends back in Canada. I miss Allie, my best friend, more than words. I've been meaning to talk to her. I repeatedly scroll down to her number and almost call her only to end up talking myself out of it every time. I want to tell her about the deal and the craziness that now comes with my life, but I can't. I can't involve her in Kendrick's mess.

I also haven't heard a peep from my mother since I moved in with Maria. Not that I expected to. Lauren Kingston isn't exactly known for her outstanding parenting skills—especially when it comes to me.

I step into the already packed classroom and sit down at the first desk I see.

"Are you going to Bianca's party?" I overhear a brunette ask her friend. This party is literally all everybody's been talking about recently. I think back to the warning Kassidy uttered in her car on my first day. *Bianca Reed and her minions. Definitely don't give them a reason to hate you.* I don't think I've met Bianca, the so-called mean girl of Riverside High, yet.

The bell rings as Ms. Jenkins, my English teacher, walks into the room, going off about the previous week's homework.

I look at the forty-year-old woman standing in front of the class. Dark circles under her eyes give away that she's exhausted. All I see is her lips moving, but I'm unable to listen to a word she says. I've always had trouble paying attention in class, but luckily for me, I was blessed with a photographic memory that gets me amazing grades without having to listen to a word the teacher says.

No, I'm just kidding. I had to get extra tutoring during my early high school years because I couldn't bring myself to listen in class. Call it a learning problem, a complete incapacity to focus on something that doesn't interest me, or an amazing ability to get distracted by literally everything and anything. I call it the *"look, a butterfly"* syndrome. My mom called it her own personal nightmare.

My thoughts hold me hostage as I look out the window next to me. The sound of the door opening startles me. Ms. Jenkins stops talking abruptly, and whispers rise in the back of the class.

My eyes jump to the person who walked into the room and interrupted the class with no shame.

Haze Adams.

His entrance is enough for the oxygen in my lungs to say *"Oh hell no. I'm out."* Looks like he finally decided to bless Riverside High with his presence. He's wearing a white shirt, the tight fabric defining his perfectly sculpted body and muscled torso. For God's sake. How is this even legal? There should be a limit of beauty allowed for one person and a fine to pay for being too attractive.

The sleeve of tattoos on his left arm immediately catches my eyes. How many tattoos does he have? I've always wanted to get one but never had the guts. I remember asking my mother if I could get a tattoo when I turned sixteen. She called it auto-mutilation and threatened to kick me out if I ever did.

Great woman, my mother.

"Mr. Adams. You're late." Ms. Jenkins tries to sound as credible as she can, but we both know she's completely helpless against him. If the rumors are true, his parents pretty much own the school.

"Sorry. I had to find my dog." He snickers, not even bothering to look at her.

"Last time, you said your dog died." She raises an eyebrow.

"Must be why I didn't find him."

The entire class bursts out laughing at his remark. Ms. Jenkins rolls her eyes and proceeds with whatever it was she was talking about.

As he walks toward one of the last desks available, I find myself holding my breath. Being in the same room as him again isn't as scary as I thought it would be. It's worse.

I look down, hoping he won't notice me. Then, like he's

reading my mind, his eyes stop on me.

Of course they do.

I can feel the weight of his stare on my shoulder as he stops in his path. What is he waiting for? I look up to see him glancing at something.

And that something…

Is the empty desk next to me.

He wouldn't dare.

When he sits down by my side, I curse under my breath. I look straight ahead, acting like Ms. Jenkins's class is the most interesting thing I've ever witnessed. I can still feel the weight of his eyes on me. Is he trying to look at me to death? One thing is certain: the whole don't-look-people-in-the-eyes thing doesn't apply to him.

I let out a breath when he gets his phone out of his pocket. Finally. He must have gotten bored. Or maybe he finally learned to take a hint. I try to focus on what the teacher's saying, but my phone silently vibrating in the pocket of my hoodie stops me from it.

There's no way.

A text from an unknown number awaits me.

> It's been a while, gorgeous.

Never mind, he still can't take a hint.

The first question that crosses my mind is how the heck did he get my number? Although, I'm not at all surprised that he found a way. Refusing to give him the satisfaction of an answer, I put the phone down without texting back. It doesn't take long for my phone to vibrate again with another text from him.

> Ignoring me, I see.
> That's not very nice

I don't reply, yet again, hoping that he'll eventually go away. In other words, I do exactly what I've been doing with my problems ever since I was born.

He doesn't budge, still waiting for a reaction. This boy is persistent, I'll give him that. I find a bit of comfort in the fact that we're in a classroom packed with people. I mean, what could he possibly do?

"Hey, do you have a pencil?"

This.

He could do this.

I quickly hand him the first pencil I can get my hands on, still denying him eye contact. Our fingers briefly touch when he reaches for it, and I can tell he did that on purpose.

"Thanks, beautiful." His voice is deep, raw.

God damn it, even his voice is attractive.

"I heard you've been hanging with the East Side lately."

I still don't answer, thinking about what Kendrick said to do if he ever did talk to me. *Ignore him at all costs.*

"Yes, I might have been asking around about you. Sue me." He smiles, making me want to slap the cocky grin off his face. "You do know they can't protect you forever, right?"

He gets a big bowl of silence as an answer.

"Listen, Kendrick probably told you that you're safe and that he's going to win the fight, but you're a smart girl, aren't you?"

Ignore him at all costs. Ignore him at all costs.

"I'm going to win that fight. You know it. I know it. Kendrick knows it. So how about we skip the part where you pretend to hate me and jump straight to the part where you show me some Canadian kindness?"

Then I can't help myself.

"I'd much rather skip the part when you were born."

His lips part, the shock in his eyes worth a thousand dollars. He quickly gathers himself. What's wrong, Adams?

"Oh my God. She speaks," he teases.

Inhale. Exhale. Deep breaths, Winter.

"Still arrogant, I see?"

"Seems like it," I reply.

"You know, it's funny that your name is Winter. You try to be cold." He leans toward me like he's going to tell me a secret. "But you're still hot."

I literally hate myself when a small smile creeps onto my lips. Like I've never heard that one before.

"Did I just get a smile?" he says, this stupid victorious grin on his face. "Don't worry. I'm going to pretend I didn't see that since you're supposed to hate me and all."

"You need to stop confusing your dreams with reality."

"Trust me, I know this isn't a dream. If it was, you'd be a lot nicer to me and a lot more naked."

Don't stab him with a pen. Don't go to jail—orange isn't your color.

I'm about to answer when Ms. Jenkins's annoyed voice rings out in the classroom. "Adams, Kingston. Do you mind?"

Haze leans back into his chair and crosses his arms.

"Not at all," he spits.

She stiffens up. "Do you ever stop talking?"

"Do you?" He arches an eyebrow.

The class breaks into laughter yet again. Most people would never dare talk to a teacher this way. Most people would have their asses sent to the principal's office for a lot less. But Ms. Jenkins doesn't react, ignoring him and carrying on with the topic of the class. I guess the rules don't apply to him.

After all, Haze Adams is not most people.

I AM IN HEAVEN WHEN THE bell rings, marking the end of fourth period. The students start pouring out of the classroom like a herd of animals. I honestly have no idea how I manage to get out this quickly. I guess the desire to run away from Haze is strong enough for my super speed to wake up.

Of course, it couldn't wake up all these years ago during gym class.

I am ripped away from my thoughts when I run into someone on the way to my locker. I look up. Two dark blue eyes are staring right at me. I almost sigh in relief when I see him. Anyone who isn't Haze Adams is now officially my best friend.

"Wow, what's got you in such a rush?"

"Blake. Hi." I smile.

"What are you running from?"

"The question is who am I running from."

He immediately puts the pieces together.

"Did he talk to you?" Blake glances around, looking for Haze. "Do I need to go kick his ass?"

"No. I mean, yes, he did. But it was nothing. He asked for a pencil," I lie, trying to avoid useless drama. That's when I realize I forgot my pencil.

I loved that pencil.

"Are you okay?" he asks, worried.

"I'm fine. What is he going to do? Get up and attack me in the middle of English class?" I laugh as we walk side by side.

"It's Haze." He laughs. "With him, we never know." He looks down at me. "Hey, what's your next class?"

I narrow my eyes, trying to remember.

"History." I groan.

Blake stops in his track and steps in my way. I can tell that he's got something in mind.

He smirks. "Want to get out of here?"

Every nerve in my body is screaming yes.

"I wish. Maria would kill me if she found out I was skipping."

Blake's smile doesn't budge. I have the feeling that he knows something I don't.

"Who said you were skipping?"

FEELING THE SAND IN BETWEEN MY toes is officially a "must do" I never knew I had on my Florida bucket list. No, scratch that—on my bucket list, period. Blake took me to the beach. For the first time, as we're walking on the shore, I feel free. Like nothing—not even Haze Adams—could possibly hurt me.

"This is amazing. Why haven't I come here earlier?" I look at the calm and clear water on my right.

"Because you didn't have me in your life, duh." He smiles, revealing his white and aligned teeth.

"I can't believe you got someone to call the school and justify my absence."

"This girl owed me one. Don't worry about it."

"I sure don't miss snow." I close my eyes for a brief moment, letting the sun rays caress my skin.

"I hear you." He nods. "So, how are you feeling about the fight? Not too nervous?"

"Of course I am. But I try not to think about it. If I let myself think about all the horrible scenarios that could happen for just one second, I'll lose my mind." I laugh faintly.

"We have to win. God, even if we lose, I'm not sure Kendrick will let Haze spend a second with you."

"He won't have a choice."

Blake sighs, running a nervous hand through his hair. "I don't think you realize how dangerous Haze is."

"Says the street gang member. You're just as dangerous as far as I'm concerned, Mr. East Side."

My statement seems to amuse him. "Trust me, I'm nothing compared to Haze Adams."

"He wouldn't actually..." I pause. "Try anything, would he?" Images of Haze's lips colliding with mine flash through my mind. I push the thought aside, trying to ignore the conflicted feelings washing over me.

I need to sanitize my brain for thinking that.

"Oh, God no. Haze isn't that type of guy. He doesn't need to force the ladies if you know what I mean."

I wince.

"Oh, come on. Deep down, you must find him a tiny bit attractive. Even if it's just a little. No girl hates Haze Adams forever. They all fall under his spell eventually." He shrugs. "I guess girls like bad boys, huh?"

"Really? Have fun being a single mom."

As soon as the words escape my lips, Blake explodes with laughter, and I can't help but join in.

"God, Winter, where have you been all my life?" he says in between chuckles.

Although I tried to deny it, it's become quite obvious that he's flirting. Blake is a great guy, but getting involved with one of Kendrick's fighters is the last thing I want right now. I'm already way more involved in Kendrick's world than I want to be. Not to mention that my cousin won't let any of his friends date his sister, and I'm guessing that bro code also applies to me.

According to what Kendrick told me a couple of days ago, Alex and Kassidy dated for a while against Kendrick's better judgment. He was afraid it would put Kass in danger. And so every girl in the family is off-limits to his friends.

"So... Alex and Kass, huh?" I change the topic. "I heard they used to be a thing."

"Yeah. They were. But not anymore. They broke up. Something about Kendrick disapproving of their relationship." He seems slightly uncomfortable. Perhaps he doesn't like being reminded of the code he's currently trying to break.

I look straight ahead at the mesmerizing sea.

"Can I just ask what you were thinking following us?" he asks. He gives me a look that clearly says *what's wrong with you*.

"Not that my cousin was going to a creepy meeting with Haze Adams, obviously." I shrug. "Look at me. Two weeks in

Florida and I'm already hanging out with criminals."

"Not trying to make it worse, but you live with one, too."

"You're totally making it worse." I put my hands up.

"I think I know why you followed us." He pauses, his eyes scanning the almost empty beach as we walk.

"You do?"

"The danger. The thrill. The mystery. You had to know what Kendrick was lying about. You know what they say—we want what we can't have. It's way better when it's forbidden."

I look down at my feet and mentally curse.

He's right.

And I hate it.

WHEN BLAKE'S CAR PULLS UP IN Maria's driveway, I'm relieved to see Kendrick isn't home yet. I have a feeling he wouldn't approve of me skipping school, especially with Blake. Kassidy's red car, however, is already neatly parked in her usual spot. She beat Kendrick home as always. I reach for my backpack and unbuckle my seat belt.

"Thanks for taking me to the beach. I needed it." I smile and open the door.

"Hold on." He grabs my arm gently.

I turn around, analyzing his face. His eyes are a dark shade of blue. Deep, sharp. They remind me of the ocean on a rainy day. He's cute. But I don't have it in me to get any more involved in Kendrick's mess. He's kind. He's friendly. That's as far as I'll allow myself to go.

"You coming to the party tonight?"

Remembering the conversation I overheard in English class, I know he's talking about Bianca Reed's party.

"A party? As in a real one—no dark alley and creepy meeting?" I tease.

He grins. "It's a real one this time. I promise."

I'm about to open my mouth to decline, but he cuts me off.

"And before you try and make up an excuse, no, you don't have to be invited. Everybody just shows up. And yes, Haze will probably be there because he's invited everywhere, but that doesn't mean we'll let him anywhere near you. Now you can answer," he says, satisfied.

I sigh. Am I really that predictable? He's right though. I was going to make up an excuse. I did have specific plans tonight: do absolutely nothing while watching my favorite TV shows for the billionth time and eating a bunch of crap I'm going to feel guilty about later.

"All right, all right. Count me in."

Blake smiles victoriously. I step out of the car and shut the door behind me. He rolls down the window and hits me with a brief "Pick you up at nine" before his car is nothing but a small dot in the distance.

I push the front door open, sending my bag flying down the

hall as I kick off both my shoes in a swift movement. In the kitchen is Kassidy. Sitting on one of the stools surrounding the marble counter, she's eating cereal.

I can't seem to hide the joy in my face. Overall, today's been a good day.

"Hey, stranger. What are you so happy about?" she asks.

"That obvious, huh?" I make my way to the fridge and grab a water bottle.

"As obvious as an elephant in yoga class," she mocks. "Come on, spill the beans." She gets up to put her bowl in the sink.

"Fine. I'm going to a party tonight. Who knows? I might meet people who see more when they look at me than the girl who looked Haze Adams in the eyes," I say, making fun of the ridiculous reputation my first day in school owed me.

"Someone invited you to Bianca's party?"

"Yeah. Blake."

I expect her to be as excited as I am, but boy, am I wrong. Color drains from her face as she looks away. What just happened?

"What's wrong?" I ask, worried.

"Nothing. I didn't know you were that close with Kendrick's friends, that's all." She looks away, obviously lying.

"Kass. Seriously, what is it? Did I do something?" I step closer. If there's one thing I learned from all the summers I spent in Florida when I was a kid, it's that both Kendrick and Kassidy are horrible liars.

"No, of course not. Don't worry about it." She is one stubborn girl.

"Kass." I glance at her severely. She knows I'm not going to let it go.

She sighs. "I didn't think he'd move on so fast."

"Wait, what? Who are you talking about?"

She remains silent for a while like she's trying to decide whether or not she's ready to say more.

"Blake. I'm talking about Blake."

My face must give away how clueless I am because she doesn't wait for me to ask another question and carries on.

"Alex and I were never a thing. Never," she adds. "I was dating Blake. Kendrick didn't want Blake to date his sister, and I get that, but... Blake and I loved each other, or at least I loved him. Kendrick approves of Alex a lot more when it comes to girls, so I pretended to date him, constantly asking Kendrick to drop me at Alex's only to end up going to Blake's."

My eyes widen. I'm unable to form a sentence. He literally lied straight to my face. And I thought he was such a great guy.

"What happened? Why did it end?" I ask Kass, hoping for his sake that he didn't do something stupid like cheat on her.

"Alex said he was done lying. That we could either break up or tell Kendrick. And, well, Blake chose option number one. He refused to give me a solid reason. He said we should go our separate ways, and he sure didn't seem to feel guilty about lying to his best friend for six months."

Six months? That's a heck of a long time to be lying to your good friend. I can't help but feel a bit disgusted that he would hurt Kassidy like that. Clearly, he doesn't care about the bro code Kendrick asked him to respect.

"How long has it been since he ended things?"

I can tell she's fighting the tears. "Three weeks."

I cover her hand with mine, feeling her pain. I get that she's heartbroken. It's so recent.

"Well, you know what? You're coming with me tonight."

She raises her eyebrows. "What?"

I look at the clock, mentally making a list of all the things we have to do before 9:00 p.m. comes around the corner.

"'You heard me. We're going to that party together, having fun, and showing this guy what he lost."

THE SOUND OF A CAR HONKING is all we've been hearing for the past couple of minutes. Will, Kendrick, and Blake's impatience is growing by the second. Those guys clearly never had to wait for anything in their entire lives.

Maria calls out our names for the millionth time and tells us the boys are leaving without us if we're not outside in two minutes. It took everything to convince her to let us go. She only agreed because we promised to be home before midnight.

Standing in front of the ceiling-high mirror in her room, Kassidy is staring at her reflection. She looks perfect. I feel proud knowing I have something to do with it. I did her hair, her makeup, and even chose her outfit. She needed a little confidence boost, which I was happy to provide. She deserves better than this.

"You ready?" I ask, opening the door.

She nods, unsure. Next thing I know, we've entered Blake's car. Blake seems a bit taken aback when he sees Kass hop in his car but doesn't comment. Instead, he shoots me a smile that I make sure not to return. Kendrick says something about Alex meeting us at the party. The ride there is painfully silent. Will tries to crack a joke or two, but it's no use. Nothing and I mean nothing—not even his ridiculous sense of humor—could make the awkward tension go away.

After what seems to be a never-ending torment, Blake's car finally slows down in front of a house I can positively say is American party–worthy.

This is the kind of house you'd expect to see in a movie— the big house with so many drunk teenagers inside that it makes you wonder if the kid throwing the party has parents.

Shortly after, we walk into her overcrowded living room without knocking, and the one thing I feared happens. The boys dissipate into the large crowd.

Sure, go ahead. Leave me alone in this house where I literally don't know a soul.

I turn to Kass, thankful she hasn't left me. She leans in and whispers something into my ear about needing a drink. Then— wait for it—she disappears into the crowd, too. Just when I'm certain all hope is lost and I'm officially alone, I look to my right and see Blake.

Great! Just the person I want to be stuck with right now.

"I'm sorry about that. I'm sure they didn't mean to leave you alone."

It's a shame I can't see him the same way anymore. Now that I know he lied, I can't believe a word he says.

"Sorry about them leaving me alone? Or sorry about lying to my face?" My words catch him off guard.

"What?" He acts like he has no idea what I'm talking about, which only irritates me more.

"Alex, Kassidy. Does it ring a bell?"

His face drops. He doesn't answer, running a hand through his hair nervously. "Listen, Winter, I just didn't think it was a good idea to tell you all about my past with your cousin. I knew you'd think that I'm a jerk."

I can't hold back a laugh. "Well, you got that right. I do think you're a jerk. How could you do that to her? Just leave without an explanation? Not to mention you've also been lying to your so-called best friend for six months."

Blake's eyes become very good friends with the floor. He

keeps his head down, clearly ashamed. That's right, be ashamed, idiot.

"Do you have any intention of telling him?" is all I can say. He doesn't answer. His silence is my answer. "You really should, Blake. If you don't, I will."

I turn away, squeezing my way through the crowd. Deep down, I know I'm overreacting. This is none of my business, but the fact that he broke my cousin's heart truly bothers me. You don't mess with my family. My subconscious wakes up.

You know that's not the only reason you get so upset over people leaving without an explanation, Winter.

It brings you back to your father.

To the explanation you never got.

Subconscious?

Yes?

Shut up.

"Where are you going?" He raises his voice as I dive deeper and deeper into the crowd. "You barely know anyone in here."

"I'm going to get myself a drink. After all, this is a party."

I can't help but think I should've opted for my initial plan, which was staying home to watch the same shows on replay. I sigh, scanning the crowd of unknown faces that were supposed to be my fresh start. As I struggle to make my way to the bar, all I can do is pray that what I'm running toward… isn't worse than what I'm running from.

FOUR

The Enemy

You know how in the movies the girl and the boy get into a fight and you hear dramatic music as she leaves?

Well, my movie scene sucks.

Walking away from Blake seemed like a good idea at the time. But now? I'm forced to admit that Mr. Liar was right. I barely know anyone in here. Some faces I recognize from the school halls pass me from time to time but none that I could actually call "friends." Will, Kassidy, Kendrick, and Alex are also nowhere in sight.

Is this Hide from Winter Day and no one told me?

"Come with us, he said. It will be fun, he said." I curse under my breath, the bundle of pain that used to be my feet taking me to the staircase. I look down at my heels and wince. Why did I do this to myself?

I go up the stairs in an attempt to escape the loud music busting my ears and sigh in relief when I reach the second floor. The music is still loud enough to make you deaf but somehow a bit more bearable. I glance around. Doors. A lot of them.

This house is bigger than my house and Maria's combined.

I lean back against the wall, trying to gather my thoughts. I look down at the empty red cup I'm holding. How'd I drink this disgusting rum and Coke so fast? I guess my boredom is to blame.

That's when I hear it.

Moans.

A mattress squeaking.

Immediately, my eyes jump to the slightly opened door a couple of steps away from me. Really?

Well, it sure looks like everybody's having fun but me.

Then, it stops. I'm about to go back downstairs and escape this nonintentional eavesdropping when a female voice reaches my ear.

"That was incredible."

No reply. The mattress squeaks again.

"What are you doing?"

No reply. Again.

"You're leaving?"

Then, after a long pause, she finally gets an answer. "Yeah. The party's waiting."

The voice obviously belongs to a male. I know I shouldn't be listening, but I can't help it. Plus, technically, it's not listening. It's hearing.

"But I thought maybe we could…" She doesn't finish her sentence. She doesn't need to. It's obvious that she wants to cuddle. The sound of a zipper being pulled up hints that her not so charming prince is getting dressed.

"Don't give me that look. You know I don't do that kind of thing. I told you. We have fun together. But that's all it is. Fun."

Harsh.

At least he did tell her exactly what he wanted from the start.

"Asshole," she hisses, and before I can run away or at least *pretend* that I wasn't listening to their conversation, the door swings open. She storms out of the bedroom, her heels in her left hand and her broken heart in the other.

She has mid-length dirty-blonde hair and pale eyes. She is so tanned it makes me wonder if she spends every day of her life outside.

Says the pale Canadian who can only tan three months a year.

Wearing a tight and short black lace dress that could make any head turn, she's the definition of "dress to impress." I get it though. She has the body to do it.

Then she notices me and I realize how obvious it must be that I was listening. She gives me the dirtiest look she can possibly muster, her eyes as red as scarlet and her heavy makeup smudged all over her face. She is both wasted and baked.

The golden chain clasped around her neck catches my eyes. It reads a name.

Bianca.

Realization hits me. This is Bianca Reed? The popular mean girl of Riverside High and the girl who threw this monster party?

She walks around me and stumbles down the stairs, the alcohol flowing in her veins obviously getting the best of her.

I'm still looking at her drunkenly walk down the stairs when someone else exits the room and the door closes.

I stop breathing, my eyes widening.

Haze.

Of course, it had to be him. Am I even a bit surprised?

His messy brown hair and the lipstick mark on his neck literally make me want to puke.

We got it. You had sex.

Do you want a sticker? A medal?

I try and subtly walk toward the stairs, hoping that by some unknown miracle, he won't see me. But I know way too well that I'm not that lucky. I'm the girl who follows her cousin to his gang meeting and becomes the ultimate target to her family's enemies because she was curious, for God's sake. His clear blue eyes stop on me.

"You really can't stay away from me, can you?" He smirks.

I don't reply, still quickly making my way to the stairs. Before I can take another step, his hand captures my wrist, stopping me. My whole body becomes tense when his fingers meet my skin.

He literally just touched Bianca with those hands. *Germs.*

"You going somewhere?"

Yeah. Somewhere you're not.

I don't reply, remembering Kendrick's words.

Ignore him at all costs.

"Your mother never taught you that it's rude to ignore people?"

"She did. But you know what she also told me? She said to never talk to creeps."

I want to slap myself for being unable to keep my mouth shut when it comes to this guy. I can't help it. He irritates me that much.

"You know you're probably the first girl to try and get away from me?" He gives me a seductive smile, stepping closer. I step back instinctively.

"First time for everything," I say.

"Speaking of first time… I almost forgot what you look like without your watchdogs next to you. Where did your bodyguards go?" He looks around.

"I don't know. They're around here somewhere getting drunk. Which reminds me, I should g—"

"They left you alone?" He shakes his head, obviously amused. "I knew they were stupid, but this is something else."

I frown. "What is that supposed to mean?"

"Not every guy is nice, Kingston. You should be careful. Who knows who you could run into tonight?" The cocky grin on his face says a lot more than a thousand words ever could. He knows all too well that the most dangerous kid in this house is him.

"You're right. Thanks for the advice. I should go find them."

"Look at you. Playing hard to get when we both know how this is going to end."

That's when I know I've had enough.

I bite my lower lip and smile as I take a step forward. I get on the tips of my toes—since he's a good six foot four of wannabe bad-boy attitude—and watch his face change as shock and surprise flash in his eyes. Quickly, it's replaced by a satisfied smile.

When I lean in until my lips are next to his ear, the disbelief in his eyes is on display for the world to see. Then I whisper.

"Careful, Adams. Your last booty call is showing."

His eyes widen as he brings his hand to his neck where Bianca's fresh lipstick mark is waiting. I jump on the opportunity and disappear down the stairs. Diving deeper into the thick crowd of drunk teenagers, I'm unable to hold back a laugh. His face was priceless.

For someone who's such a player…

He easily got played.

I NEVER WOULD'VE THOUGHT WHEN I entered this party that a red cup would turn out to be my only friend. So much for meeting new people, huh? Staring down at the bottom of the plastic cup in my hand, I lean back against the kitchen counter. Kass should be here by now. She said she'd be here in ten. Problem is, it's been thirty minutes. Plus, my phone is almost dead, and I have no idea how I'll contact anyone without it. If these heels weren't so painful, I'd be walking home right now.

The clock on the wall reads 11:54. I can already hear Maria's speech about missing the curfew. She's been calling for the past twenty minutes, but I can't bring myself to pick up. What could I possibly tell her? I'm sorry, I'm trying to go home, but I can't find the others as they're probably making out with people they just met or about to throw up?

"I've been looking everywhere for you."

I jump, turning around to see who the voice belongs to.

Standing behind me is Blake. With one hand in his jeans pocket and the other holding a beer, he gives me the puppy eyes that clearly say *please don't still be mad at me*. The alcohol in my system is probably to blame for how happy I am to see him right now. I was angry at him. But now? I'm just relieved to see someone I know.

"Where have you been?" He leans on the counter next to me.

"You know, here and there. Desperately looking for a familiar face." I try a joke but can't even muster a smile.

"How's that working out for you?"

I draw a breath. "Not well."

"Listen. I'm sorry for earlier. I shouldn't have lied to you."

"Don't worry about it. I might have overreacted. It's none of my business. I'm sure you had your reasons for breaking up with Kass. It's just... I know what's it like to have someone leave without an explanation, so it hit close to home. Plus, you really need to tell Kendrick." I take a sip of my drink.

"You're right. I'll talk to him. I'll talk to both of them. I promise. I'm just waiting for the right moment." He looks down, clearly anticipating Kendrick's reaction. "So, we're okay?"

I let our eyes meet, unsure. He truly seems sorry.

"Sure."

He's about to speak when the loudest noise I have ever heard cuts him off. Distant screams and footsteps make it clear that something is happening. I jump, my heart crawling up my throat.

What the hell is this?

Blake and I exchange looks, frowning.

"Cops! Everybody out!"

People start running, pushing each other carelessly as they try to get out of the house. How could I not see that one coming? The music is so loud the entire neighborhood probably can't sleep. Plus, the amount of underage drinking in this place is unbelievable. When I finally take my eyes off the madness unraveling before me, I look to my left at Blake. Let me rephrase that—I look to my left where Blake should *be*.

He's gone. In the blink of an eye. He left me. How did he manage to disappear so fast? I have no idea. My mind starts racing as I try to think of a logical explanation. What do I do?

"What the hell are you waiting for? Move," a deep voice says.

I barely have time to recognize Haze Adams standing tall next to me. Where the hell did he come from?

He grabs my arm and starts running, dragging me along with him against my will. I desperately try to keep up, my feet hurting so bad I curse the day heels were invented.

"What the hell are you doing? Let me go." I try and remove my arm from his grasp.

"Trust me, you *really* don't want me to do that right now," he says, looking straight ahead.

"Why? What's going on?"

"Whatever you do, do not stop, you hear me?"

"But we could get arrested for running if…"

All it takes is one severe look from Haze to shut me up.

"Winter, they're not cops, okay? Run."

That's when I hear it.

The sound that makes my blood turn cold.

A gunshot.

Haze takes a little side street, distancing us from the frantic crowd. The numerous blisters on my feet make it seem like we've been running forever. The streets are empty. Silent. We can still hear the panic from afar, but the sound decreases with every step.

A black car is parked a couple of steps away from us. Haze

doesn't say a word, but his eyes tell me everything I need to know.

"No." I shake my head.

"Get in the car."

"I'm not going anywhere with you."

"Winter, get in the damn car," he barks. "Now."

I look at him, unsure. There are a million reasons why I shouldn't get in the car. But none of them are as powerful as the fear that infiltrates my entire being when I hear distant footsteps coming our way. I don't want to stick around and find out who they belong to.

I get into Haze's sports car and slam the door loudly. It doesn't even take a second for the vehicle to take off in a roar. I hold on to the leather seats so tight my knuckles turn white. I glance at him from the corner of my eyes, trying to breathe properly. Key word: *trying*.

He keeps glancing in the rearview mirror as if he's afraid someone might be following us. I don't dare speak or move for a good five minutes, unable to fully process what just happened.

"We're clear," he finally says.

He seems to relax like a huge weight's been lifted off his shoulders.

"Who were they?"

He doesn't answer, not even bothering to look at me.

"This is kidnapping, you know that?"

Like his ability to speak just returned from an unexpected trip, he scoffs. "Not exactly the answer I expected."

"And what in the world did you expect?"

He looks at me for a brief second. "Oh, I don't know. Something like 'thank you for saving my ass, Haze. You're amazing. To show you my gratitude, I'll give you a—"

I cut him off. "Don't you dare finish that sentence."

He stifles a laugh.

"Listen, I don't know what you smoked tonight, but my ass is doing very well and doesn't need your saving, thank you very much."

He doesn't reply, taking a very tight and abrupt turn.

"Slow down, please."

"Not until we get you somewhere safe."

"What the hell does that mean? I'm not in danger. Dangerously close to smacking you in the head maybe, but that's all. Please drive me home."

"Love is weakness. Kendrick loves you. Yes, you're in danger."

I freeze, my thoughts racing each other.

"So these people…"

"They were after you."

A million memories start spinning around in my head as I remember Kendrick's words. If word gets out that I have someone to protect, horrible things could happen. Fear slams against my chest.

"It was a gang, wasn't it?"

He doesn't reply. I know his silence means yes.

"Is everybody going to be okay? The kids from school?"

He sighs. "They'll be fine. That's not how they work. They only wanted you. They're probably already out of there, looking for you."

"But there was a gunshot? And how did they even know who I am? I thought that if we agreed to the deal, your guys wouldn't tell anyone about me. I—"

He interrupts me. "We didn't."

"Then how?"

"I don't know, Winter. One of my guys must've disobeyed. I'll have to take care of them."

I don't answer, terrified to even think about what "taking care of them" means.

"Why did you help me?"

"Because your idiot of a cousin left you all alone," he hisses.

"Yeah, but what's in it for you?"

"For God's sake, do you ever stop asking questions?"

"Do you ever answer them?"

His jaw is clenched, and his fists are tightly wrapped around the steering wheel. Call me crazy but...

It almost looks like he doesn't know the answer to that question himself.

AFTER A LONG AND HORRIBLY AWKWARD ride, Haze pulls up into the driveway of a house that's—for the second time tonight—so big it looks like it came right out of movie.

"Where are we?" I frown, glancing at the brick-built house.

"Somewhere safe."

I roll my eyes. "Thank you. I feel much better."

"We're at my house." He steps out of the vehicle. "You're spending the night."

He shuts the door and walks around his rich-kid car to—believe it or not—open my door and hold out his hand for me.

"Haze Adams opening doors. What a gentleman." I don't move, ignoring his hand.

"Well, I can't exactly let you sleep in my brand-new car, can I? I have a 'no drool on my leather seats' policy."

I look down at my phone. Ten missed calls from Maria. Seven from Kendrick. Five from Kass. This is really bad.

"Listen, thank you for what you did. But I really need to go home now. Kendrick's probably worried sick, and my aunt will literally murder me if—"

He cuts me off. "I can't. As much as Kendrick hates me, he'd much rather have you here than back at the party, trust me." His hand hasn't moved. He's waiting for me to take it. "It's too risky being out in the streets after the attack. I'll drive you home tomorrow. Come on."

I stay still for a few seconds, hesitating. Then, after mentally making a list of every option presenting itself to me, I step out of the car while making sure to ignore his hand held out in my direction.

Do I trust him? Never in a million years.

But I don't have a choice.

I turn off my phone to save the battery as Haze unlocks the front door to his castle—I'm sorry, *his house*. I follow him as he casually walks into the impressively big living room, making it clear that he's used to it. It's an everyday thing for him.

I can't stop myself. "You are literally the definition of spoiled, you know that, right?"

He turns around and flashes a smile. Only this one is tainted with a distant sadness. "Yeah, well, it's not all it's cut out to be."

Kicking off his shoes, he removes his jacket and sends it flying onto the leather couch next to him. My eyes instantly connect with the lean back muscles peeking through his T-shirt. Oh freaking hell, is the perfect body necessary? As if the pale blue eyes, perfect smile, and undeniable charisma isn't enough.

Winter, stop checking out the enemy.

"Come on. Your room's this way." We pass through the kitchen to reach the stairs. As I glance around the high-ceiling room that's surprisingly clean, I wonder if he has a maid. Probably.

The second floor is as spacious as the first. But the lack of decoration and white walls give it an impersonal vibe, like no one lives there at all. That's what differentiates a house from a home.

Haze finally stops in front of a door and pushes it open. Behind it is a very empty room with, yet again, white walls. A bed and a nightstand are neatly placed in the center of the room.

"Your parents won't mind that I'm spending the night?"

He scoffs. "It would require for them to be here in the first place."

I look down, so many possibilities colliding in my mind.

"I'm so sorry. I didn't know."

"Winter, stop." He half-smiles. "They're not dead. We just don't live with them."

"Oh."

Oh is also code for *"I have no idea what to say, but I have to say something before it gets awkward."*

"Wait, you said we?" I remember what Kendrick said. Haze is the best fighter there is, and his brother is next in line.

"My brother and me." His eyes become cold, an obvious sign that he doesn't want to talk about it anymore.

"I'm sorry. I don't mean to be nosy."

"Don't worry about it."

"Whose room is this?" I narrow my eyes, still analyzing my surroundings.

"That's my brother's."

I frown. His brother's? Unless his brother is a ghost, I can't believe anyone actually sleeps in here.

"Is he okay with me taking his room?" I look up at him.

"Of course. I hope you don't mind sharing the bed though." My mouth drops.

He bursts out laughing. "Chill, I'm kidding. It's a guest room." He mocks, "You should've seen your face."

"Jerk." I mutter the first insult that comes to my mind under my breath.

"Prude," he says right back.

I sit down at the edge of the king-sized bed.

"I'll get you a pair of sweatpants and a T-shirt." He walks out. Shortly after, he's back with clothes that look very comfortable although they are clearly way too big for me. I get up, taking the clothes from his hands.

"I swear to God, if I wake up tomorrow and you're not here, I will kill you. Don't think I won't."

"Oh, so you want me to stay?" He gives me an annoyingly charming smile, tilting his head to the right.

One step is all it takes for the distance between us to disappear. I don't step back, refusing to let him think for even a second that he has any control or effect over me.

"Because that can be arranged," he whispers.

Oh, he's good.

I'm sure that trick usually works for him.

"I'm just saying. I don't want to wake up alone in this completely unknown house. Plus, I don't know where I am and…"

"Relax, Winter. Of course I'm staying. What kind of guy would I be dropping you at a stranger's house and taking off?"

"I don't know. Let me see. You'd be the Haze kind of guy."

He smirks. "Point taken."

"One night, Adams. That's all. Then you drive me home first thing in the morning." I try to sound as threatening as I possibly can, well aware that I'm probably doing a very bad job. He nods, a small smile tugging at the corner of his lips.

"Under one condition."

I sigh. "What?"

"I want a kiss."

"Excuse me?"

"You heard me. A thank-you kiss if you will. I mean, I did save your ass. As cute as that ass may be, it was still a lot of work." He steps forward until I can smell his cologne.

Smooth, Haze. Real smooth.

He stills smells disturbingly good. Just like I remember.

He offers me his Colgate commercial smile. I place my hands on his chest and force him out of the room.

"Of course. I'll give it to you tomorrow."

His eyes widen.

"Really?"

"No." I slam the door in his face.

"And they say I'm mean," he says from the other side.

I suppress a laugh. "Good night, Haze."

"Good night, Kingston."

The sound of his footsteps fade out down the hall, a sign that he's going to bed, too. I quickly throw on the clothes he got for me and, just like I expected, they make me look like I'm wearing a potato sack. I can't help but wonder how the hell I went from bored and drunk at the party to sleeping in Haze Adams's guest room. As I crawl up under the cold covers, my eyelids so heavy it's a miracle I didn't fall asleep midconversation, I can't help but think that maybe, just maybe, the all-powerful leader of the West Side isn't as bad as he'd like people to think he is.

MY EYES FLY OPEN AT THE sound of a door closing. My vision takes unbearably long to adjust to the light. I glance around the white room as questions invade my brain. Where am I? How did I end up here? What happened? I rub my heavy eyelids, looking down at the clothes I'm wearing, and my memories come rushing back.

I'm at Haze Adams's house. He saved me yesterday. I'd hoped that this was a dream. Or should I say, a nightmare. I wince at the pounding in my head. Alcohol and I do not get along. I reach for my phone on the bedside table. Problem is, there's nothing to reach for.

Where the hell is my phone?

Panic takes over me. I get out of bed, my mind racing. Haze is the one who took it. It has to be. I throw on the clothes I was wearing yesterday, neatly fold his T-shirt and sweatpants and step out of the room. No one. I can't hear a single sound. The house seems empty.

Haze didn't leave, did he? I need to get home before my aunt calls the police and files a missing person's report. I go down the stairs. Still no sign of Haze. I enter the spacious living room, taking in my surroundings.

"You must be Winter."

I jump, startled, and quickly turn my head to see a guy looking at me. Casually sitting on the leather couch, he's analyzing me carefully. I instinctively bring my hand to my chest as if it'll somehow steady my frantic heartbeat.

"I'm Tanner. Haze's my baby bro." He stretches his arms and flexes his muscles, making me want to roll my eyes. Yeah, definitely in the same family these two. Tanner seems older than Haze—maybe twenty-two—but I can totally see it: the smirk, the messy hair, the muscled body. Tanner's hair is darker and his eyes are green, but apart from that, he has that same "I'm going to break your heart and destroy your innocence" look to him.

Guess it runs in the family.

"Hi." I shift uncomfortably. "Where's Haze?"

"You just missed him, actually." I think back to the slammed door that woke me up. If I'd just been up ten minutes earlier, I could be on my way home right now.

"He had an emergency," Tanner adds. "Told me to tell you not to go anywhere. He'll be back soon."

I curse under my breath. God damn it, Haze. Sticking around for breakfast wasn't part of the plan.

Although, I must say I am not at all surprised that he went and did exactly what he promised not to do.

"This might sound weird, but have you seen my phone by any chance?"

"Yeah. Haze took it. Said it was to make sure you waited for him."

Bastard.

"Oh. Well, I really have to go. I think I'll just walk." I nervously fidget with the fabric of my clothes, wondering how the hell I'm going to find my way back home.

He tenses up. "I can't let you do that."

"What am I? A hostage?" I force a laugh and spot the closest exit.

The seriousness in his eyes dissipates gradually. "Listen, I don't know what my brother wants with you, and you clearly don't either. So why not stick around and find out?"

I sigh. I guess I don't have much of a choice. Plus, as crazy as it may sound, something about the way his eyes darkened when I tried to leave tells me he's not the right person to mess with.

"Thanks for letting me spend the night."

"Don't thank me. Haze is free to bring home whoever he wants." He grins, insinuating that I did more than "spend the night."

I'm about to tell him he's wrong when he speaks again.

"So what exactly are you to my brother?" He narrows his eyes, staring at me intently. "Friend? Special friend?"

I make a face. Even the word friend sounds like too much.

"We're not sleeping together if that's what you're asking. And I don't really know, to be honest. We're acquaintances at most."

"So he invited you over because you're nothing to him?" He frowns, clearly not buying my story.

"I was in trouble, and he offered me a place to stay. He was trying to help. Nothing more. Is the interrogation over?" I try a joke, and he laughs faintly.

"I'm sorry. It's just…" He pauses. "My brother never, and I mean never, brings a girl home. You can't blame me for being curious."

If I was drinking water right now, I'd probably be choking.

"Oh, come on. You can't seriously expect me to fall for that?" I shake my head, the conversation I overheard between Bianca and him yesterday coming back to me. Haze is no saint.

"I know what you're thinking. You'd assume with all the girls throwing themselves at him, he'd bring a different girl home every night. Well, he doesn't—he goes to their place. But bringing them here? Don't even think about it."

Well, that's weird.

I don't reply, smiling awkwardly.

"Do you know about him?" He raises an eyebrow.

"You mean, do I know about the fights? Yeah. I do."

He nods. "Good. I thought I'd have to make up stories."

The familiar sound of a text message coming through interrupts us. Tanner reaches for his phone in his pocket and unlocks it. I can't tell what he's looking at, but when uncertainty crosses his face, I know something's wrong. Realization seems to hit him. Then he looks up as any trace of kindness quickly drains from his emerald-green eyes.

"Hold on. You said my brother offered you a place to stay because you were in trouble last night. What kind of trouble?"

I mentally debate on whether or not I should tell him.

"Listen, it was great talking to you, but I really have to go. It's getting late," I stutter, walking toward the kitchen where the closest door is screaming my name.

He gets up as well, a hatred I've never seen before occupying his gaze. Then he says the two most dreadful words I've ever heard.

"You're her."

"What?" I step back, desperately analyzing my surroundings

for an object I could use as a weapon.

"You're the East Side girl."

I don't even have time to react when he rushes toward me, his eyes as dark as night. The oxygen is knocked out of my lungs when he pushes me against the wall, his hands circling my throat roughly. I hit him as hard as I can to get him off me, but it's no use. He's a good six foot five of muscle and obviously stronger than me.

"You're that girl he made the deal about, aren't you?" he hisses, barely an inch from my face. "Listen, I don't know what the fuck is going on with Haze or why he's messing with the enemy, but this is never going to happen again. You stay the hell away from my brother, do you hear me? You tell the East Side their pathetic attempt to screw us over is not going to work."

Then I do the only thing I can think of. I lift my leg up and knee him as hard as I can where the sun doesn't shine. He lets go of me almost instantly, groaning in pain. I sprint to the exit, slam the door open, and rush out onto the street. I have never run so fast in my entire life. Unable to see my feet hitting the ground, I look back to the Adams house that keeps getting smaller. In the end, I was right. What I was running toward turned out to be so much worse than what I ran away from.

FIVE
The Point Of No Return

"Where the hell were you?" Kendrick throws a million questions at me the very second I get into his car. I don't have it in me to answer. Not after everything I've been through.

As soon as I got far enough from Haze and his psycho brother's house, I found myself on a hunt for a good citizen willing to let me use their phone. The nice cashier at the convenience store turned out to be my savior. Kendrick picked up on the first ring, and I'll admit, when I heard his voice, I almost cried in joy.

"Winter, answer me. Where were you?"

I don't speak, completely drained from the rush of adrenaline I previously had.

"What happened to you? Are you okay?"

"I'm alive, aren't I?" I let out, not bothering to look at him.

"Gee, Winter. Do you have any idea how scared we were? I had to tell my mom you were sleeping at a friend's place, and she wasn't easy to convince. I thought something horrible happened to you. You could've called—I was worried sick."

"I lost my phone," I mutter.

"Oh please, cut the crap. You treat that thing like it's your child. Someone stole it or something?"

"Something like that."

Haze just had to take my phone. Asshat.

"I'm going to ask again. Where the hell were you?"

"You really want to know? Fine. I was at Haze's."

Color drains from his face. "What?" he shouts. "What did you just say?"

"I slept at Haze's place, and if you really want to know, he's the one who took my phone."

"How could you let that happen?" Kendrick's accusing eyes are pointed right at me.

"I didn't let anything happen. I didn't have a choice. He saved me when you guys left me to fend for myself. Thank you for that by the way. A heads-up about the gangs coming after me would've been appreciated." I can't stop the resentment from growing.

"He…" He pauses, in disbelief. "He saved you?"

"Seriously? That's the only part of my sentence you remembered?"

"You're right. I'm sorry. We have no idea how it happened. No one was supposed to know about you. Haze might be a piece of trash, but he usually keeps his word."

"It wasn't him," I whisper.

"Is that what he told you?"

I nod faintly.

"And you believe him? For all we know, he's the one who set this whole thing up."

"Why would he do that?"

"Gee, I don't know. Let me see—to get you killed?"

"Is that why he helped me escape? Or maybe that's why he found me a place to sleep? Because he wants me dead. Are you even listening to yourself?" I rest my head against the car window. The headache is officially here to stay.

"I don't know why he did it, Winter. All I know is, no matter what he did for you last night, you can't trust him. Ever. It's all a game for him. Nothing he does is out of the kindness of his heart."

"Yeah, yeah. I got it. He's bad. Do we have any idea who did it?" I wince and shift in my seat. I know from the burning sensation that Tanner's handprints must be quite obvious under my hair.

"We're on it. We suspect the North Side, but it doesn't add up. Ian is Haze's ally. He wouldn't pull the trigger on an attack like that without consulting him first." He glances at me. "We'll figure it out. I promise."

I'm slightly amused by the way Kendrick talks to me like I'm supposed to know who the hell this Ian is. I need a "street fighters for dummies" lesson *fast*.

Kendrick's car pulls up into Maria's driveway, and I'm relieved to see her white car is nowhere to be seen. I'll have a lot of explaining to do when she comes home from the hospital tonight. My cousin shuts off the engine and we walk to the front door side by side. Kendrick tells me about Kass not coming home either. Apparently, she texted him not to worry. He says he suspects it has something to do with a boy.

"Good for her," I reply. After everything Blake put her through, she deserves it. Of course, I refrain from saying the last part out loud as Kendrick isn't aware of Blake and Kass's secret.

We stop on the porch to unlock the door. When a cold breeze blows my hair off my neck, Kendrick stops dead in his tracks. I frown.

"What the hell is this? What happened to you?"

Shit. Shit. Shit.

"What is what?"

"Your neck. Oh my God."

He brushes the hair off my neck swiftly before I can step back. He balls his hands into fists, making them look like white-knuckled weapons.

"The bastard attacked you?" he says through gritted teeth, the look in his eyes making my skin crawl.

I consider lying for a second. I don't want to cause any more problems than I already have. When I get a quick glance of my reflection in the kitchen window, I'm forced to face the obvious truth—nothing can get me out of this one. What could I possibly say to justify the bright red marks on my neck? *I got into a fight with a curling iron?*

"It wasn't Haze. He was gone when I woke up. He wanted me to wait for him." I finally come clean, my eyes dropping to the ground.

"Then who?" Kendrick shouts, anger flowing out of him profusely.

"Kendrick, calm down, please."

He's about two seconds away from punching the wall.

"Who?" he screams again.

I give in. "Tanner."

"I'm going to kill him." He unlocks the front door and rushes inside the silent kitchen. I follow him, terrified that he might do something stupid. Against all expectations, he gets his phone out of his pocket and starts typing.

"What are you doing?" I try and see the screen.

"Texting you," he grumbles.

"But Haze has my phone."

Kendrick looks up from his phone, and we lock eyes.

"Exactly."

I glance over his shoulder, finally getting a clear shot of the message.

> Your brother lays a finger on my cousin again. You're both dead. - K

Lovely.

I remember turning off my phone last night, and although I'd like to think Haze won't see it, I also know I'd be dumb to think he hasn't tried to snoop. Even if—thank the Lord—my phone has a password, the locked screen will allow him to read Kendrick's text. My cousin storms out of the room seconds later and I collapse onto a chair, cursing.

It's official, life hates me.

"WHAT ABOUT THESE?" KASS INTERRUPTS THE foreign thoughts spinning around in my head for the billionth time today. I look at the heels she's holding up in front of my eyes.

"I tried walking in heels once. I made a new friend—the floor."

She doesn't laugh, instead she looks at me sharply.

"Think of how great you'd look."

"Maybe, but my feet would never forgive me. I tried yesterday at the party. It's not worth it."

I glance around the crowded mall and wonder why on earth I let her convince me to go shopping. I guess I needed something to take my mind off the whole Haze mess. Shortly after Kendrick sent him that very kind text message, Kassidy walked into the house with a cheeky smile on her face. Kendrick left almost immediately after. I followed him outside to beg him not to do anything he might regret. He nodded briefly before taking off.

Do I feel better? Not even a little bit.

I grimace at the pain emanating from my neck and adjust the silk scarf I'm wearing. I am not risking Kassidy seeing the handprints on my skin and losing her mind, too.

I tried to get her to tell me where she was all night, but she sticks to her obviously false story which is that she was at a friend's. She seems lighter than usual, happier, less controlling, less moody.

Less Kass.

It's a boy. It's got to be.

After a good thirty minutes, I end up convincing her that she's bought enough clothes for the day, although I practically have to drag her out of the mall. Resting my head against the car window, I watch the passing houses in the rearview mirror. We come to an abrupt stop, and Kassidy sighs, stretching her neck in an attempt to see the reason behind the blocked circulation. That's when she hits me with the one sentence I did not want to hear.

"So… About the party."

"What about it?"

"Rumor has it you slept at you know who's?"

I chortle. "You can say his name. He's not Voldemort."

"Haze," she says, anxiously glancing around as if she fears

he's going to come out of one of the cars next to us in traffic.

"Yeah. I did."

But it's actually a funny story, you see? My life was in danger, and that's why Mr. I'm-too-handsome-to-be-human slash don't-look-me-in-the-eyes had to come to my rescue. Not to mention that his psycho brother ended up attacking me.

Ah, memories.

"What's the deal between you two, Winter? He's dangerous."

"No shit, Sherlock," I mutter under my breath.

"I'm serious. You need to be careful. I can't believe you let him take you to his house. You need to stay away from him."

"I'm trying to."

"Oh, really? Is that why you keep hanging out with Kendrick and his trouble-magnet friends? They're involved in... some stuff."

I pretend to be surprised when in fact, I already know exactly what she's talking about.

"Stuff?"

"Stuff." She makes it clear she is not willing to discuss this any further. "Do you know what happened yesterday? I was already gone, but I heard it caused a panic."

I look down. "Cops."

I hate lying to her.

"I know that's what everyone said, but it seemed like a lot more than that. Some people said they heard a gunshot."

"Cops these days." I pray that she won't ask any more questions.

"Yeah." She shrugs. "I'm just saying to be careful. Haze Adams is not one to do romance and—"

I cut her off. "Wait a minute. You were gone? With who?"

"With… with a friend."

"Oh, come on. Who's the boy?"

"There's no boy. Don't try to change the subject. What were we talking about?"

"You were lecturing me about Haze."

"Right. All Haze wants is fun. Like what he does with Bianca. He keeps sleeping with her even though the poor girl's head over heels in love with him. Just don't let him fool you, too."

"Believe it or not, I'm actually not a fan of heartless douchebags. I'm one of the girls who don't enjoy when a man doesn't give a crap about them. Yes, we do exist."

"Says the girl who literally just let him take her home."

I can't hold it in anymore.

"Okay. You know what? I did not sleep at his place willingly. Something happened to me, and I was in trouble. Haze helped and offered me a place to stay."

She seems a bit taken aback by my sudden change of tone and doesn't reply for a while, mentally debating on something.

"Some street gang trouble?"

My face drops.

"You know?"

She nods faintly. "I've known for a while now. I'm not blind. Neither is my mom. She knows Kendrick is involved in something she can't control. I hear your fights at night. Kendrick needs to stop taking the world for idiots. Not to mention Blake's behavior was so weird back when we were dating. Eventually, I put the pieces together."

"Why didn't you say something?"

"Because it's better to pretend not to know certain things, Winter. I don't want to get involved in his mess, and I've managed to do that successfully until..."

I finish her sentence. "Until me."

"Well, don't get me wrong, but you literally threw yourself into the fire. What were you thinking following my brother when he goes out?"

"Seriously? You heard that, too?"

"You guys are pretty loud when you argue at night." She puts her hands up in surrender.

We don't speak for a couple of minutes. We haven't moved one bit, still stuck in traffic. I look out the window and spot a woman dancing like no one's watching in her car. Singing along to the radio, she doesn't have a care in the world. I can't suppress a smile.

"Look at her." I rest my chin in the palm of my hand.

"Can't. I'm driving." She keeps her eyes fixed to the road.

"You're sitting in an unmoving car, actually."

She exhales. "What?"

"I hope I can be this carefree when I'm older."

Kass stiffens. "If and only if you live beyond the age of eighteen."

I raise my eyebrows. How could I not see that one coming? "Harsh."

"I know. I know. I'm being an asshole, I'm sorry. It's just… Haze Adams is only as nice as he needs to be to get your trust. Promise me that you'll stay away."

I find myself locked in her persistent gaze.

"I promise."

The traffic picks up the pace, and Kass's face softens. She focuses on driving, pleased by my response. As I tap my foot, eager to get home, I can't draw my thoughts to a close. Something tells me that if I make it my mission to avoid Haze, he'll somehow be in my life even more. It doesn't matter if I promise to stay away from him.

I'm not sure he will stay away from *me*.

SIX

The Date

"Finally! Alex, they're back," Will shrieks the very second I enter the house and drop the bags I'm holding on the floor.

"Aw, did someone miss us?" I tease, going back to the door to let my shopping addict of a cousin inside. Kass lets her bags hit the floor, as well, not even bothering to acknowledge Will's presence. She wasn't kidding when she said she'd made it her life mission not to get involved in Kendrick's mess.

Then, as if our return is the most awaited event of the year, Alex rushes inside the room with nerve-wrecking anxiety flowing out of him.

"What's up with you?" I ask.

"You've been gone for like two years, that's what's up," Alex replies, eyeing the now-covered-with-shopping-bags floor.

Kass deigns to look up from her phone. "We've been gone for like four hours."

"What the hell were you doing at the mall for four hours anyway?" Will mocks.

"Hunting elephants." Kass retorts, "Isn't it obvious? We were shopping. What do you think we were doing?"

Will arches an eyebrow. "Shopping for what? And don't tell

me shoes. You already have 2,433 pairs."

"That's not true," I say.

"Thanks, Winter." Kass smiles at me.

"She has 2,435."

Alex and Will both suppress a laugh as my cousin rolls her eyes and picks up as many bags as humanly possible. She departs the room and disappears up the stairs into her room.

I shrug, kicking off my shoes. "Why were you guys waiting for us? And where are Blake and Kendrick?"

Their faces become even paler than they already are—if that's even possible—as their eyes seem to develop a sudden passion for the floor.

"That's kind of what we wanted to talk to you about." Alex nervously rubs the back of his neck.

"What did you do?" is all I can say.

"Well… You remember Tanner, right?"

"Oh yeah, the guy who violently attacked me. Nice guy. What about him?"

"Promise you won't freak out," Alex replies.

"That's exactly what not to say to me if you don't want me to freak out," I blurt.

"Kendrick told us about what happened. He called us right after he dropped you off and… he was really angry. We had no way of knowing what he was going to do. He—" Alex cuts himself off.

"He what?" I insist.

"He went to find Tanner. Problem is, he wasn't alone, and let's just say it ended badly. Kendrick looks awful right now. He'll have to crash at Blake's until he doesn't look like his face was used as a punching bag. We need you to cover for him."

I can't find the words to say how I feel, unable to get the images of me begging Kendrick not to do anything stupid before he left out of my head. Guilt washes over me. He went there to fight Tanner for what he did to me, and I know it technically isn't my fault, but he wouldn't have gotten hurt if it weren't for me following Haze. He told me he was going to kill him. And I went shopping. I went shopping for God's sake! I didn't think he was serious.

I'm about to speak, but Will cuts me off, raising his finger in my direction. "And before you say no, just remember that Kendrick and Haze have a deal. If Maria sees her baby boy looking like he got ran over by a truck, Kendrick will have to break it, and you know what happens in the community when you break a deal? You're considered a coward, and the prize is automatically given to the other person. In other words…"

"Haze," I finish.

His words hit me pretty hard, and although I was going to help without this bit of information, it certainly doesn't hurt in the motivation department.

I nod. "What do you need to me to do?"

"Just tell Maria he's staying with me to uh… help me deal with depression or something," Alex babbles.

"Why would you be depressed?"

"I don't know. Because my cat died?"

I can't hold back a small laugh. "Oh come on, there's no way she's buying that."

"Just make up something. You girls are good at that kind of stuff." Will shrugs.

"That kind of stuff? Like lying?"

"No. Talking shit."

Will's outstanding skills with the female population will never cease to impress me.

Alex hits the back of Will's head quickly. "You really know how to convince a woman, don't you?"

"Ouch." Will winces, grinning.

"When can I see him?" I ask.

"He says he wants to wait until he's better. He'll give you a call when he's ready," Alex says.

"Here's the plan. We set up a date tonight with Haze through your phone. All we need you to do is use your…" Alex pauses as if he's looking for the words he could say not to sound like an asshole. "*Charms* to convince him not to tell everyone. The last thing we need is for our enemies to know our leader got beat up. We're weak at the moment. You have no idea how many people would like to get rid of Kendrick."

"You want me to convince him to cover up for his enemies? Are you kidding? Why the hell would he do me this favor?"

"Because he's obsessed with you, duh," Will exclaims like it's the most obvious statement in the world.

"What Will is trying to say is that Haze's the one who stopped Tanner and his fighters. He basically saved Kendrick and let him escape."

I can't stop my jaw from dropping. "He did what?"

"Believe me, we know." Will makes a face, an obvious sign that he's as confused as I am. "We got there just in time to get him out of there. When we realized what he had in mind, it was too late."

I can't stop a feeling of uncertainty from growing.

"This might be our best and only shot, Winter," Alex says. "You might be the only one who can convince him. He definitely sees something in you."

Will scoffs. "Yeah. His dick. That's what he sees in you."

Alex elbows him in the stomach.

I like Will. Always so sweet and polite.

Something tells me this banter's an everyday thing for them.

It's become quite obvious that Will is the immature, prankster, funny guy with inappropriate jokes, and Alex is the nice "dad" who constantly apologizes for his son's behavior.

"How do you know he's even going to show up at all?"

Will shrugs. "Because he thinks you're the one who set it up.

He'll be there. Trust me."

"I don't have to go alone, do I?"

"Of course not. Kendrick would kill us." Alex says.

"Well, technically, it would require for him to be able to walk," Will adds.

My worries increase tremendously.

"It's that bad?"

"It is. I have no idea what Kendrick expected. That he could take down four guys at once? Not to mention he thought Tanner wouldn't have backup. Tanner was expecting him. Kendrick's good. But no one's *that* good." Will glances at me. "We're leaving in a couple hours. Wear something a bit more…" He pauses, analyzing me from head to toe. "Revealing."

"In other words, wear almost nothing."

I look down at my oversized sweatshirt and leggings.

"Yeah, pretty much."

This results in another blow to the stomach from Alex.

"Don't listen to him. What he means is that we want all the help we can get. If you seducing Haze can save Kendrick, we have to try."

So basically… I'm meeting Haze Adams late at night, wearing almost nothing, with gangs potentially trying to kill me.

Sounds fun.

SITTING IN A CAR THAT'S TAKING me to a meeting

with Haze isn't exactly what I had in mind when I thought about my Saturday night. Will is driving while Alex is tapping his foot to the music playing on the radio. Am I the only one completely freaked-out here? It sure looks like it.

I look down at the red dress I'm wearing. It's tight and something I bought a while ago for my nonexistent boyfriend. I thought I might need a dress like this one day. I just never expected that day would be now. My cleavage is a lot more exposed than I'm used to, and I can't help but constantly try to fix it.

When Will parks the vehicle a couple of blocks away from the creepiest park I've ever seen, my response is immediate.

"Seriously? You just had to pick the creepiest park in the history of parks, didn't you?"

"That's the farthest we go." Alex says.

"What? But you said you were coming to watch over me."

"We are. Just from afar. We can't risk Haze seeing us," Will motions to get out of the car. "Come on. He'll be there soon."

"Here goes nothing," I sigh, closing the door and walking toward the completely empty and silent park. I sit down at one of the unoccupied benches, every single noise—as small and ridiculous as they may be—scaring the living heck out of me. Ten minutes go by.

Then I hear it. The sound of an engine in the distance.

I don't know if I should be relieved or nervous when I spot

a motorcycle speeding toward me, its gleaming headlight so bright it temporarily blinds me. It gradually slows down in front of me until it comes to an abrupt stop. Haze kills the engine and hops off his bike, removing his helmet. He runs a hand through his waving-in-the-night-breeze messy hair, still managing to look like he came right out of a movie, might I add. *Cue the slow motion and music.*

"Hey," he says.

I can't tell what he's thinking. Our eyes meet for a second, but his hastily abandon mine when I get up from the bench. He's looking at my dress. No, scratch that—he's staring.

"Well, someone is enjoying making an entrance."

"Get on." His tone makes it clear he's not asking.

Houston, we have a problem. That was not part of the plan.

"Why?" I ask.

"This place is the ultimate place to get attacked, Kingston. That's why." He hands me a spare helmet. My thoughts are going a thousand miles an hour.

I try to buy myself some time. "What makes you say that?"

"It's empty. Isolated. You're lucky nothing happened to you." His eyes fall to my dress again as he bites the inside of his cheek. "Especially dressed like that."

I feel my face heat up as my gaze drops to the floor. Well, he definitely noticed.

"Why would I trust you? If I recall, last time I followed you, your brother—"

"My brother was wrong," he interrupts. "And I'm sorry for what he did to you, but if you want to talk about it, you'll have get on and let me take you somewhere safe."

I glance at the helmet in my hand.

What choice do I have? If I insist on staying in the park from hell, he might get suspicious and figure out that we're not alone.

"Fine."

Next thing I know, I'm sitting on the back of his motorcycle, holding on to him tightly. Haze Adams or not, I don't want to die today.

We take off in a roar as I hold my breath. I don't dare turn around to see if Will and Alex are following us. I'm afraid even just the slightest movement would mean falling off and possibly breaking every bone in my body. Because that's how lucky I am.

Our speed increases with every turn, and it almost seems like he enjoys my grasp getting tighter around him.

Then he says the one thing I feared.

"I think we're being followed."

I take a deep breath and finally turn my head to see the glimmering lights of Will's car in the distance. They are keeping a huge gap between us. I have no idea how Haze even noticed.

"Why do you think that? They're so far away."

"That's the best way not to be noticed while following someone. Plus, they started their car at the exact same time we left. They're following us."

"What do we do?" I mentally curse. He has no idea how much better I feel knowing they're following us.

"Now…" He pauses. "Hold on tight."

If I thought we were going fast before, I'd obviously never experienced Haze's "getting away from the bad guys" driving. My breath gets lodged in my throat when he takes an unexpected turn to lose them. The car manages to turn, too, but not without difficulties.

"I'll lose them, don't worry," he says.

Oh the irony.

"Just so you know, if you kill me, I'm coming back to haunt your ass," I let out, holding on to him so tight I'm guessing it must be hard to breathe.

"Don't worry. I'm going to need you alive for that deal." I can picture him smirking.

"How can you be so sure you'll win anyway?"

"Have you seen Kendrick? Go see him and you'll understand."

Heart squeeze.

I try to brush off the guilt, well aware that if I let it in, I'll drown in it. Haze carries on with his "let's see how fast we can go without dying" game for a little while. Then he finally slows down.

"They're gone."

The fear infiltrates my entire being. It's just me and him now.

"Where are we going?" I ask.

"Somewhere crowded."

I sigh. "What's with the mystery?"

"The ladies love it."

And the best question avoider award goes to Haze Adams.

When he pulls up in front of a restaurant that looks like it came right from the '50s, I glance up at the sign that reads Debbie's Diner. It does look as crowded as it could possibly get. We walk into the restaurant where everything reminds me of the movie Grease. A kind-looking waitress walks up to us, and before I know it, we're sitting in a red booth, waiting for her to return with our coffees.

"Nice place," I begin. "You come here often?"

"I used to." He avoids my eyes, apparently not interested in discussing this topic any further.

I don't reply, wondering why he always does that. Any question that's even a little bit personal turns him into this cold, unreceptive person. Then as soon as the subject changes, he's back to his regular annoyingly charming, overconfident, and mocking self.

"You wanted to talk. Let's talk." He takes his jacket off, revealing a black T-shirt that makes his buff arms unmissable. The ink on his left arm captures my eyes. He has numbers tattooed on his forearm. *04/16.* I wonder what it means. A date maybe?

"Is it true?"

"Is what true?" He leans back into the booth, crossing his arms over his chest and glancing up at me with a familiar grin on his face.

"You stopped the fight?"

"Maybe."

"Well, thank you for saving my cousin."

"I didn't do it for him. Don't thank me."

"Then why?"

"The only reason Kendrick was stupid enough to attack my brother is because of what Tanner did to you. I shouldn't have left you alone with him. It was a mistake. People may call me heartless, but I have a code, and there's nothing I hate more than seeing a woman get hurt."

His words catch me off guard. They bring me back to the night of the party when I heard him say to Bianca that he warned her about only wanting casual sex. Yes, it isn't okay to keep sleeping with her even when he knows she loves him, but making sure that she knew where they stood before getting involved with her is better than telling her he wants a relationship to get into her pants. He has this sort of "honor" to him that I never would've suspected.

"Too bad your code missed a generation." I can't help but wince, my neck still sore.

"Can I see?"

His penetrating blue eyes collide with mine, and I find myself unable to move away. I nod, unsure.

He leans in over the table and gently pushes my hair off my neck with his hand. I shiver at the contact. His eyes darken when they meet the marks on my skin.

"Does it hurt?" If I didn't know any better, I'd say he actually looks concerned.

Coming back down to earth, I shake my head quickly and move away, bringing my hair back to the front. "A little. But it's nothing I can't handle."

"Listen, I know it might not mean much to you but..." His gaze descends to the wooden table like he's looking for the right words to say. "I just want you to know I wouldn't have left if it wasn't urgent."

Somehow, he looks sincere. And part of me wants to believe him. But I know better. Kendrick warned me he had a way with words.

"He was right, though, wasn't he?" My words seem to surprise him. He doesn't speak, waiting for me to continue. "I'm the enemy."

Still no reply.

"So why did you save me?"

He looks conflicted. Then after a few seconds of silence, he speaks.

"Somebody had to."

I'm about to argue and say this isn't an answer when a high-pitched voice interrupts me.

"Excuse me."

We both look up at the same time. Next to our table is a girl that's a good five foot nine. She has long ginger hair and green eyes. Her beauty is undeniable. Her cleavage is on display in the short white dress she is wearing. She happily squishes her breasts together by resting both her arms on the table.

Something tells me she's not here to talk to me.

Her eyes stop on Haze. "Hey. So, I saw you from afar and..."

She pauses and looks at me, probably wondering if I'm his girlfriend and about to pounce on her.

"Here's my number." She hands him a crumpled piece of paper with her perfectly manicured fingers.

Haze's face turns into a seductive one as he takes it.

"Well, thanks." He smirks. "What's your name, gorgeous?"

My stomach drops.

"I'm Natasha." She cackles, obviously appreciating the attention. "Maybe we could go somewhere else, you and I..." She gives him the "let's make babies" look.

Okay, that's enough.

I clear my throat to remind them of my presence. Natasha glares at me. "I'm sorry, is this your girlfriend?"

"Oh no. Don't worry. You two can go and do your thing in a minute. I just need to know the answer to the question I asked you earlier."

Haze's eyes widen. His face says *don't you dare*.

"Have you told Samantha about the STD yet?"

His jaw drops while color drains from Natasha's face. Disgusted, she walks away without a word. As soon as she is out of range, I burst out laughing. I can't stop no matter how hard I try. Haze glares at me.

"What? You've got to admit her face was priceless." I put my hands up in surrender.

"You couldn't have found something else to get rid of her?" he asks but I can tell he's repressing a smile.

"It's the first thing that crossed my mind."

I carry on laughing, and eventually he starts laughing, too.

"You're unbelievable, you know that?" He shakes his head. "And who the hell is Samantha?"

"It was my grandmother's name. Also the first name that came to my mind."

"So, correct me if I'm wrong, you're suggesting that I'm sleeping with your grandmother?"

"You just infected my brain with images." I bury my face in between my hands.

"That was the point." I peek through my fingers and catch his smirk.

We're still laughing when the waitress brings us our coffees and rests them in front of us. Ruining one of Haze Adams's possible hookups? *Check.*

WE'RE ON OUR THIRD COFFEE WHEN the waitress comes to tell us they're closing in thirty minutes. We've been talking about anything and everything for close to two hours, and to my great surprise, it's actually been a lot less awful than I expected. Haze knows how to hold a conversation. Not to mention the guy's actually really funny when he's not in "street fighter" mode.

"All right. Enough." His voice interrupts my thoughts.

"What?"

I have a little idea of what he's going to say.

"The evening's been great. You've been lovely. Now spit it out."

"Spit what out?"

"The question you obviously came here to ask me."

Busted.

"I'm not dumb, Kingston. You wouldn't be here with me after what happened to Kendrick if it wasn't important."

I hate how he sees so clearly through my game.

"Is it so hard to believe that I could just be a nice person who wants to spend time with you without getting anything in return?" I rest my hand on my heart and pretend to be offended.

He laughs.

"Winter, come on."

"Fine, smartass." I sigh. "I was wondering if maybe you could do something for me."

"Try me."

"Here's the thing." I take a deep breath. "Kendrick's at his worst right now, thanks to your brother and his fighters. The last thing we need is for word to spread that the East Side is vulnerable especially a month before the f…"

He doesn't say anything. But he doesn't have to. The look in his eyes is more than enough to cut me off. I press my lips together, uncertain.

"That's a lot you're asking from me." He glances around the diner as if he fears someone might be listening. "I know I owe you after what my brother did to you. But I think I did my part to repay you when I saved your cousin. You're asking me to cover for my enemies. I can't do that. I won't." I feel in my bones that his answer is final.

I can't believe how stupid the guys and I were to think that a nice little coffee date would be enough to convince Haze Adams to show kindness.

"Even if I wanted to, I couldn't make any promises."

"Wrong. You can promise me one thing." I gather every ounce of courage I have left and let our eyes meet. "You can at least try and talk to your brother. And when the fight does come, don't be too violent."

Haze smirks. "So you do think I'm going to win, huh?"

"Haze, please."

"And what makes you think I would do such a thing for you?"

His words feel like a slap. He's right. I have no idea why we thought he would somehow act civilized and do something right for once. And for some girl he just met?

"Nothing. I'm just hoping you'll use the heart you pretend not to have and make the right decision for once because if you don't give Kendrick time to get better, he will die and you know it."

He leans back into the booth and exhales. Irritation can be seen in his perfect features.

"They sent you to sweet-talk me, Winter. Do you realize what that means?" he hisses, "They think they can mess with my head. They think *you* can mess with my head, so let me clarify something."

Any trace of kindness drains from his light-colored eyes.

"I am not going to go soft. I don't care how badly the East Side gets hurt, I don't care if something happens to them, and I sure as hell don't care if they're vulnerable at the moment. Am I making myself clear?"

Feeling rage and disappointment take over me, I nod and get up, not even bothering to look at him.

"Winter, sit."

"Why? You're clearly not going to help, so why waste my time trying to find some humanity in Mr. Bad Boy?" I head for the door.

"And how do you think you're going to get home?" he calls.

"I don't know. I guess I'll just walk. Or maybe I'll call Kendrick to come pick me up. Oh no, wait. Your brother beat him up." I rush out of the restaurant, blinded by my anger.

The sudden burst of rage Haze created in me seems to have been enough for my common sense to go missing. I look around me and see I'm standing next to some sort of abandoned factory. I'm pretty far from the restaurant already and in a part of town I don't know. I have no choice but to admit that I should've probably waited for him to drive me home before I made a scene. I instinctively reach for my phone in my pocket, and I'm mortified when I realize that Haze still has it. I completely forgot to ask him to give it back. How in the world am I going to get home?

"You're an idiot."

I almost feel bad for being this happy when his voice reaches my ears.

I turn around to see him looking at me with mocking eyes. With both hands in his pockets, he's shaking his head in disapproval.

"Yeah. I figured that out when I realized I have no idea

where I am, thanks."

"Oh please. Don't pretend like you're not relieved that I came after you to save your ass again. Notice the word again," he teases, slowly stepping closer to me.

"I would thank you but…" I analyze my surroundings. "Saving me would require a danger of some sort, you see?"

"You got lucky this time, but take my advice: don't storm out into the night like that again. You're hanging out with the bad kids now. That makes you a target."

The distance between us decreases by the second. He stops a little too close to me for my liking. The darkness of the night somehow makes his piercing eyes a bit more bearable. They're slightly less hypnotizing at night.

"So what? You made it clear that you don't care one bit if something happens to me, remember?"

"Has anyone ever told you how stubborn you are?"

"I'm not stubborn. Just realistic. Those are your words, not mine."

"My words? Are you sure about that?" He's staring at me intently.

I try to find some hidden message in the sentence he so kindly said to me earlier but can't find any. Probably because the idiot is messing with me and there is none.

"You said, and I quote, 'I do not care if the East Side gets hurt.' So yeah, I'm pretty damn sure."

He steps closer until I can feel his breath against my skin. We don't move, staring deeply into each other's eyes like we're waiting to see who'll look away first.

"I said I wouldn't care if something happened to them."

Then he pauses for what seems to be an eternity.

"I never said I would let something happen to you."

THE SILENT STREETS WELCOME THE ROAR of Haze's motorcycle but also welcome unwanted thoughts into my head. The neighborhood's asleep. It's late. Too late. Maria is probably worried sick right now. Not to mention I already owe her an explanation about not coming home yesterday.

After Haze left me speechless, he started walking and told me, "Let's get you home," like it was nothing. I have no idea if he meant what he said. But I can't deny that it's been on my mind ever since.

Everything about him is so incredibly confusing. He's like burning ice—might be cold, might be hot. You never know which one you're going to get.

I ask him to stop a couple of houses before mine, and he nods. My aunt would lose it if she saw me get off the back of some guy's motorcycle.

"Thanks for taking me home." I get off his bike, removing my helmet.

"And?" He does the same.

I give in, a bit amused. "For not leaving me to die in front of some abandoned factory."

"That's a weird way to end a first date, but I'll take it."

My eyes widen. "Did you just say the D word?"

A perverted smile spreads across his face.

"Oh for God's sake, not that D word."

"We had coffee, we talked. So yes, it was a date."

"Only because I was trying to get you to do me a favor—did you forget that part?"

"Good reasons or not, it still happened, Kingston." His fingers slip into his pocket. He hands me something. My phone. "There. You might need it next time you do something stupid like rush out onto the street alone at night."

"Or next time I'm trying to run away from you," I say. He smiles. "Gotta go. Time to get grounded for the rest of my life."

"Hold on."

I turn around.

"You may want to cover up before you go in there and pretend you were out studying," he says, analyzing me from head to toe. He bites his lower lip slightly, then looks away.

I flush, ignoring the thick tension that suddenly decides to bless us with its presence. My gaze drops to my dress. He's right. Whatever excuse I find to justify my absence, Maria's not going to buy it if she sees me walk into the house wearing this.

He removes his jacket and hands it to me.

"Here. Take it."

"You don't have to," I say.

"Don't worry about it. Call it a guarantee."

"Guarantee of what?"

He smirks.

"That I'll see you again."

I don't reply, unable to find the words to say, and take the leather jacket from his hand. He starts the engine and looks at me one last time before disappearing down the street in a roar that echoes long after he's gone.

I find myself smiling when I glance down at the jacket in my hand and put it on. It smells like him.

For a short-lived moment, I almost forget about the million questions Maria's going to ask me as soon as I walk through the front door. What am I going to say to her? The closer I get, the stronger the urge to run in the opposite direction becomes. Her car is in the driveway. All the lights are on even though it's close to midnight. She's probably waiting for Kendrick and me to come home.

Problem is, Kendrick's not coming home anytime soon. And something tells me I'm going to have a hard time justifying it.

SEVEN

Liar, Liar

"Where the hell were you?"

Two seconds. That's how long it took for the first question to come bursting out of her mouth. Sitting at the kitchen table in her nightgown, she was waiting to pounce on whoever would walk through the door. She's the definition of angry. The dark circles under her eyes tell me that she's exhausted. She came back from her shift at the hospital at eight. She's probably been sitting there and calling us for hours. I would've sent her a text before but didn't have my phone until now.

"Out," I say, well aware that she's not going to let it go.

"I'm not going to ask again. Where were you?"

"I was at a friend's."

"It's past midnight. You can't seriously expect me to believe that?"

"We were studying. We have a big test on Monday. I didn't realize how late it was. I'm sorry. I won't do it again."

Her face softens although she is still upset. "And about last night? What happened to coming back before midnight?"

"One of my friends wasn't feeling well, so I took her home. I ended up falling asleep there. I would've called, but my phone was dead. By the time I woke up, it was way too late to walk alone, and I didn't want to wake you." I hate that I have to lie to her. But she can't know the truth. She can't be in danger, too.

The anger slowly dissipates from her stern face. She lets out a long and discouraged sigh. "You never do that again, you hear me? I'm supposed to be watching over you while your mother's gone. When you move out, you'll be free to do what you want, but for now, you live with me. If anything happens to you, it's on me."

"I know. I'm so sorry. I won't do it again. I promise."

She nods and opens her arms in my direction. I walk into her welcoming embrace, relieved that she bought it. At least, for now. Maria has always been like a second mother to me. Lying to her breaks my heart.

"Whose jacket is this?" She pulls away.

"Kendrick's. I was in a hurry, so I grabbed whatever I could find."

She nods, but I can tell she's not a hundred percent convinced. She did his laundry for so long, something tells me she knows every piece of clothing he owns.

Karma is going to hit me really hard for this.

"I'm exhausted. I'm going to bed." I smile and attempt to walk around her. I can't believe I avoided the Kendrick questi—

"Do you happen to know where Kendrick is?"

Dang it.

I turn around, my mind racing. "Yeah. He asked me to tell you…"

Think, Winter, think.

"His friend's parents got divorced. He's staying with her to help her cope with it. She's very sad."

Maria's face lights up.

"You mean…" She pauses. "My little boy has a girlfriend?"

Shit.

Why did I use the term "her"?

Of course she would think they're more than friends if he's staying with her because she's depressed.

"Yeah." I force a smile.

"I can't believe he didn't tell me. This is great. I think a girlfriend might be really good for him. Might set him straight. I'll call him tomorrow morning." The excitement in her voice is unmissable. "Good night, sweetheart."

She smiles warmly and exits the kitchen. I drag my feet toward the stairs and curse under my breath.

Life hates me—the return.

FOR THE PAST HOUR, I HAVE been doing two things I am proud to say I excel at: lying in bed and procrastinating. I can't bring myself to call Kendrick to tell him that I messed up again. Maria's going to want to meet his girlfriend, but there's just one slight problem—she doesn't exist. I keep on reaching for my phone to call him but end up talking myself out of it every time.

As soon as I walked into my room, I saw I had ten messages from Will and Alex. I texted them that I was fine. They completely freaked out when Haze lost them. All they could do was trust that he wouldn't hurt me. A notification pops up on my screen, interrupting my thoughts.

I have a new message.

Just realized I forgot to give you your pencil back.

Speaking of Haze.

I find myself smiling, I forgot about the pencil I handed him in English class. I'm surprised he remembered.

You know what else you forgot?

?

To take a hint.

Ouch. And I thought tonight went well.

Sorry. Had to. It was too easy.

How'd it go.
You still alive

Barely. She bought it for now. Thanks for the jacket.

No problem, gorgeous.

He might be a decent person after all.

When can I give you your pencil back? How about tomorrow night ;) Your place.

And... *he's back.*

Sure. Come over at 9 ;)

Really

No.

Why you gotta be so cruel

I already see you in my nightmares, Adams. Don't need you in my house, too

You know I'll never stop trying

Why are you texting me?

Why are you replying

You're not answering my question.

Neither are you.

-.-

:D

I click out of the text conversation and push all Haze-related thoughts out of my head. *Focus, Winter.* I have to call Kendrick. If I don't, he'll find out about my mistake tomorrow when his mother calls him, and something tells me he'll be even more angry.

I dial his number with a shaky hand. It rings a couple of times before he picks up.

"You owe me big-time. I think I've lied more in one night than I have in my entire life."

A dreadfully long silence follows.

"Who is this?"

The voice is deep, masculine. But it's not Kendrick's.

I immediately know something is wrong.

I hang up as fast as humanly possible, my fingers automatically selecting Blake's number in my contact list. There's no way the boys are asleep. It's 1:10 a.m.; they're not anywhere near going to bed. They're either training or playing video games and being sore losers.

One ring. Two rings. Three rings. Pick up, damn it!

"Hello?" Blake says on the other end.

"Does Kendrick have his phone?" I blurt.

"Well, hello to you, too, Winter," he chuckles.

"Blake, I'm serious. Answer the question."

"Of course not. He lost it during the fight with Tanner. We're confident a gang has it by now."

I freeze.

"You can't be serious. Tell me you're kidding."

"Why? What happened?" Blake says. "Winter, what did you do? You didn't call him, did you?"

Crap.

"Some guy answered. But I didn't tell him anything and hung up right away. How the hell was I supposed to know? No one told me."

"What?" Blake brings the phone away from his mouth. "You didn't tell her about Kendrick's phone?" he says to Alex and Will, I assume.

I hear Will's voice in the background. "Of course we did. Alex told her, right?"

"What? I thought you did it," Alex answers.

"You dumbasses, she called him. Listen carefully, Winter. You're going to tell me exactly what happened."

"I told you. I called him and some stranger picked up. But it's not a big deal, right? It was just a phone call—right?"

"Winter…" He pauses. "We have no idea who has it by now. It could be anyone that's an ally to Tanner. Chances are they're not Kendrick's biggest fans. If they try to locate the call, you could be in danger."

Panic takes over me. "But why would they do that? Try and locate some random girl calling Kendrick?"

"Because that's what they do. Any chance they get to hurt us, they'll take. Not to mention the attack at the party got people talking. There's rumors of an 'East Side girl'—a girl that Kendrick cares for. We have enemies. A lot of enemies. What Tanner did to you is the mere example of that. You have to get rid of your phone. They can't find you if there's nothing to locate."

"What?" I exclaim, mortified. "Y-You can't ask me to do

that. Isn't there another way?"

He raises his voice. "Do you want to go to sleep tonight wondering if someone's on his way to your house? No? Then stop arguing and do it."

Blake tells me to write down his number and to call him with the house phone as soon as it's done. I do as I'm told. Then, like I'm no longer in control of my body, I run toward the bathroom that's directly linked to my bedroom and slam the door open, my breathing shallow and irregular.

"Forgive me," I say to my brand-new phone before throwing it in the toilet and watching it sink to the bottom.

The screen glitches and turns pitch-black. Poor baby. I run to the house phone, frantically dialing Blake's number.

"Did you do it?" he asks as soon as he picks up.

"It's done. Can they still find me?" I pant, out of breath. All this running is making me realize how out of shape I am.

"We can't know for sure. But thank God you called us right after."

Realization hits me when I instinctively reach for my phone in my pocket but can't find it.

"What the heck am I going to do without a phone? My entire life was in there."

"We'll take care of that tomorrow, I promise. Why were you calling Kendrick by the way?"

"Promise you won't get mad." I pause, overwhelmed. "I

might have told Maria that Kendrick is staying with his depressed girlfriend whose parents just got divorced. Okay, bye." Then, before he can get a word in, I hang up, not emotionally able to deal with their criticism right now.

The words poured out of me so fast, I'm assuming he could barely keep up. I collapse onto my bed and stare at the ceiling, a feeling of shame weighing on my conscience.

Not so long ago, my biggest worries were not making friends and getting lost in my new school.

Now, I'm afraid my simple mistake will hurt not only me but my entire family.

When you think things couldn't possibly get any worse, life looks at you with a smile and says, *"Challenge accepted."*

WAKING UP TO THE SOUND OF the idiots my cousin calls friends rushing into the house and screaming my name isn't exactly how I wanted my Sunday to start. Way to do it, guys. Fortunately, the lack of complaints from Maria and Kass tells me that they left for work already.

"Canada, where you at?" Will screams. I roll my eyes at the stupid nickname.

"Upstairs," I shout.

Last night was probably the worst I've had in a while. After I canceled my phone via internet, I kept on tossing and turning, alerted by every single noise. Like not having a phone anymore isn't bad enough, I also couldn't call for help if someone did track me down and showed up at the house.

No one did. Thank God.

"Good morning, sunshine!" Will walks into my room without knocking. I consider yelling at him but decide against it. This is Will we're talking about—it'd go through one ear and right out the other. Alex follows not so far behind him.

"You still in bed? What's wrong with you, woman?" Will says and walks to my window, opening the curtains. I wince, covering my eyes with my hands.

"Well, excuse me. It's not like I spent the entire night afraid someone was going to track me down and murder me or anything." I rub my heavy eyelids. "What time is it?"

"Eleven," Alex replies. "We got you a gift."

He drops something on the bed. I blink a couple of times, my sight struggling to adapt to the light. As soon as I can see clearly, the first thing that comes to my mind is, are they serious?

"An alarm clock. Gee, thanks."

Because buying me a new phone isn't the least they could do after not telling me that Kendrick lost his.

"Would you rather have no way to wake up for school tomorrow?" Will mocks. "We canceled Kendrick's phone. Kass's old phone still works if you want it. Now come on, get dressed. We've got a long day ahead of us." He turns away, heading for the door. When did Will have time to talk to Kass?

No, scratch that.

When did I-hate-the-East-Side Kass find time to talk to Will?

"What? Why? Where are we going?" I yawn, running a hand through my knotted morning hair. Thanks, Mother Nature, for the *"she'll look like a troll every morning"* curse.

"Fake girlfriend hunting. Kendrick called his mom this morning, and guess what? She's dying to meet her. Thanks for putting us in even more trouble than we thought possible, by the way."

"Thanks for not telling me calling him was dangerous and forcing me to throw my new phone in the toilet." I smile slyly. "We're even, don't you think?"

Alex apologizes like the overly nice guy he is while Will completely ignores me and comments on the posters hung up on my wall.

"Okay, out. Both of you." I get up and push them out of my bedroom, into the hall. I slam the door in their faces.

"You have fifteen minutes," Will says from the other side.

Yesterday, I was on a "date" to seduce a guy into doing me a favor, and today I'm casting a fake girlfriend for my cousin who got beat up because of me.

Another regular day in my life.

"THANK YOU." ALEX SMILES POLITELY AND shows the redhead the door. She smiles back, her eyes full of hope, and leaves like the ten other girls we've seen today. Alex's living room has been operating as a casting room for hours now, and we're not anywhere near close to finding a girl that's right for the job.

"How many other girls do we have?" I ask, leaning back into my seat.

"Four," Alex says. "The next one just texted me that she's on her way."

When the boys called up a bunch of girls they know and got repeatedly turned down, they had no choice but to opt for the last resort: the wonderful world of Craigslist. Unfortunately, they weren't very specific, and the girls are either too old, too young, or terrible actresses.

"I need a break," I tell them. They nod. I get up and step out onto Alex's impressively big balcony that overlooks the pool, basketball hoop, garden, and waterfall. The billion family pictures scattered all around his house make it clear: Alex has it all.

Kind of makes you wonder what on earth pushed a kid who grew up in the definition of a "good family" to take part in illegal street fights. According to Kendrick, Alex's entire life has been mapped out for him. He's to be a lawyer like hbis father was before him and his grandfather was before that. I think back to what my stepfather always says: The more you try to lock your kids into a cage, the harder they'll try to get out. The more lines you draw, the more they'll want to cross them.

I lean forward and rest my arms on the railing surrounding the wood-built balcony. I let my mind wander to the complete madness I've been thrown in during these past few weeks.

Kassidy's prehistoric phone is officially registered to my number. It is as basic as it gets. It's also very old. And not the "didn't come out this year" kind of old—it's the "you can't even downloads apps on it because it can't take the server updates anymore" kind of old.

It serves the main purpose of a phone, which is to call and text, but that's all it does. Realizing I haven't checked it all day, I turn it on and unlock it. I have seven unread messages.

Is this your way of telling me you don't want to be friends anymore

But it was going so well :(

Hi

Bonjour

Hola

Aloha

> I'm running out of languages to say hi which means you should probably answer soon

I mentally curse when I realize I'm smiling. He's still texting me? He's right though. I never answered him. If he only knew why.

> How obnoxious can you possibly be?

It only takes a couple of minutes for my phone to light up with a response.

> 1. Very.
> 2. You answered;)

> 7 texts? Seriously? Can you please stop blowing up my phone? I'm busy ignoring you

> And live without your heartwarming messages. How will I ever survive

> I'll block your number, I swear.

> You'd miss me too much.

What do you want? Don't you have STDs to catch?

That stung.

STDs tend to do that.

Look at you trying to convince yourself that you'd never sleep with me;)

Don't you have better things to do -.-

Better than annoying my favorite Canadian. Nah.

Lucky me

I have a question for you.

Consider me afraid.

Are you a virgin

No. I'm a Scorpio.

Virgin. Not Virgo.

> What about you? I bet you're a Sagittarius.

God, you're annoying.

> That's something a Sagittarius would say.

How long can you dodge questions like that

> I can go all day

> My turn to ask questions.

> What do you have against question marks?

Nothing. I'm just lazy.

> Right. But you're not too lazy to text me 7 times.

He stops replying. I put the phone down, a feeling of guilt burdening me. What's happening to me? I feel bad for texting him. But mostly, I feel bad for kind of *liking* it. I shake my head as if it'll somehow restore much-needed order to my obviously disturbed mind. Then, after a good ten minutes, my phone lights up with a reply.

> I'm never too lazy
> when it comes to you.

He probably says things like that to a thousand different girls. He can't expect me to fall for his lines. *I won't.*

Acting on impulse, I do something I shouldn't. But what's new? I stare at the message I just sent and regret it immediately. This probably seems like an invite into my life.

Maybe it is.

> All talk. No action.

I stare at the conversation intently, afraid of his answer. To say I don't hold my breath when he replies would be a lie.

> Is that a challenge, Kingston

"Winter?"

I jump, my heart suddenly on a mission to be heard by the entire world. I turn around, bringing my hand to my chest. Blake is staring at me. How long has he been standing there?

"Blake, you scared me."

"Sorry. You seemed so focused. What are you doing out here?" He walks toward me.

I instinctively shove my phone deep into my pocket like I've been caught doing something wrong.

I guess, in a way, I have.

I shouldn't be answering his texts at all. This needs to stop.

"Nothing. Just texting some friends." I feed him a lie which he's happy to swallow.

"Two of the girls bailed, and the other two weren't great. No luck today. Come on, I'll drive you home."

"Thanks."

I say my goodbyes and follow Blake to the driveway where his car is patiently waiting for us. We both get inside. The entire car ride feels heavy, awkward even. Blake is trying his best to create small talk, but it feels forced. I can tell he's flirting with me again.

I didn't want to get involved with him *before* I knew he'd dated my cousin and lied to his best friend for months. I'm not sure what makes him think I'm interested now.

"Do you mind if I drop you off here?" he asks, stopping the car a couple of houses before mine. He explains that he has an appointment he completely forgot about.

"Of course not. Thanks for the ride," I say gratefully and reach for the car handle, but he stops me.

"Winter, hold on."

Please don't ask me out.

"I was wondering if you wanted to do something next weekend."

Dang it.

I play dumb. "Like with the boys?"

"No. Just you and me."

I hate that moment. I hate having to turn someone down. It's honestly so uncomfortable and painful for both people.

"Blake, listen…You're a great guy and I like spending time with you, but I just don't think it's a good idea for me to get involved with one of Kendrick's friends and fighters. I mean, I'm already way more involved in this mess than I ever wanted to be."

His smile fades.

"Oh. Of course. Don't worry about it. I get it." I can tell that it stung even though he's trying to be nice.

"It has nothing to do with you, I promise."

That's a bit of a lie. The fact that he's a liar who dumped Kassidy without a solid reason doesn't especially help his case.

He nods faintly, and I don't see what's left to do except get out of the car. I watch him take off.

It's almost five o'clock, and I honestly have no idea what I'm going to do for the rest of the day. Maria's coming home at midnight, and Kass works at the pet store until eight. I look down at my phone at the text conversation with Haze and then look up.

That's when I see it.

A motorcycle. Parked in my driveway.

But that's not the worst part. The worst part is the annoyingly charming guy that comes along with it.

Casually leaning against his bike with his arms crossed, he's staring right at me.

"You've got to be kidding me," I mutter under my breath, walking toward him. "What are you doing here?"

"Well, *someone* told me that I was all talk and no action, so I had to come and prove that *someone* wrong."

"That *someone* never told you to show up at her house, and that *someone* is thinking you're running out of excuses to stalk her."

"Fine." He steps closer. "I wanted to see you."

"Well, you saw me. Goodbye now."

"I liked our date yesterday," he whispers.

"It wasn't a date," I retort.

"Sure it wasn't."

One step closer from him.

One step back from me.

I jump when my back comes in contact with something—his motorcycle. Great. Haze fills the remaining distance between us, and I find myself at a loss for words when his pale eyes capture mine. It's like I can't think when he's too close.

"Stop it," I let out.

"Stop what?" He smiles.

"Trying to seduce me."

I push him off and step back until we're at a bearable distance.

"Can't you just act normally? The flirty looks, the cocky attitude, and overconfidence. It's getting old."

He half-smiles. "Oh, so you want to see the real me?"

"That's not what I said. But if you're going to show up at my house, I'd rather not have to deal with your player attitude."

He seems a bit taken aback but quickly gathers himself.

"As you wish, Kingston."

He does the one thing I did not expect.

He hands me a spare helmet and starts his motorcycle.

"Where in my sentence did I say I wanted to go somewhere with you?"

He grins.

"Where in my sentence did I say I was giving you a choice?"

I shake my head. Definitely not getting on that thing again.

"Come on, take a chance."

His insistent gaze refuses to leave me. I feel his eyes piercing through my skull. I can't go. It would be wrong. This is Haze Adams, the guy who started this whole mess by making the deal. My mind screams no.

But my body isn't listening.

"Give me that," I sigh, and he smiles victoriously when I put on the helmet.

There's something about him that makes it hard to say no.

That could be the title of a movie about teenage pregnancy.

I mentally laugh at my own joke and realize if people could read my mind, they'd probably think I'm crazy.

For the first time, I'm not following him by obligation. I have no excuse. But I tell myself that maybe I'll get him to cancel the fight. That if I get closer, we might avoid all of this. In that moment, as much as I hate to admit it, I want to follow him.

It's all me.

"You want to get to know me? Fine."

I don't reply and hold on to him.

"Just remember you asked for it."

EIGHT

Rooftop And Confessions

"I can't believe I'm trusting you right now." My words come out in a whisper.

We've been on the road for a good twenty minutes. I try and gather as much information as I possibly can to at least get a small idea as to where we're going, but the truth is, I've never been in this part of town before. A quick glimpse of my surroundings is all it takes. I only have one word to say: *wealthy*. Everywhere I look, there are tall edifices with ceiling-high windows and rich families flaunting their gated houses with high fences.

Haze turns right, revealing an old washed-out building in the distance. The architecture and design give away that it's a school. To say it stands out from the perfectly mowed lawns and brand-new cars would be an understatement. It's quite obvious that it was abandoned many years ago. The closer we get, the less apparent it becomes that we're in a rich-kid neighborhood. The houses downgrade by the second as middle-class vibes find their way back to me.

"Let me guess, this is where we're going."

He doesn't reply.

"Is this the part I realize I followed a murderer?" I force a laugh, analyzing the edifice hovering in front of us.

There's something familiar about it.

"I already told you. I'm going to need you alive for when I win the fight."

I roll my eyes.

"Oh and for the thank-you kiss you owe me."

"I already told you, that's not happening."

"We'll see about that." The confidence oozing off him makes me blush.

"Where the hell are we?"

"My favorite place in the world."

The rumble of the engine wears away as the motorcycle comes to a stop near the creepy building. When I look up, all of my interrogations are drawn to a close.

The color and neat look of the bricks on the left side of the school bring it all back. They're new. Or at least, less old.

I recall a conversation between my mother and my aunt when I was younger about a high school that was almost destroyed by fire. Something about a rebellious student smoking inside the school and accidentally lighting it. Eight lives were lost. Tragic. They rebuilt the part that got completely destroyed but ended up shutting the school down anyway almost right after. I wonder why.

It's a bit surprising that it's still standing considering the neighborhood it's situated in. You'd assume they'd have gotten rid of it and replaced it with a mall by now.

"This is the abandoned high school, isn't it?" I say.

Haze and I both get off his bike. "The one and only."

"Your favorite place in the world is high school?" I can't hold back a chuckle.

"Its roof is my favorite place, smartass."

"And how are we supposed to reach it?" I glance up. It isn't exactly something you can easily climb to.

"I'll show you. Come on." I squirm when his hand drops to my back. He gives me a small push to get me to start walking. I try to ignore the goose bumps crawling all over my skin.

I wish he was ugly.

It would make things so much easier.

When we reach the back of the school, I'm quick to notice a cemetery is situated right across the street.

Cruel coincidence.

We stop in front of an incredibly old-looking ladder.

"No." I say.

"You're the one who wanted to know me."

"Technically, I never said that."

"Ladies first." He motions for me to climb. I raise an eyebrow in response. "Come on, what's the worst that can happen?"

"Gee, I don't know. I can fall, break my back, break a leg, get arrested for trespassing. I can—"

He cuts me off, grinning. "Okay. Okay. You've made your point."

"Is this even legal?" I take a step forward.

"Of course. I've done it multiple times and never got into trouble."

"Says the guy who gets away with everything."

"You scared, Kingston?" He raises his eyebrows, a challenging smile spread across his face. "I didn't take you for a quitter."

I stare at him intently, his blue eyes getting the best of me. I can't deny this irresistible need to prove him wrong. This guy knows exactly how to push my buttons. I take a deep and long breath and begin the climb. By the time I reach the roof, I am confident that I just beat the world's record for fastest ladder climbing. Haze follows right behind me.

"Show's this way," he says, getting onto the roof.

Confused, I turn around. My mouth drops. I guess I was too busy trying to breathe properly again to notice the picture-postcard view before my eyes. The mesmerizing and distant landscape make the biggest buildings look like tiny dots and the cars like grains of salt. I can only imagine how amazing it must be at night. The city lights must be to die for.

"Wow." I let out.

"Tell me about it."

We don't move or speak for a couple of seconds, both in complete awe. He breaks the silence. "Come on."

He leads the way toward the edge of the brick-built school and casually sits down, his legs hanging off the building. He stares blankly ahead of him, completely unaffected by the fact that the only thing separating him from death is a few feet.

"What are you waiting for?" he beckons.

I sigh and hesitantly step in his direction.

"What's to say you won't push me off?"

He smiles. "Who would insult me through text messages, then?"

When I sit down next to him, it takes everything I have not to look down at the void under me. I make sure to keep an acceptable distance between the two of us, not about to let him break the touch barrier any more than he already has.

"How does that make me know you better, if I may?"

He doesn't answer at first, throwing a rock down the abandoned building.

"I never brought anyone here. Just knowing this exists makes you know me better than a lot of people."

When his sharp eyes meet mine, I understand them—Bianca, the random girl at the restaurant, and the group of girls in math class who swoon over him even if he is the definition of trouble.

There's something about him.

Something about the way he talks that could make any girl

feel special. Maybe it's the way he looks at you like you're all he sees. Or the way he knows exactly what to say to get your heart racing. This boy could convince anyone that he cares if he wanted to.

And that's probably the most dangerous thing about him.

"I come here to think," he continues.

"Does it help?" I pick up a rock lying next to me and throw it down the building, as well.

"The silence usually does."

I smile. I'm giving him everything but silence. "Sorry."

He lets out a laugh. "That's not what I meant."

"I'm pretty sure a lot of buildings provide a good view. Why here?"

"I used to go to this school before… you know."

Part of me wants to ask a million questions, but the other fears it might be a bit of a sensitive topic. I decide to try anyway.

"Did you know anyone that—"

I don't have to finish my sentence. Our eyes connect. He knows that I'm talking about the victims.

"A couple." The usual coldness that always fills his tone whenever a somewhat personal question is brought up comes rushing back.

"So…" I try and think of a different topic. "Why don't you live with your parents?"

"They're annoying, that's all." Sharp. Blunt. He is not in the mood to discuss his life. As always.

I stiffen up, a bit taken aback.

He gives me his version of an apology. "It's just… I don't like talking about them."

"Just like you don't want to talk about this school. Got it," I mutter more to myself than to him.

The truth catches up to me. There will never be a way for me to know him better. Haze Adams obviously isn't the leader of the West Side and an unbeatable fighter for his honesty and social skills.

This is wrong. Me spending time with him, him taking me to his "secret" spot. This is all so wrong.

"You want to get to know me? Let's play ten questions."

I sigh. He's trying in his own way, I guess.

"You first."

He pauses, waiting for the right words to come to him. "Favorite color?"

"Red. Yours?"

"Black."

I smother a chuckle. This is the most predictable answer he could've possibly given. He is almost always wearing black.

"Biggest fear?" he asks.

"Serious life-changing one or dumb one?"

"Both." He raises his eyebrows. "Start with the dumb one."

"That's easy. Clowns."

I am not surprised when he howls with laughter.

"Shut up, it's not funny."

"It's a little funny considering that you're hanging out with criminals and the only thing that crosses your mind is your fear of clowns."

He's not wrong.

"It sounds way worse when you put it like that."

His smile only grows wider. "And the serious one?"

"It's a very deep and complicated road you're taking, Mr. Adams."

He doesn't speak at first, looking deeply into my eyes.

"Maybe I like complicated."

His eyes drop to my lips for a little too long, and my heart decides now is the perfect time to pretend it's a drum in my rib cage. I flush and break the eye contact, repressing the many conflicted emotions running in my veins. What was that?

"I think I'm afraid of regrets," I mumble.

He doesn't say a word, waiting for a backstory of some sort, until he finally blurts. "Oh come on, no explanation?"

I sigh, the shadow of a smile tugging at my lips.

"I'm talking about the 'down the road' regrets. You know, the 'I failed at life' regrets," I confide. "I'm scared of that moment when you wake up in bed with your boring husband that you haven't had sex with in months and curse because you have to go to that job you hate that you only got to pay your

145

bills. I'm afraid of the moment you look around and realize you fucked up. The moment you realize that you settled for something you knew wouldn't make you happy because it seemed like the right thing to do. Or maybe you settled for this guy you knew wasn't the love of your life, but he was here, emotionally available, and he was stable. So you stayed. I'm afraid of not trying everything I want and choosing a routine over an adventure. I'm afraid, no—I'm terrified of surviving instead of living and doing all the right things for the wrong reasons."

I finish my speech and narrow my eyes, realizing that I basically just told Haze her story—my mother's. My biggest fear is to end up like her. Angry, unsatisfied, bitter, knocked up at sixteen by the neighborhood's trashy boy and kicked out to the curb by her own parents. She was a single mother for years before she found a "great guy" to marry. Deep down, I know she'll never look at my stepfather the way she looked at my biological one. Harry was convenient, stable, and he loved her. She said yes, but her heart screamed no. That's probably why she's always been so cold to me. To everyone.

Because she did all the right things for the wrong reasons.

Haze presses his lips together, the silence surrounding us as thick as it could ever be.

"That was deep."

"I warned you." I crack a smile. "What about you—what's

146

your biggest fear?"

"That's going to be a tough speech to follow." He lowers his head, getting a clear shot of his feet hanging above the emptiness. "It's probably to end up alone."

"Do tell." I rest my chin in the palm of my hand, giving him my undivided attention.

"There's not much to say really. My family is the living proof that it's not worth having material things if you don't have what matters. Nobody's standing up at your funeral to say that you had a big house and an expensive car."

To say his words don't resonate deep within my core would be a lie. He's right. Having things will not make your life complete. Friends and family will. Under all the attitude, cocky comments, and jaw-dropping smiles, there's a guy with decent values and fears like everybody else.

Something tells me it's been a while since he had a chance to show it.

"And the other one?"

"I don't have another one."

"Come on. I don't care if it's silly."

He sighs, a small smile covering his face.

"Fine, but you have to promise not to laugh."

"I won't, I promise." I put my hands up.

He takes a breath. "I'm afraid of spiders."

All of my good intentions vanish as quickly as they appeared when the words escape his lips, and I break into uncontrollable laughter. I cover my mouth with my hand.

"You can't be serious?" I say, laughing so hard I can't breathe.

"Shut up. I wouldn't say afraid—it's more of a hate thing. I swear I can kill it, but if somebody else can do it, I'm not going anywhere near that thing even if you pay me."

"So you're not afraid of illegal street fights that put your life in immediate danger, but you have a problem with a tiny innocent spider?"

"You're no better with your fear of clowns, Kingston." He says, a hint of a smile on his lips.

A silence that's oddly reassuring follows. We don't speak for a good minute, but it doesn't feel uncomfortable. My mind isn't racing, and I'm not desperately looking for something to say. It's like we know that we don't have to. That we don't *need* to.

"What happened here?" I look down the building that's obviously been the victim of time. "Doesn't make sense. Why would you spend that much money on rebuilding a school that you're going to close anyway?"

"That's the thing. They never intended to close it."

I frown.

"They thought they could carry on until multiple lawsuits from the parents who'd lost their kids were dropped on them. Something about the school not supervising their students enough and letting the kid light the cigarette that accidentally killed his classmates. Not to mention the lost lives didn't exactly owe them the best enrollment record. They closed it, blocked every entrance, and it's just been rotting there ever since."

"How old were you when it closed?"

"Sixteen." He shrugs. "Then I got into Riverside High."

I nod, understanding that this is as many questions as he'll accept to answer on this topic. I'm relieved when the conversation drifts to lighter subjects. We discuss so many things, such as favorite animal or favorite meal, slowly learning more about each other.

I can't lie. Haze Adams is far from an open book. It's hard to know him. Or at least, on a deeper level. It's like he's terrified of letting someone, anyone, close to him.

I can't imagine how lonely that must be.

It almost makes you wonder if anyone even knows him at all.

When I realize that night has set upon the city, I glance down at my phone and gasp.

We've been talking for three hours.

"Oh my God," I say. "It's 7:30 already? We have to go."

"Why? You have a date or something?" he teases.

"Wouldn't you like to know?"

The truth is, Kass is coming home at eight. If she sees I'm not home then, she'll know I was out, and if she finds out who I was out with, she'll never let me hear the end of it.

We get up and head back down the creepy ladder. When my feet hit the ground, I let out a breath of relief and look up, thanking the Lord. Haze makes fun of me for being a chicken, and I don't hesitate to bring up his fear slash hate of spiders.

I glance at the wooden ladder one last time, surprised that it hasn't collapsed yet.

I look back at him, and my smile fades when I notice the frown plastered on his face. He seems to be on the lookout, staring straight ahead of him at something in the distance.

The cemetery on the other side of the street.

That's when I see them.

The silhouettes.

There's four of them. They're tall, broad-shouldered, and dressed in black from head to toe. Every nerve in my body is telling me that something might be wrong. When they start walking toward us, I don't just think something is wrong—*I know it.* Haze's actions confirm my thoughts when he turns around abruptly, and I find myself locked in his gaze.

"Keep your head down, and don't say a word. If I tell you to run, you run and you don't look back. Do you understand me?" His eyes are dark. Severe.

Fear consumes me as I glance up at him.

"Winter, do you understand? I need you to say it."

I nod. "I understand."

He steps in front of me, blocking the view I have of them.

150

His tall and broad physique operates as a human shield between the four strangers and me. He's suddenly a completely different person from who he was barely a couple of minutes ago. He clenches his jaw and his fists, ready to fight.

When they stop a couple of steps away from us, I keep my head down, ignoring the weight of their hostile gazes on my shoulders. Darkness has set upon the neighborhood, which makes it hard for me to see their faces clearly.

"Haze." The taller one speaks. He seems to be around twenty-five and the leader of the four, somehow radiating power and violence.

"Ian," Haze says.

I frown. I think I've heard that name before. But where?

"What are you doing around here?" he asks, trying to look over Haze's shoulder.

"Remembering."

"I see you're with a friend." Ian smiles.

And when I say smile, I mean a "I want no trouble with you, but I would kill you in a heartbeat if I had to" smile.

"Congratulations, you have eyes."

"Isn't that the East Side girl?" Ian glares at me.

"That's really none of your business, is it?" *Cold* is the word to describe his tone.

"Considering our…" Ian pauses, searching for the right words to say. "*Situation*, I think it is." The tension keeps on growing by the second.

Haze takes a menacing step forward. "I'm sorry. Am I crazy, or did you just question me?"

Ian seems to forget how to properly speak English, his gaze meeting the ground. "No, of course not. I would never. Just making sure we're on the same page, that's all."

Haze tilts his head to the side. "Are you sure? Because that's not what it sounded like."

"Let's forget that this happened," Ian mumbles.

"Yeah, let's do that," Haze spits.

He's scared of him. No, he's terrified. How can a twenty-five-year-old be terrified of an eighteen-year-old boy? Kendrick wasn't kidding when he said Haze is the best fighter of them all.

Realization crashes against me. Kendrick. That's where I heard Ian's name. Ian is the leader of the North Side. They're Haze's allies. But that means...

Haze risked ruining his alliance for me.

But why?

The four guys give us one last killer look and turn away, gradually disappearing into the night. There are so many ways that this could have gone wrong. So many ways I could've gotten hurt. If Haze hadn't protected me, who knows where I'd be right now? I curse, fighting the urge to slap myself. Why'd you even let yourself get into this situation at all, Winter? Why did you follow him?

"Are you okay?" he looks down at me.

"Why did you bring me here?" The words fall out in a more hateful manner than I intended.

Haze doesn't budge, apparently unaffected.

"Because I wanted to."

"Is it to get my trust? To upset Kendrick? Because it's already done. You got what you wanted."

He breathes out a sigh. "Why are you being like this?"

"Why are *you* being like this?" I say right back. "They're right. You're my cousin's enemy. You can't hate him and spend time with me, Haze. You can't have both. That's not how it works."

His wandering gaze carefully avoids mine. He doesn't speak. He knows I'm right.

"This bonding thing we have going on, it has to stop. Just drive me home, please."

The silence that follows makes it clear the conversation is over.

He walks toward his parked motorcycle, an unreadable expression covering his face. I follow not so far behind. One second, he's this funny, kind, and charming guy, and the next he looks ready to rip someone's head off with his teeth.

I can't figure him out, and I hate myself for wanting to unravel him. For wanting to understand the secrets hidden behind his blue eyes.

The ride home is painfully long. He doesn't speak or make

flirty jokes that trap me in a fluster like he usually does. I make it a point to remind myself that this is wrong. That I can't be friends with him or trust him. Kendrick said it so many times. It's probably an act, all of it. If it is, if Haze really is playing me, the boy deserves a goddamn Oscar.

When I get off the killing machine he uses as his main way of transportation, I mentally curse in anticipation of the most awkward goodbye in the history of goodbyes. I reach for the helmet and try my best to remove it, already picturing the dramatic scene that's coming.

But there's just one slight problem. The helmet refuses to come off, vowing to love me until death do us part.

"Come on," I mutter under my breath, using all of my strength to get rid of the unwelcomed guest now living on my head.

Haze doesn't say a word, watching me struggle for a couple of minutes.

Please, not now.

On failed attempt number three, Haze finally reacts—but not the way I want him to.

He starts laughing.

"Seriously?" He kills the ignition and gets off his bike. "Stop moving. You'll rip your head off."

Feeling my cheeks heat up from the sudden burst of embarrassment, I do as I'm told. He steps closer in an attempt to set me free. He tries once. Then once becomes twice. Still, the helmet doesn't budge.

He presses his lips together, hardly suppressing the mocking smirk remolding his lips.

"Haze, just get it off."

"I'm trying, I swear. When did you grow such a big head, Kingston?"

I roll my eyes, ignoring his comment. When the helmet wins round number five, Haze has no choice but to admit defeat.

"We need soap. Or water. Anything to make it slippery."

I squirm. "What? Tell me you're kidding."

"Would you rather go to the hospital?" I can hear the amusement in his voice.

Horrifying images of me walking into the emergency room with a helmet stuck on my head wash over me. I don't think my ego can take that today. *Or ever.*

I'm assuming that the sight of me with a helmet stuck on my head is enough to destroy any trace of attraction Haze might've ever felt toward me, if it ever existed at all.

I glance at the empty driveway and hesitate.

"I don't exactly have a choice, do I?"

Haze and I walk side by side, making our way toward the entrance. He snickers. "Looks like the Universe doesn't want the bonding to be over just yet."

In that moment, I look up to the sky and all I can think is,

"STOP MOVING FOR GOD'S SAKE," HAZE complains for the billionth time.

"Easy for you to say. You're not the one with this thing stuck on your head," I say. "Which, by the way, isn't exactly weightless."

"Oh, I'm sorry, princess. I shouldn't have given you a helmet. It's not like it can save your life or anything."

It's been like this for the past fifteen minutes. The bonding session quickly turned into a sarcasm battle. He's been doing everything he possibly can to remove the helmet from my head, rubbing soap and water all over my neck. I'd probably be affected by the physical contact if this heavy-ass helmet wasn't weighing down on me and giving me a headache.

"We might have to go to the hospital," he says. "I mean, you can't exactly keep it on your head forever, can you?"

I find myself laughing at that. Yes, laughing. At this point, I'd much rather laugh about it than cry. This whole situation is the definition of ridiculous, and although right now it sucks, I'm sure I'll laugh about it one day.

"They could make a documentary about me."

He clears his throat. "Helmet girl. When Winter was eighteen years old, her head got stuck in a motorcycle helmet. People were never able to get it off. She's been living without makeup

156

and hasn't brushed her teeth ever since."

I laugh harder at his narrator voice.

"Winter?"

My heart crawls up my throat when a familiar voice interrupts us. I turn around and see Kassidy through the tinted glass of the helmet. Standing in the doorway to the bathroom, she is looking at us with an expression that's worth a million dollars. I completely forgot that she was coming home at nine.

"This isn't what it looks like," I say instinctively.

Haze smothers a laugh. "Tell me, what exactly does this look like?"

I look up at the broad-shouldered guy next to me. His hands are covered in soap, while I'm wearing a motorcycle helmet. I have no idea what scenario popped up in her mind, but I'm pretty sure that whatever she thinks she saw, she's wrong.

"You know what? I don't even want to know." She shakes her head in disapproval and exits the bathroom before I have a chance to justify myself.

As soon as the door is shut closed, Haze and I share an awkward look and burst out laughing

This day just keeps on getting better and better.

"If she tells Kendrick, I'm dead," I say.

"What could she possibly tell him? He had soap in his hands and she had a helmet on her head?"

He has a point. I can't think of a credible way to explain this.

Haze goes back to trying to free my poor head. After a painfully long while, the helmet finally decides that it's done fucking with me and cooperates.

"Oh my God," I say, staring at myself in the mirror.

"What?"

"I have a face."

We laugh again.

His gaze drifts from me to his phone. "I hate to put an end to our second date, but I have to go."

I consider fighting him on the D word again but decide against it. He's right, and although I profoundly hate myself for it, I did go out with him for the second time tonight.

"I'll see you at school?" I can tell from the way he chews on the inside of his mouth with a hesitant stance that he's debating on something.

He glimpses at my lips but rips his eyes away shortly after.

I hand him his helmet, or should I say my own personal nightmare, and watch him stride toward the door. Just as he's about to open it, he turns around, smiling,

"Hey, Kingston?" he says quietly.

I look at him.

"Thank you for getting to know me."

I try and ignore the feeling of warmth spreading deep within me.

I smile as he reaches for the door handle.

"Hey, Adams?"

His blue eyes collide with mine.

"Thank you for showing me you were worth knowing."

A smug grin widens across his strong features. He looks at me one last time and walks out of the room. Seconds later, I hear the front door being shut. I walk out of the first-floor bathroom and come face-to-face with Kassidy. She doesn't say a word at first, but the look she gives me is full of blame.

"Thank you for showing me you were worth knowing? Seriously?" She raises her eyebrows, her tone judgmental and cold.

I don't reply, walking around her in an attempt to escape her speech.

"When you catch feelings and he drops you, don't say I didn't warn you."

I enter my bedroom and shut the door, hearing the roar of a motorcycle fade out outside.

His words echo in the back of my head. *Thank you for getting to know me.* He's right. I know him... and it could turn out to be the worst thing that's ever happened to me.

NINE

Gone

My favorite part of the day has always been when it ends. Don't get me wrong, I've never particularly hated school, nor have I ever particularly liked it, but I always loved that feeling of knowing that you're done for the day and going home. I walk toward the exit with Kass. My cousin's words sound distant although she is right beside me. She's been going on for the past five minutes about how her science teacher, is completely nuts, but I can't seem to focus.

He wasn't in class today.

Or yesterday.

Or the day before that.

I know I shouldn't care or even notice, but the only empty desk in the class was pretty dang hard to ignore. Especially when it's been three days since he gave me any sign of life. He said, "See you at school," didn't he? I think he needs to work on his definition of "see you." It usually requires both people being in the same place.

I haven't texted him. If he wanted to talk to me, he would. I'm guessing the sight of me with a helmet stuck on my head finally did the trick and he lost interest.

"Are you even listening to me?" Kass waves her hand in front of my eyes.

"I'm sorry, I was…" I begin but then realize I have no idea what I could possibly say to her. I was thinking about Haze? "What were you saying?"

She picks up from the start, but I stop listening again, barely two words in.

Tonight I get to see Kendrick for the first time since he got beat up by Tanner. The guys said he looked better. Or at least, less awful. Will's supposed to be waiting for me in front of the school so we can ride to Blake's place together.

I still can't believe that Kendrick convinced Maria to justify his absence for four days while he's staying with his depressed "girlfriend." He promised that the guys—who he shares every class with—would bring his homework over every day.

I think she's either blinded by the hope that her son might actually be in love and ready to walk a straight line, or she knows a lot more than she lets on.

"So, what do you think?" Kass finishes her speech, and her gaze shifts to me.

"Uh…" I have no idea what she's going on about. "You're right. That sounds great."

"Really?" She bounces up and down in excitement. "Thank you, thank you, thank you. I promise you won't regret it."

Damn it. What did I just agree to?

"I know you had a crappy experience last time, but it's different since it's a pool party, and I promise I'll stick with you all night long. I just need to get my mind off some things."

Great. I agreed to a party.

God knows the last one went so well.

I do understand why she wants me to come though. Kass's friends aren't the best wingwomen. I eat lunch with them and Kass regularly, and although they're great, they're polar opposites. Morgan is a bit awkward, big on books and hell-bent on getting into a great school. She's never had a drink or gone to a party before. As for Zoey, she's boy and fashion obsessed, loves to party, but always ends up ditching Kass halfway through the night to make out with the football team. She's in her rebound phase. She just got out of a three-year relationship.

"Where did you say it is?" I ask.

"I didn't. It's at Natasha's house—you've might've heard of her? She's a friend of Bianca. Redhead, tall, gorgeous."

Natasha. I know where I heard that name before. She's the girl who hit on Haze at the diner last weekend. But why would she hit on him if she's friends with Bianca? Wouldn't she know that Bianca's crazy in love with him? That's harsh.

"Does she go here?" I analyze my surroundings, looking for her ginger hair in the moving crowd.

"Nah. She's in a private school. Rich daddy and all."

I nod. We reach the front door and walk out, pushed around

by the students who are all as eager as I am to get this day over with.

"Anyway, I've got a shift at the store in thirty minutes. You're okay to get home?"

"Yeah, Will's driving me."

An unreadable look crawls into her eyes. "He is?"

"Yeah. Something wrong?"

"No. Just surprised that he knows what a nice gesture is, that's all." She purposefully ignores my eyes set on her. "I'll see you at home. Don't forget. Tomorrow, 9:30 sharp." She turns away, heading for her car that's parked in its usual spot.

I watch her stride across the parking lot and shake my head, trying not to overthink her confusing behavior. *That's just Kass being Kass.*

On a positive note, the party is not today. I have a whole day before she drags me to hell. There's no school on Friday this week. So, of course, that means a massive pool party on a Thursday.

I'm ripped away from my racing thoughts when I see Will's car in the distance. I march toward him and slide into the passenger seat.

"What took you so long?" he asks.

"Kass begging me to go to a party I don't want to go to. What's new?"

He doesn't laugh, the smile on his lips fading away. "A party, huh?" He slightly clenches his jaw, his fingers tightly wrapped around the steering wheel. What's with him? "Didn't you use to have to drag her to those?"

"Yeah. I guess she had a change of heart. Something about needing to get her mind off some things. Whatever that means." I stare out the window.

Will doesn't reply, giving off a vibe that's positively frosty. It's no secret that Will and Kass don't really get along, but I didn't know it was to the point of drastically changing attitude at the mere sound of each other's name.

"How's Kendrick doing?"

"Not too bad. You'll see for yourself." He turns on the radio, making it clear he is not interested in small talk.

I have no idea what caused this mood swing, and frankly, I don't even have the energy to overthink it. I bury my earplugs in my ears and throw my head back, my worries vanishing with every note.

That's when my phone lights up with a text message.

> You looked gorgeous today.

I stare at the screen in shock. I have no idea what he did these past three days, but the fact that he didn't try and annoy me until now tells me he must've been really busy. But doing what? Maybe he was with Bianca. I haven't seen her much at school either. The thought leaves a bitter taste in my mouth.

Why the hell do I care?

Says the guy who didn't show up to school.

I don't need to. I know you looked good.

Does that line usually work for you?

Usually, but you're not like other girls.

Violently vomits at how cheesy you are

Violently keeps on being cheesy

Give me one good reason why I shouldn't kill you as it seems it's the only way to get you to leave me alone.

There's no Netflix in jail.

I can't help but laugh at his message. It comes out a bit louder than I'd anticipated, raising suspicion from Will, who peeks at me from the corner of his eyes. Thankfully, he doesn't go as far as to question who I'm texting.

> Why haven't you been at school?

I had stuff to do.

> Like what?

Like not be at school. Badum tsss.

> You know, if you put as much energy into your studies as you put into dodging questions, you'd be a freaking genius.

Did you just give me a compliment

I sigh. He's never going to answer me. It's no use.

> Why are you still texting me?

Because I like talking to you.

> Well, you shouldn't. I meant what I said Sunday night. We need to stop.

"We're here." Will's breathy voice brings me back to reality.

I look up to see Blake's washed-out apartment complex ahead of me. Will pulls up into the guest parking spot and motions to get out of the car, which I do, dragging my feet and trying my best not to check if Haze replied. Then, as Will leads the way toward the main entrance of the brownstone building, I can't help but give in to the curiosity.

What if I don't want to

I text back that I'll talk to him later and bury my phone deep in my pocket. I can't keep doing this. I need to get this boy out of my head and focus on what's really important here: Kendrick.

We go up the stairs, heading for the fourth floor. I try my best to ignore the throbbing guilt I've come to know very well in the past few weeks. There are a million reasons why I should get him out of my life.

But my stupid self still tries and find the one reason not to.

BLAKE'S LIVING ROOM IS SUN SOAKED and barely furnished. You'd assume with the money he makes from the fights, he'd be able to afford a kitchen table. A red couch is pushed up against the wall of his one-bedroom apartment, and a lamp is placed in the right corner next to it. I'm guessing his excuse of a couch is where my cousin has been sleeping. Blake lives alone, which is convenient for Kendrick, but two guys living by themselves also means dishes in the sink, unwashed floors, and empty beer bottles.

I'm so relieved when Kendrick walks out of the bedroom that I pull him into a hug. He isn't as bad as I thought he would be; the dark bruises on his face and neck are still very much visible but they're starting to fade. I've tried asking Blake why he's not living with his parents, but he remains very secretive about it.

"I'm hungry," Kendrick says, his hand on his stomach.

"Me too. You guys want to go get some food?" Blake asks.

"Sure. I just need to shower first." Kendrick gets up and winces in pain. Tanner got him good. He enters the bathroom, shutting the door behind him.

Will turns to us. "We still haven't found a girl to play Kendrick's girlfriend."

"I know," Blake sighs. "We tried everything, but no one's up to the task."

"Well, then, we don't have a choice." Will shrugs, sliding his hand into his pocket to get his phone out.

"What are you doing?" I frown.

"Desperate times call for desperate measures," he says, dialing a number.

I look at Alex and Blake in confusion. "What's he doing?"

168

"Will, we can try again. You don't have to do that." Alex begs.

"We've been trying for days now. Plus, Maria already knows her. It's perfect."

I raise my voice. "Knows who?"

Alex scolds. "Kendrick made it clear he never wants to see her again."

"Oh please. We both know they have that weird 'I hate you but want you' chemistry going on." Will rolls his eyes.

"Who are you talking about?"

They remain silent like they're scared to say her name.

"We're calling Nicole."

Cue the dramatic music.

Although I have absolutely no idea who this Nicole is, so it's not dramatic at all.

"Kendrick's ex-girlfriend," Blake adds when he sees how clueless I am.

It all comes back.

"Oh my God, you mean…"

"Yeah, the one you think we're talking about."

Kendrick only had one serious girlfriend in his life, and it did not end well. Will puts the call on speaker.

Nicole picks up. "Hello?"

Will grins. "Hey, Nicky, it's been a while."

"For the love of God, what did Kendrick do this time?"

Will spends close to thirty minutes with her on the phone. He proceeds to explain it all to her, and even though she isn't easy to convince, she gives in and accepts to help us out.

William hangs up, the guys glaring at him.

"Now, how are we going to tell Kendrick?"

I stop listening.

Hiring Kendrick's ex-girlfriend—which ended with a horrible breakup—to hide from his mother that he got beat up and can barely walk?

What else could I want to do on a Wednesday night?

LOCKING MYSELF UP IN MY BEDROOM and stepping into a scorching hot shower, just the way I like them, is the first thing I do when Will drops me off in front of my house. It's close to eleven already.

We went out to eat and ended up spending hours trying to get a fry out of Will's nose. He thought he was so funny when he put it up his nostril but quickly changed his mind when the fry decided it felt at home. I haven't checked my phone since I came back.

Only one message awaits me.

What are you wearing?

Of course.

> Creep.

As always, he texts back almost right away.

> Just answer.

> Pajamas. Why?

> I think this would look really good on you.

Haze Adams sent a picture.

I click on the attachment and frown in confusion. Something must've gone wrong. He sent me a blank picture.

> It didn't work. It's a picture of nothing.

Minutes go by.

> Exactly

It hits me.

> OMG. Stop!

> Never;)

Did you really ask me that just so you could plug in your stupid joke?

Maybe...

You're unbelievable.

My phone chimes again.

Call me now.

Hi Now. How are you?

You think you're so funny, don't you?

As a matter of fact, I do.

I'm serious. Call me. You don't even need to say anything. I just need an excuse to leave

What do I get out of it?

I'll stop texting you for like 2 days.

One week.

5 days.

And you cancel the deal.

Don't push it.

One week without texting
or you find another excuse.

Fine. One week.

Good boy.

Holding my breath, I divert my fingers to the call button. He picks up on the first ring.

"Hey. I know I'm late. I'm coming. I'm sorry, I got held up," he says before I can get a word in.

"Do you really have to leave so soon?" I hear a female voice say in the background.

Bianca.

"Yeah. Yeah. I'll be there in ten."

"But—" she says, but she's cut off by Haze hanging up.

He's with Bianca. That's probably where he's been these past few days. I should've known. A new message comes through almost right away.

Thanks. I owe you one.

You do know she's head over heels in love with you?

I mean... It's not my fault I'm irresistible.

You need to stop playing with people's feelings.

It's not playing if I'm completely honest with her. She knows I don't do romance.

But she does. She loves you. How would you feel if you were constantly around a person you like without ever truly being with them?

Idk. Never experienced it.

You keep telling yourself that. No texting period begins now.

:(

I turn off my phone and rest my head on my pillow, the burning ache in my chest spreading. I shouldn't feel this way.

I shouldn't care.

But I do.

TEN
Back For You

I've always wondered what it would be like to not have to go to school. Or work a full-time job. Or do anything that requires spending years of your life doing something repetitive for survival reasons. What would we do with our time? If there was no such thing as "money," would we go back to desperately fighting for our food? How quickly could a well-balanced society turn into a war zone if we all truly were equals and numbers didn't define our ability to see another day? If you could just go to the store and pick up what you wanted without paying for it, would chaos enfold our world?

My guess is yes.

Our entire lives basically consist of giving away our time so that we can have more of it. And in the end, that time we earned will also be given away in exchange for more time. It's a never-ending cycle. Money is not the main thing a job gives you. A job gives you a tomorrow. A future. *Survival.*

I have no idea why I'm thinking about this right now. My packed high school cafeteria isn't exactly my first choice for a moment when I'm questioning everything and anything. But then again, my random and philosophic thoughts might have something to do with my desperate need to not let my mind be consumed by other things.

And by other things, I mean Haze Adams.

I haven't checked my phone since yesterday. If he doesn't want to stop and I don't want to stop, all that's left to do is remove the choice from the equation.

I know if I read his messages, I'll be tempted to answer, and I don't trust myself not to.

Still no sign of him at school. If his three days of ghosting tell me anything, it's that he probably won't show today either.

Kass has been talking for an unbearably long ten minutes about how incredibly excited she is to attend Natasha's party. Zoey squeals in agreement. As for Morgan, to my great surprise, she actually seems invested in the conversation, too. Looks like the straight A student grew a sudden interest for the dark side.

I wish I could reciprocate Kass's excitement, but all I can think about is the risk I'm taking by going to another party after what happened. The boys said it should be fine. That it's actually better to be in a large crowd than to stay home like a sitting duck. But still, Will, Blake, and Alex decided to come along to keep me safe just in case.

Because it definitely has nothing to do with the free booze and the multiple girls running around in their bikinis.

The clock reads that only fifteen short minutes separate us from the beginning of next period. I tell the girls I'll see them later and exit the cafeteria. I know that getting to my locker is going to be much harder than I anticipated when I see the crowd of students gathered in the hall. I make my way through the sea of teenagers and freeze.

What is he doing here?

With his back against my locker and his hands deep in his pockets, he's glancing around, obviously waiting for someone.

Me.

He's wearing a black T-shirt, the tightness of the sleeves complementing the ripped and perfectly defined muscles of his arms. This is ridiculous. He looks like he stepped off the cover of a freaking magazine

Stop drooling.

The absence of anxiety in his features throws me off. He's relaxed, casual, while I am the very definition of a nervous wreck.

His gaze travels up to my face, his eyes so sharp they could cut through the toughest diamonds. I consider walking in the opposite direction for a second but decide against it. It's too late. He's already staring at me.

And he's already smiling.

That goddamn smile.

"Look who decided to rise from the dead." I stop in front of him.

He smirks. "Well, hello to you, too, Kingston."

"What do you want?" I try and push him off my locker but fail miserably. He barely moves, crossing his buff arms against his chest. I sigh as my eyes stick to his tattooed arm where the numbers *04/16* are on display. I still have no idea what it means. I doubt he'd tell me if I asked.

"I came to ask you what you're doing tonight."

"Seriously?" I scoff. "You're not going to acknowledge the fact that you disappeared for three days at all?"

Does he really think a couple of text messages magically make up for his disappearance?

He tilts his head to the side and shrugs. "I had business to take care of. I told you."

Still no real answer.

"I see." I sigh. "Can you please move?"

He doesn't budge. "I know a place if you want."

"A place for what?"

"For your phone. It's obviously broken since you're not texting back."

I can't stop a grin from growing across my face. Dang it. I'm supposed to be mad at him.

"We're in a no-texting period, remember?"

He pouts. "What? But I thought you were kidding."

"I wasn't. Plus, you can't just show up to my locker like this. Kendrick may be gone for now, but the boys still go to school," I warn, well aware that he doesn't care.

"What are they going to do? Attack me in the hall?" He snorts and glances around. "Let them try."

Students pass us, making sure to stare for as long as humanly possible. I can literally hear them thinking, *What the hell does Haze Adams want with the new girl?*

"What are you doing tonight?" he asks.

He's not going to let it go.

"My cousin's dragging me to a party."

"You mean the pool party? You're actually going to that?"

I can discern a hint of shock in his features. He's probably surprised that I'd risk going to another party after the first one.

I nod as an answer.

"Do you really think it's safe after… you know." He doesn't finish his sentence, but he doesn't need to.

He steps out of the way, letting me access my locker. I open it, while he leans against the one next to mine.

"I can't hide under a rock for the rest of my life, can I?" I try to deny the raw edge of anxiety burning in my chest. "Plus, I could use a night off. My neighbor's dog's new thing is to bark until 3:00 a.m."

We lock eyes.

"You know if you need a place to stay, you can always sleep at my house."

"And sleep in the same house as your psycho brother? Sure. Sounds great. I haven't been strangled in a while."

He laughs and steps closer until his disturbingly addictive cologne reaches my nostrils. He doesn't speak, lowering his eyes to the tiled floor for a brief instant. He hovers over me, so tall I have to stretch my neck to get a good look at him.

"You know damn well I'd never let him lay a finger on you again."

My heart jolts in my chest.

I open my mouth to speak when—

"There you are."

Haze and I both jump and step away from each other. We turn our heads simultaneously. Next to us is Bianca. I take in her delicate features. She looks a hundred times better than she did the last time I saw her. But I mean, she'd just finished having sex with Haze so...

Ugh. *Vomit.*

Her eyes remain fixated on him as she completely ignores my presence.

"What happened to you last night? You left in such a hurry. You disappear for three days and then show up only to leave after ten minutes?"

I can't ignore the relief that pours over me. He wasn't with her these past three days. But then where was he?

Uncomfortable is the word to describe Haze's facial expression.

"I was busy." He shrugs.

Only then does Bianca deign to look at me. She looks me up

and down, obviously tearing me to pieces in her mind. I'm not sure if she recognizes me from her party.

"The party's tonight. You're coming, right?" She steps closer, biting on her lower lip in an attempt to seduce him. "I thought we could finish what we started last Sunday."

Realization punches me in the face.

That's why he had to leave on Sunday after he helped me remove the helmet. It was to go see her. I look down, a painful pit forming in my throat.

Haze's lips part as he stares at me, helpless. I pray that he won't try to explain himself. After all, he doesn't owe me anything. He is free to do what he wants.

Or, in this case, *who* he wants.

"Winter—"

I cut him off, grabbing my books and shutting my locker. "I have to get to class. I'll let you two talk."

The bell rings seconds later. I try and soothe the twinge of discomfort taking over me. Now that I think about it, a party might be just what I need.

"SHE DID NOT SAY THAT?" KASSIDY slurs, her fingers white-knuckled around the glass bottle she's holding.

Morgan chortles. "Yes. She did. I swear."

I can't even count how many times Kass has spilled beer on herself so far tonight. Bright side is she's wearing a bathing suit.

I look down to my outfit. I wasn't sure how to dress, since pool parties aren't exactly a common thing in Canada, so I opted for a simple tank top and shorts. I'm wearing my bathing suit under it but highly doubt that I'll go for a swim tonight. I think someone threw up in the pool already. Or is it the hot tub? I'm not sure.

Everywhere I look there are girls wearing very small pieces of fabric they call bathing suits, with red cups in their hands, and teenagers making out or grinding on each other.

Morgan decided to tag along and is currently drinking alcohol for the first time. Her tolerance is pretty much nonexistent, which makes it all the more hilarious.

Alex, Will, and Blake fell off the face of the earth almost as soon as we walked into Natasha's modern house. They said they'd keep their phones close if I needed anything, but something tells me that if they have to choose between my call and the open bar's call, the choice won't be hard.

"Kass, Luke's staring at you." Morgan giggles, taking another sip she'll probably regret tomorrow.

I turn around, scrutinizing my surroundings for Luke Jenson, a football player from school. I spot him, drinking out of a red cup and staring at Kass like she's the only girl in the room. Luke's actually a decent guy. He hangs out with the varsity team, which automatically means that he's friends with some douchebags, but overall, he's a nice kid. He's pretty cute, too.

"He's totally checking you out," I confirm, but Kass doesn't seem too excited about it.

She exhales. "He asked me out two days ago."

"What'd you say?"

"No."

Morgan is scandalized. "What? Why?"

I stop listening, my eyes roaming the room. I haven't seen him anywhere, and we've been here for a while now. Might have something to do with what happened in the hall.

I finish my drink in one gulp. "I have to go to the bathroom."

Natasha's house is slightly smaller than Bianca's, making it even harder to circulate around the house freely. When I spot a ridiculously long line of people, I assume that's where the bathroom is. But what I also know is, there is no way that this big-ass house only has one.

Too bad the geniuses in line haven't figured that out yet.

I go up to the third floor and sigh in relief. The party's still going strong downstairs, but as I predicted, the only people interested in coming here are the wasted couples looking for a hookup spot. Four doors surround me. I have no choice but to open them all until I find what I'm looking for. I mentally prepare myself to see drunk couples making out and eating each other's faces off.

At door number three, I begin to lose hope. I take a hesitant step toward the last door and reach for the handle with an unsteady hand.

What I see behind it leaves me speechless.

It doesn't matter how prepared I thought I was, I certainly wasn't ready for this. Their eyes land on me immediately. I make eye contact with Haze but quickly look away. I can't imagine what they must be thinking right now. I probably look like an idiot, standing in the doorway with my mouth agape.

Sitting on the edge of the bed, Bianca seems pissed. Her eyes are bloodshot. But this time, it has nothing to do with illegal substances.

She's holding back tears.

Haze's standing tall in front of her.

"Winter," he says, a bit surprised.

I speak rapidly and turn away. "I'm so sorry. I was looking for the bathroom."

"It's fine. We were done anyway," Bianca says and gets up.

She stops in front me, her eyes plunging into mine. I can tell she's going to say something.

And I can tell I'm not going to like it.

"I see the look in your eyes. I've been there, too. But take my advice—run. You're a phase. We all are." She turns her head and glares at him.

"Bianca…" Haze blows out a discouraged breath.

"I'm not done," she hisses. "You think you're so special, don't you? That you'll somehow be that one girl who makes him fall in love? News flash: you're not. And in the end, he'll get sick of you. Because guess what? You're not different. Or special. *No one is.*"

She walks around me, radiating rage. Her words sting, no matter how hard I try to deny them access to my heart. I have no idea what he said to her, but it certainly wasn't what she wanted to hear. Haze's gaze tries to connect with mine, but I ignore him and walk out of the room, striding down the long hallway.

"Winter, wait."

Here we go.

"Let me explain." He easily catches up to me, walking by my side.

"You don't have to explain yourself to me. You're free—"

He cuts me off. "I didn't sleep with her."

I stop in my tracks.

I hate to admit it, but I want to hear what he has to say.

If he carries on, we'll be crossing the line—the "let's pretend we're both unaware that there's something going on here" line.

"She showed up at my house on Sunday. I sent her away. Nothing happened. She just couldn't take a hint."

"Oh."

We don't speak for a couple of seconds. That still doesn't explain why he was with her when he asked me to call him.

"What'd you say to the poor girl to get her this mad?"

"I told her the truth. That I'm not interested in her. We can't keep doing this when she has feelings for me."

I half-smile. "How considerate of you."

"I know." He steps closer. "See? I'm a good guy sometimes."

"You just ended things with a girl that you *literally* only used for sex—don't push it."

"Oh come on, I don't even get a couple points in your redemption board for the noble gesture?"

"Nah. You actually have to earn the redemption points. You're going to have to do a lot better than that, Adams."

He smiles, following me down the stairs. When we reach the first floor, the loud music and the scent of a mixture of sweat and vomit overwhelm us. The bass crushes my chest unpleasantly. I wince.

Haze and I exchange a look. It says, *Are you thinking what I'm thinking?*

He looks down at me. "Want to get out of here?"

I'd like to say that I hesitated. That the multiple sirens going off in my head were enough to restrain me. But they didn't. I wanted to go. For the first time in forever, I didn't care if it was wrong. Because nothing had ever felt more right.

"I DON'T BELIEVE IT FOR A second." Haze shakes his head, the squeaking of the swing ringing in my ears.

Blatantly staring down at my feet, I try to remember the last time I swung in a park. I must've been around six years old. The streets are empty, enfolded in silence. I'd never be outside at this hour if Haze wasn't with me.

"I swear." I put my hands up. "I was alone for hours washing her car for Mother's Day. I was so tiny I could barely reach the windows."

"How old were you again?"

"Five."

"You were one determined kid, that's for sure. Was she happy?"

I shrug. "I don't know. She never really said anything."

Gratefulness would require for her to have a heart instead of a block of ice in its place.

"Sounds like your mom sucks."

His bluntness amuses me.

"I wish I could hate her. I really do. But even after all of this, she's still my mom, you know?"

He stares into the emptiness. "Yeah, I know the feeling."

"What about you? Any good childhood stories?"

The chances of him actually confessing something to me are slim, but I try anyway. He opens his mouth to speak and closes it.

"Let me guess, you don't want to talk about it?" I mentally chastise myself for hoping I could get something out of him. What was I thinking?

"It's not that." He looks conflicted. "It's just…"

I wait for him to speak, holding my breath.

"I can't think of a good memory."

Ouch.

Then, like he got too close to a forbidden place, he shakes his head, trying to remove the unwanted thoughts from his brain. There are so many questions I want to ask, so much more I want to know.

"Want to go for a walk?" He gets up from the swing.

I nod, following him on the empty sidewalk that borders the park.

I watch the cars pass us. "You're not who I thought you were."

"And who is that, may I ask?"

"A big-headed Mr. Know-it-all, player, daddy's spoiled little boy."

"And who am I now?"

"A *decent* big-headed Mr. Know-it-all, player, daddy's spoiled little boy."

He laughs. "How kind of you."

"I know." I laugh along with him.

"If we're being honest, you're not who I thought you were either."

"How come?"

"I thought you were wild when I met you. You know, since

you basically broke every single rule. But you're not. You're the definition of a good girl. A prude," he teases.

I jolt around to face him. I hit him in the arm, trying to hurt him, but end up hurting myself instead. What's his arm made of? Bricks?

I make a face. "I am not."

"Yes, you are."

"I'm not," I retort. "How am I a saint? I'm secretly hanging out with a street fighter, not to mention my cousin's nemesis, aren't I?" Guilt burdens me when the words leave my mouth. It sounds so much worse when I say it out loud.

He scoffs. "Oh come on, when's the last time you did something crazy? And I mean really crazy? Like the 'I'll tell my children this story' kind of crazy?"

"That's easy. Last week, I followed this guy onto the roof of an abandoned high school."

"That doesn't count. I practically had to carry you there."

"Whatever," I huff. "I'm not a prude."

He steps closer until his strong physique hovers over me.

"Then prove it."

The small proximity between us makes it hard to think.

Reboot the computer. I repeat, reboot the computer.

"And how am I supposed to do that?"

Haze glances around, analyzing the area. Then, after a good ten seconds, he speaks.

"Jump." He points at something.

I turn my head to see a public pool. At first, I crack up. One, because I expected something a bit more challenging, and two, because I'm wearing my bathing suit right now. It's perfect.

"All dressed," he adds.

Shit.

He walks toward the fenced pool where a large sign says "$10 for adults. $5 for kids." I follow him, my heart thumping loudly against my rib cage. The fence is high and surrounds the entire property. I'd have to do way more than get into a pool all dressed. I'd have to jump the fence and break in. That's a crime.

"Absolutely not."

"Then you admit that I'm right?"

If there's one thing I hate about Haze, it's his ability to make me want to do the craziest things just so I can prove him wrong. I'm not sure what it is. In every way, he's the bad influence I never knew I craved. The devil on my shoulders who tells me to let go.

To be wild.

"One minute, tops," I mutter.

A satisfied smile remolds his lips as he nods. I can't believe I'm doing this. Haze and I look around carefully, making sure we're alone. I struggle to climb over the fence while he watches me, already on the other side, and snickers. When I finally make it, his pale eyes lock with mine.

"On three," he says.

A violent wave of second thoughts hits me. The severity of the situation overcomes my fleeting moment of madness, and I realize what I'm about to do.

"Haze, I'm not sure this is a good idea. Maybe we should go."

He doesn't reply, frowning. His gaze rapidly shifts from the pool to me.

"Yeah, you're probably right. But before we go, can I use your phone for a second? I need to make a call, and I left mine in the car."

"Sure."

I get my phone out of my pocket and hand it to him. He captures Kass's prehistoric phone in his large hand and briskly drops it on the grass surrounding the pool.

"What are you d—"

Before I have time to comprehend the events unraveling before my eyes, he runs toward me, picks me up like I'm weightless, and throws me into the freezing water.

Bastard.

He jumps, too, making sure to create a splash as big and obnoxious as humanly possible. How could I not see that coming? I gave him my phone like a freaking idiot. At least he thought about protecting it.

The water is freezing. I hold back a scream, goose bumps

erupting over my skin. I come back up to the surface, gasping for air and trying my best not think about all the kid pee I probably just swallowed. I didn't even have time to close my mouth.

"You piece of sh—" I cut myself off, coughing.

No words can explain how grateful I am that I wasn't wearing makeup.

"I can't believe you just did that."

He laughs. "I can't believe that you thought I wouldn't."

"I hate you." I splash him.

He splashes me right back, and thanks to his considerably stronger and wider arms, I'm practically hit by a tsunami. We keep on splashing each other, struggling to hold back our laughter as our clothes go from wet to soaked.

"Hey! You!" a man's voice screeches in the distance. A glimmering light catches my eye. It's a flashlight. It has to be.

"Shit," Haze growls. "Shit, shit, shit."

Security.

We hurry out of the pool as fast as lightning. I scoop my phone off the ground.

"Come on, we have to go. Now!"

Jumping the fence suddenly seems like the easiest thing I've ever had to do. As soon as our feet hit the ground, he traps my hand in his and starts running.

I always hated exercise. In gym class, the teacher would find great pleasure in threatening to fail me because I refused to do anything that required running. News flash: almost every sport does. But now that it's the only way to *not* end up in jail tonight, I'll run for two hours straight if I have to.

The man screams to stop, but we don't look back, dodging everything that dares stand in our way. Haze is a fast runner. We're very different in that department. Anyone who sees me running should start running, too.

After a never-ending five minutes of cardio, Haze pulls me behind a trash bin next to a store and motions to stay silent, his finger pressed to his lips.

We see the flashlight wandering around the darkness of the smelly alley for a couple of minutes.

"Damn it," we hear the man curse.

The footsteps decrease, gradually becoming more and more distant until they disappear altogether. We catch our breath, our eyes colliding.

Then, we can't stop ourselves.

We break into laughter, holding on to our stomachs while our shoulders shake uncontrollably. I can't believe I'm laughing at this. It could've gone extremely wrong. We could've gotten arrested. We could've gotten hurt.

We could've died.

So tell me why I've never felt more alive.

"DON'T WORRY ABOUT IT. MY AUNT'S working at the hospital tonight, and Kassidy's still at the party." I unlock the front door to Maria's house and walk into the completely silent kitchen that's usually crawling with Kass and Maria's yappers. Haze follows me hesitantly.

When we finally managed to stop laughing, we started shivering. The water was so cold, it's a wonder we didn't catch hypothermia. I suggested that we go to my house, which was closer to where we were, to dry ourselves up. Haze's place is around thirty-five minutes away, and I don't want him to stay in his stone-cold clothes and get sick.

"Come on." I guide him to the bathroom upstairs and hand him a clean towel. When realization seems to hit him and his eyes grow two sizes, I frown.

"What is it?"

No reply. He dives his hand into the back pocket of his pants and gets something out of it.

A phone. It's dripping on the floor, completely soaked.

"Crap. I thought you said you left your phone in the car."

He looks up at me. "I did."

"Then whose phone is this?"

"Kendrick's."

"What?"

"I completely forgot to give it back to you when I took you to the rooftop, so I brought it tonight but… then, I also forgot that it was in my pocket when we jumped in the pool."

"Okay, hold on. Why do you have Kendrick's phone?"

"He lost it when he attacked my brother. They wanted to use it against him, but I stole it to give it back to you. I thought you had enough going on," he glances at me. "What's up with hanging up on people, by the way?"

Everything falls into place.

Haze is the one who picked up when I called Kendrick.

"But…" I stutter. "They made me throw my phone into the toilet in case someone wanted to locate the call!"

It takes a couple of seconds for the information to register into Haze's brain. Then, after silently staring at me with his mouth wide open, he bursts out laughing, for the billionth time tonight.

"You did what?"

"Shut up." I cover my face with shaky hands. "I can't believe it was you. God damn it."

Haze doesn't stop laughing, nor does he seem to have any intention to.

"You threw your phone in the—" He cuts himself off, laughing louder. "I can't believe you. It's impossible to be bored with you, Winter, you know that?"

I shake my head, unable to take any more humiliation. I threw my phone in the toilet. How was I supposed to know?

"You're dripping everywhere. Don't move. I'll be back with

some dry clothes."

He nods, still laughing.

I walk into Kendrick's room, which is messier than I thought possible, and grab whatever clean clothes I can find—God knows that's rare in my cousin's room. *Boys will be boys.* These two are around the same size. It should fit.

When I walk back into the bathroom, I see Haze managed to get his laughter under control and is drying his hair off with the towel. One of his toned arms holds the towel up as the other one ruffles his messy brown hair. I swear, this boy could make the simplest actions look attractive.

"There you go," I say, a shy smile forming on my lips. "Take off your clothes so we can throw them in the dryer."

Haze grins and proceeds to do the one thing I did not expect. He tugs at his shirt and removes it with absolutely no shame.

Don't look at his abs.

Don't look at his abs.

Don't look at his a... *Dang it.*

My cheeks heat up when I take in every inch of his Adonis body. My wandering gaze can't seem to stay in one place, drifting from his pecs, to his biceps, to his obliques, to his six-pack.

Don't even get me started on his six-pack.

He's... infuriatingly hot.

Street fighting and training close to every single day will do that to you. It's hard to believe he's only eighteen. According to what Kendrick said, he's been training with his brother ever since he was fourteen years old. Well, it shows.

I giggle nervously, looking away. "I didn't mean right now."

"Oh, I'm sorry. Is my sexiness making you uncomfortable?" He smirks, stepping closer.

My pulse quickens with every step. As the distance between us decreases, my ability to breath does, too.

"Is there a better way to react to someone stripping in front of me?"

He laughs, staring right through my soul.

"There are *many* ways to react to someone stripping in front of you."

Barely four steps separate us now.

The cockiness drains from his face and is replaced by something darker, eager. I know that look. I know that lust.

Three steps.

His gaze drops to my lips

Two steps.

For the first time, he doesn't rip his eyes away. He stares. Hard.

One step.

He stops, refusing to take the last step. We both know that would be taking *us* to the next step, as well. We don't move a muscle, looking at each other in silence. My head is a freaking whirlwind. His eyes say that it's up to me. That he won't make a move unless I want him to. Do I want him to?

Yes, you do.

Shut up, voice of reason.

I have no idea why I do it. Why I take the last step. Maybe it's the four drinks running in my veins, or maybe it's my heart and its annoying tendency to disagree with my brain.

His breath lightly fans my lips. He smells like mint. I'm confident that my heart is going to burst out of my chest any second when he lifts his hand and cups my face gently. I shiver at the touch, welcoming the warmth of his skin.

He leans forward, his lips dangerously close to mine…

"Who left a trail of water around the house?"

I jerk away from him in a sudden move. It's like coming out of a trance. Or waking up from a dream.

A really, *really* good dream.

I panic. "My aunt's here early. You have to go." Then, yelling loud enough for her to hear, "It's me. I'm sorry. I'll clean it up in a minute." I turn back to him. "Come on, you can sneak out my bedroom window. It used to be Kendrick's room. He did it all the time."

Haze is as overwhelmed as I am, but he doesn't budge. He throws his wet shirt back on and follows me. I unlock the window with a shaky hand and open it.

Our eyes meet. We're thinking the same thing. Should we say something? Probably. But we don't have time.

"Go." I whisper.

Then, without a word, he exits through my window, hustles down the vines growing on the side of the house, and disappears into the pitch-black night.

Seconds later, Maria comes up the stairs, complaining about the trail of water Haze and I left all the way from the kitchen to the second floor. I apologize and tell her that someone pushed me in the pool, which technically isn't false.

I refrain from telling her that it wasn't at the party but in a public pool that the town's bad boy and I broke into. I don't think she'd like that part very much.

She says to clean it up and hugs me good night, exhausted from her day at work. I sit on my bed, my skin burning where Haze's fingers used to be.

I almost kissed him. I almost kissed my cousin's worst enemy. He's the one who made the deal. He is the reason Kendrick is hurt. I should be crippled with guilt. I should feel awful. I stare at the window that Haze just escaped out of, and I hate myself.

Because I don't hate myself at all.

ELEVEN
The New Girlfriend

"Guys, I'm begging you, just drop it. It's not too late to turn around." I shift in the back seat, staring out the window at a neighborhood I've never been to before. None of the boys reply, bumping their heads along to the music playing on the radio.

"Fine, ignore me. But when Kendrick finds out and kills all of you, don't say I didn't warn you." I put my hands up in surrender, gently pressing my forehead to the tinted glass.

"He told us to do whatever it took to fix it. That's what we did. We fixed it. He'll give us his blessing. You'll see." Will says, his eyes locked on the road.

"We're talking about hiring Kendrick's ex-girlfriend, which was a very messy breakup, may I remind you, to play his new girlfriend in front of his mother. The only thing I see him giving you is a broken nose."

"Well, he's going to have to deal with it because the dinner's tonight and Nicole's the only girl who said yes," Will retorts. He claps like an overexcited child to spite me. "Look, we're here."

I glance out the window. He's right. We're in front of her house already. We got this far—might as well get it over with.

Alex furrows his eyebrows. "Remind me why they broke up again?"

"Don't know." Blake frowns. "Will?"

Will snickers. "No idea. Kendrick's not exactly big on talking about his feelings."

Then, as if they can read each other's minds, they turn their heads concurrently and gaze in my direction.

"Don't look at me. I don't know any more than you do."

"Yeah, right. Spit it out," Will says.

Will might be a complete jerk sometimes, but he's right about one thing. Kendrick rarely talks about his feelings. Everything I know I heard from Kass after she bugged him for days.

I give in. "He wouldn't tell her about the fights. She dumped him because she felt he was hiding things from her."

Alex nods. "Dating her wasn't a walk in the park either. Last I heard she was needy, controlling, and a bit crazy."

Will makes a face. "Aren't all girls?"

I roll my eyes so hard I see my brain.

Guys like him are the reason some girls go gay.

The boys reach for the car handle, ready to step out of the vehicle. I'm about to do the same when Will cackles.

"What do you think you're doing, Canada?"

"What do you mean? I'm coming with you."

"No, you're not. You don't know Nicole like we do. Let us handle it."

"What? Absolutely not. I'm not staying in the car." I'm about to open the door when I hear the unmistakable sound of defeat.

He locked the door.

The bastard locked the door.

Will has this great car that you can't get out of if it's been locked from the outside. Some call it childproof.

I call it a kidnapping car.

"Will." I knock on the glass.

"Oh, you're right. Sorry." He rolls down the window slightly, amused. "Oxygen. Kind of essential."

Freaking idiot.

My gaze diverts to Blake and Alex. Blake's laughing, and Alex is trying not to. So much for being the nice one of the three.

The guys walk toward the front door, and I watch them, helpless. God knows how long I'm going to be stuck in the car. I get my phone out of my pocket and unlock it, hoping to distract myself until they come back.

0 new messages.

I never knew three little words could sting so much.

They've been more than stubborn for the past couple of days. They refuse to budge from my screen, reminding me of the words no one wants to say to me. Today is Saturday, and it's been eight days since I heard from him.

Of course, I get texts from Allie, my best friend from Toronto, Kass, and Maria. But they don't count.

I guess what I truly see when I look at my phone is:

0 new messages from Haze.

I shouldn't be surprised, really. I did tell him to stop texting me for a week. The thing is, I didn't think he'd actually listen. Especially after what *almost* happened the last time we were together.

I've seen him at school a couple of times, which makes it even weirder. He's not ignoring me. Or at least, I don't think he is. Avoiding me is more like it. He didn't show up to the classes we have together all week. He smiles when he sees me. I smile back. But it's not a "we almost kissed" kind of smile.

The fight is getting closer every day. I forbid myself from counting the days, convinced it'll destroy what's left of my sanity.

I deleted his number to make sure I wouldn't be tempted to talk to him, but also to make me feel better.

It goes without saying that it didn't.

In a way, I thought that deleting him from my phone would be like deleting him from my brain.

I know now that it doesn't work like that.

To make it even better, since Haze broke things off with Bianca, she's been spreading lies about me at school. She says he ended things with her to sleep with me. That Haze was interested in dating her until I showed up and ruined everything.

I'm not sure if Haze knows about it, considering that I saw

him like two to three times during the week. But even if he did, I don't know if he would care.

The sound of a new message coming through rips my attention away from my complicated thoughts. It's from an unknown number.

Locking the lady in the car. How nice.

I stop breathing, glancing around. There's no one in sight. The streets seem empty, but they're not. They can't be. Not only is the message from a number that's impossible to identify, but it also comes from someone who's watching me at this very moment.

On the other side of the road is an imposing building that looks like it used to be a hotel. The broken windows and boarded entrances give away that it's been closed a long time ago. A large board that reads TO BE DESTROYED in bright red letters covers the main entrance. Next to it, another one says DO NOT ENTER. DANGER.

It only lasts a second.

But that's enough.

I see a shadow pass in front of a window located on the third floor. It vanishes almost as quickly as it appeared.

If I had blinked at the wrong moment, I would've missed it.

> **Who are youth?**

I curse as soon as I hit the Send button. Will messed with my phone yesterday. Looks like someone had wandering fingers and turned on the autocorrect.

> **Who are yogurt?**

God damn it.

> **Who are you****

The reply comes a lot quicker than I anticipated. I can feel my fingers tremble when I tap the message to open it.

> **I'll tell you who I'm not.**

Five seconds go by.

> **The guy with the shitty phone**

I keep my eyes glued to the hotel and exhale. No sign of the shadow, but I know better than to think that it's gone because I no longer see it. I desperately try and reassure myself. That's something Haze would say. It's probably him.

I begin typing a reply but turn my head when I hear a door closing. I see the boys walking out of Nicole's house with, you guessed it, Nicole herself.

She is a solid five foot eight. Her perfect wavy auburn hair falls all the way down to her stomach. She's that girl you see on the street that makes you say "I should start working out and drinking green stuff."

I understand what Kendrick saw in her.

She's beautiful. Her makeup is on point. She probably follows the fashion trends, and I bet she knows how to make even-winged eyeliner. Next thing I know, Blake has opened the car door for her, and she slides into the back seat next to me.

I smile. "Hi, I'm Winter."

She looks me up and down. "That's fascinating."

Her answer doesn't really surprise me. Kendrick didn't exactly make it his life mission to get her back when she left him. That has to mean something. Will and I make eye contact in the rearview mirror. He's right. I don't know how to handle her.

"REMEMBER, IF MARIA ASKS, YOU RANDOMLY ran into each other at the mall and—"

Nicole interrupts Alex, annoyed. "Yes, I know. I was crying, he comforted me, and we got back together."

As I sink into the couch, I fight the urge to comment. What a terrible story. Might as well make her say, "Your son lied to me for months, broke my heart, and ruined my idea of love, but he saw me crying at the mall, because the mall is such a good choice for a crying spot, and I realized I never stopped loving him and we should get back together."

The unknown number didn't text me again after I stopped replying. I decided not to tell the guys about it. I don't want to worry them when I'm 99 percent sure it was Haze.

It's probably nothing.

Creepy shadow in an abandoned building texting me that he can see me. No big deal, right?

We've been sitting in the living room and waiting for Nicole to finish covering up what's left of Kendrick's wounds with makeup for an hour. Because it turns out Nicole's a makeup artist.

Well, that's convenient.

Most of Kendrick's wounds have healed, but some of the dark bruises scattered across his face and neck have to be taken care of. It's nothing a little concealer can't fix.

To say Kendrick was pleased when he found out Nicole had been chosen by his friends would be a lie. He was pissed. Big-time. But he didn't have a choice. So, he swallowed his pride and let his ex-girlfriend do his makeup. It was obvious that she was dying to know why he was bruised. But the guys gave her one rule and one rule only: don't ask questions.

The dinner with Maria is scheduled for 7:00. She should be

coming home from work anytime now.

"Do you guys happen to know anything about the abandoned building in front of Nicole's house?" I ask as soon as the sound of Nicole's heels fade out down the hall. I had to wait until she went to the bathroom to give in to the burning curiosity.

"You mean the abandoned hotel?" Will says, grabbing a handful of chips and shoving it in his mouth like a pig.

Gracefulness at its finest.

"Yes. It used to be a gang meeting spot."

A shiver skitters down my body.

Whoever texted me was probably part of a gang. Again, all the signs point to Haze. Part of me wishes it was. But the other is desperate to get him out of my head. What can I say? I guess I got used to him annoying me every day.

Will goes back to eating and texting the same way he has for the past thirty minutes. I hear Blake say something from the kitchen about Will being weirdly secretive lately. Apparently, he put a password on his phone, which he never did before, and refuses to let anyone see it. The guys love to say it's a girl, but he keeps on denying it.

"Why?" Will narrows his eyes.

"No reason. Just curious."

Will seems suspicious, but he doesn't say anything.

"How long has it been since Adams contacted you, Canada?"

209

he asks like I said my thoughts out loud. "We're wondering if he got sick of you and found some new girl."

Alex gives him a severe look. Good old papa bear Alex.

"Man, come on. More tact, please?"

"What? Somebody had to say it."

Deep down, I know they're probably right. Bianca was, too. She said he'd get tired of me, and he did. After all, everybody keeps on saying that he's a manwhore.

It's always disorienting to hear them talk about him like he's this entirely different person. He was never that guy with me. But then again, it might've been exactly what he wanted me to think.

"It's been a week or so. Why do you care?"

"Word on the street's that the North Side's preparing an attack. We wanted to ask if Haze knew something about it. But that would require communication, you see?"

"I'm sorry that I can no longer be your little spy." Irritated, I get up from the leather couch.

"Where are you going?" Alex asks.

"To my room. I'm bored."

"You'll be back for dinner?"

They're probably worried that the story will lack credibility if I'm not there to confirm everything these two liars say.

"Sure. Just call me when it's time."

I sigh and disappear into my bedroom. This is going to be

one heck of a long night. I need some time to myself before I have to fake smiles and lie to the woman I consider my second mother. I don't know how Kendrick isn't drowning in guilt. He's been lying like that for years.

My phone chimes. I have a new message from an unknown number.

It's been a while, Kingston.

My heart skips a beat. I glance at the screen in silence for a couple of minutes. Only one person calls me Kingston. The message is from Haze. No doubt. But what scares me the most is… that the other messages *aren't*.

TWELVE
Maybe I Missed You

I prowl around my bedroom, trying to remember every single detail I possibly can about the abandoned hotel. Who could be texting me? How did that person get my number? Tanner is my guess. But then there's also Ian and the North Side.

Why would Tanner be trying to scare me? His brother doesn't care about me. He made it clear by disappearing on me twice. Tanner got what he wanted—to weaken the East Side and get me away from Haze.

> Who is this?

> You deleted my number. Harsh.

> I repeat, who is this?

> I'm the guy you seriously shouldn't be dreaming so much about ;)

> Omg. Channing Tatum?

> Hilarious

> I know. Seriously, who is this?

> I'm the guy standing
> outside your window.

> Yeah, right.

> You really shouldn't keep
> your curtains open. What if
> some creep is stalking you

There's one thing you do *not* want to see after reading a message like this and that is your curtains wide open. I gasp at the completely uncovered window. He's right. Either Haze is really standing outside my house, or he just took a really, really lucky guess. I draw a breath, my mind racing, and look out the window. The streets are calm and certainly don't contain any trace of him. The idiot is messing with me. I register his number in my contacts so I can differentiate his number from the other one.

> You almost got me. Almost.

> Careful. Just because you don't see
> it doesn't mean it's not there.

You are so creepy, Adams, you know that?

Damn it, how'd you know it was me

Only you call me Kingston, dumbass. Plus, I think I know your bad jokes by now. Why'd you decide to come back to life?

Aw, did someone miss me? You're the one who told me to stop texting for a week if I recall.

Since when do you listen to me?

Come on, fill me in. What have I missed?

Nothing much except for my new reputation. Thanks to your crazy friend with benefits. I'm a hoe now. Haven't you heard?

Don't think so low of yourself, Kingston. You're more than a gardening tool.

I find myself laughing out loud when I read his message.

Idiot.

You laughed.

I did not.

I saw you.

How could you?

I'm standing outside
your house, I told you.

The hotel this morning and
now my house? You really
are obsessed with me.

What are you talking about?

Stop. I know it was you.

What was me

The text messages.

What messages?

I can't tell if he's messing with me. I sure hope he is.

Is someone sending you creepy texts

You mean except you?

Seriously, someone's messing with you?

Oh so now you know how to use a question mark.

Winter, I'm serious.

I'd like to stay and chat but I can't. I have a dinner to go to.

Oh yeah, the fake girlfriend dinner. Am I invited

How do you know about that?

Because we haven't been talking doesn't mean I haven't been keeping an eye on you.

There he goes again with his damn lines. The boy sure has a way with words. But most importantly, he has a way with *me*. Sometimes I think he is endeavoring to seduce me. And sometimes I'm afraid that it might be working.

Creepy.

Am I invited? ;)

Never in a million years.

"Winter, honey, dinner's served!" Maria shouts from downstairs, her voice distant but firm.

"Coming."

By the time I walk into the kitchen, Kendrick and Nicole are already sitting at the table and pretending to love each other. A hint of sexual tension floats around the room, but I try my best to ignore it. These two clearly have a lot of unfinished business. And by unfinished business I mean that they still want to rip each other's clothes off. I sit next to Kass, but also the farthest I possibly can from the fake lovebirds, and pour myself a glass of water.

Ding. My phone goes off again. I look down to the message that popped up on my screen.

Challenge accepted.

Wait, what?

My blood turns cold, and the oxygen leaves my lungs when the worst sound I've ever heard rings out in the room.

A knock on the door.

"Are we expecting someone?" Maria gets up.

Kendrick shakes his head.

"Sit down, Mom. I got it." Kass motions to her mother, beating her to the door. She swings the door open, and the expression "color drains from her face" has never been more accurate when she sees the person standing on our porch. I can tell that she considers closing the door, but the unwanted guest stops her, stepping inside.

"I'm so sorry I'm late."

When we trade glances across the room and he assesses me, I swear I can hear my heart explode.

"I hope you didn't start without me."

It's official.

Tonight is the night Haze Adams dies.

I squirm in my chair as Kendrick glowers at Haze with a tight jaw that's twitching with fury. If you could stare at someone to death, he would be six feet under by now. Kass is probably the least shocked one in the room as she knows Haze and I have been… I'm not sure what the hell it is we've been doing, actually.

As for Nicole, she's just sitting there, confused.

My aunt frowns, the wrinkles on her face making themselves

known. "I'm sorry, who are you?"

Haze peels his eyes away from me, his gaze traveling to my aunt.

"Of course, where are my manners? I'm Haze." He holds out his hand, which Maria shakes with hesitation.

He looks at me, and I know from the way his eyes light up that he just had an idea. *The worst idea of all fucking time.* My first instinct is to get up, ready to pounce, as if it'll somehow stop him from carrying on with what he clearly intends to do. But it doesn't.

The words come rushing out of his mouth.

"I'm Winter's boyfriend."

I'm going to hurt this boy.

Multiple emotions take over my aunt's face. She's confused, then happy, then confused again, and finally, she's relieved. Wait, relieved? I get up, walking toward them to somehow stop this big problem from turning into a straight-up disaster we can't get back from.

"Honey, why didn't you tell me?" She pulls me into a loving embrace. "I knew something was going on. That's why you were so secretive. You've met your first boyfriend."

Two problems with this sentence.

One: She's wrong. But, just like she did with Kendrick, she'd rather believe that there's a reasonable explanation for the change in my behavior. I think me getting a boyfriend is the better option as the other one is that I somehow got involved in Kendrick's mess. Which I did. But she can't know that.

Two: Now everyone, especially Haze, knows that I never had a boyfriend before. Why'd she have to expose me like that? He's never going to let me hear the end of it. He already thinks I'm a prude.

If only I was.

Haze ignores the first-boyfriend comment, thankfully.

He grins. "I can't believe you didn't tell them about us, babe. I thought we were official."

To think that I almost missed him.

"Please, give me your coat. Welcome to my home." Maria smiles warmly. Haze takes off his jacket and hands it to her with a thanks.

"What's wrong, honey bunny? No kiss?" Haze turns to me.

"Of course. I'll give it to you in a second. I just have to show you the thing first," I lie, a fake smile plastered on my face.

"What thing?"

"You know that thing that I talked to you about the other day?" I elbow him when no one's looking, obviously saying "just go with it, or I'll make you swallow your eyeballs."

"Aren't you eating with us?" Maria asks, a bit disappointed. I bet she's just dying to get all the juicy details of our "love story."

"We'll be back. Start without us," I reassure her and quite

literally drag him out of the kitchen to escape the killer looks Kass and Kendrick have been throwing at us for the past minute. I can tell Kendrick is on the verge of losing it. But he can't do anything as long as Maria is here.

I slam the door shut as soon as we walk into my bedroom.

"Are you out of your freaking mind?"

I push him, but he barely steps back, still smirking.

"I'm sorry. I couldn't miss such an opportunity to piss off Kendrick."

So it was true. He really was outside of my house this whole time. I don't know what to think of it.

"Do you realize what you've done? Kendrick will literally crucify me, and don't even get me started on Kass and her guilt trips. You can't just show up when you want to. Especially not now," I spit, pushing him once more. "Why did you do that?"

"I was in the area and thought it had been a while."

The fact that he thinks for even one second that this is a good enough answer is what baffles me the most.

Haze is that guy who leaves for three months, then comes back and says it's because he forgot to look at the time.

"Thanks, I noticed."

"God, you're sexy when you're mad." His eyes travel downward to my dress and back up to my face. I don't usually wear dresses. It sure is different from my usual Converses and T-shirts. He chews on his bottom lip for a second, and a wave of shivers runs down my spine.

Damn you, sexual tension.

When he steps closer, I step back faster than I thought possible.

"You're going to tell them something came up and leave, am I making myself clear? We've worked too hard for this to have you come in and ruin it all."

"And miss all the fun? No, thanks. I'd much rather stay and enjoy a great family dinner with my girlfriend. But, I mean, if you really needed me to behave, I could be convinced." His voice is dripping with suggestion.

The conclusion that's brought upon me when he finishes speaking is one that I wish I never had to face. He has the upper hand. I'm helpless.

"What do you want?"

He raises his eyebrows, satisfied. "You agree to come with me somewhere after dinner."

"And do what?"

"There's something I want to show you. It only happens tonight."

I have no idea what he has in mind, as always, but if it can save Kendrick's dinner and make the hell that my cousins will put me through slightly more bearable, I owe it to myself to try.

"Fine."

A victorious expression covers his face. "I believe we have a dinner to go to." He takes a couple steps forward and rests his hand on the door handle.

"Why did you come back?"

I'm slightly surprised by my own words when they ring out in my tiny bedroom. Haze pauses, his brawny back facing me.

"You disappeared for days. No messages, nothing. Don't get me wrong. You do whatever the hell you want, and clearly, disappearing is your thing... so why bother coming back at all?"

He turns around, and our gazes meet.

"I told you I was in the area."

I nod, beating myself up. I don't know what I expected him to say. That he came back for me? We're not friends. We're not anything. He's just a lonely bad boy with attachment issues who's desperate for some company. Plus, he did tell me that he came to annoy Kendrick. Not for me.

He begins turning the door knob but stops himself. I hold my breath.

"And..."

He takes a long pause, his back still all I can see.

"Maybe I missed you."

THERE ARE MANY PLACES I'D RATHER be in the world right now. So many people I'd rather be having dinner with, too. I'd rather be eating with Gretchen, my elementary school bully who constantly stole my Capri Suns, than be here,

223

dining with Haze and Kendrick and wondering if Kendrick's going to jump over the table and rip off my "boyfriend's" head.

Indeed, I'd rather go back to the most humiliating moment of my life than be here. Like that one time I choked on my chicken nuggets at McDonalds in front of my fourth-grade crush, George Bay, and almost died.

Needless to say, Bay never became *bae*.

For the past thirty minutes, Haze has been getting the worst possible childhood stories out of my aunt, who's more than happy to provide. The only thing that's missing is the baby pictures, which I swear on my life, he will never see.

"Why did you do that to that poor little girl?" Haze says in between laughter.

"You call that a poor little girl? She was awful. She rubbed her boogers on every kid in kindergarten. She deserved it."

"But you filled her pants with bugs. Bugs, Winter. That's evil."

"Not as evil as she was, I assure you."

"How did you two lovebirds meet?" Maria asks.

"School," I say, thinking back to his stupid reputation and the way it all began.

"I saw her in the hall, and I just knew I had to get close to her." Haze smirks and reaches for my hand, intertwining our fingers on the table. I'm a bit shocked, but I don't move away.

I see Kendrick clench his fist from the corner of my eyes. I get it. Love at first sight is not the reason why he knew he had to get close to me and he knows it.

No words can explain how relieved I was when I saw Maria had ordered pizza and that we were eating off paper plates. That means no dishes and no more painfully long conversations between Haze and my aunt.

It's clear that Maria likes him.

Of course she does.

He's nice, he's funny, and he's... well, *Haze Adams.*

As for Kendrick, I bet he's wondering whether or not it'd be okay to stab him with a fork. On the bright side, Haze did behave like he promised. He's been sweet, polite, and he made sure not to do anything that might result in Kendrick slapping him with the pizza box. It's 9:30. I'm surprised we made it this far without a conflict of some sort.

"Well, thank you so much for dinner. It was great talking to you, but I'm afraid we have to go," Haze says just as we finish throwing the paper plates away.

"We?" Kendrick says through gritted teeth.

That's the first time he's spoken to Haze all night. So many questions must be spinning around in his head right now: Why did he show up? How did he know about the dinner? Is something going on between them? What the hell is this?

"Yeah, we're going on a little adventure tonight. Aren't we, sweetie pie?" Haze smirks.

I swear he is calling me the most ridiculous nicknames on purpose.

"Yeah." I press my lips together.

"You two have fun." Maria hugs both me and Haze. "It was great to meet you. Take care of my niece, okay? She's like a daughter to me."

Something shifts in his eyes. I can't tell what.

"Of course." He nods.

As Haze leads the way toward the front door, I ignore Kendrick's furious glances. I can hear Kendrick thinking, *Don't you dare walk through that door.* My eyes connect with his. I give him an apologetic look before stepping out of the house and following Haze into his brand-new car. There's so much Kendrick doesn't know or understand.

"What? No more motorcycle?"

"We have a long ride ahead of us. I thought you'd be more comfortable in a car."

Going on an adventure to an unknown location with Haze Adams? It could either turn out to be a great idea…

Or the worst one I've ever had.

THIRTEEN

I Like You

"Where are you taking me?" I ask for the third time. Haze keeps his eyes glued to the road. He's a stubborn one, I admit. But what he doesn't know is—I'm worse.

"Earth to Haze?"

Still no answer.

"I love this song." He turns up the radio to spite me.

I said it before, and I'll say it again: Haze's subject-changing skills will never cease to amaze me.

"Can you stop changing the subject?"

He arches an eyebrow. "Can you stop being curious?"

"We've been driving for an hour and a half. Can you blame me for wanting to know?"

"We're going somewhere really nice, I promise," he says, rolling the window down to let the night breeze into the car.

"Last time you said that, we ended up trespassing on the roof of an abandoned building."

"The view was worth it, wasn't it?" He carelessly runs a hand through his hair.

Oh for fuck's sake. Does he do attractive things on purpose, or is he just naturally irresistible?

Yep. Same old question.

"Why was it so important that I came with you?"

"Do you ever stop asking questions, Kingston?" A hint of exasperation can be seen in his features.

"Do you ever stop avoiding them, Adams?"

"Nope."

"Jerk."

"Prude."

I can't help but smile. I look at him from the corner of my eyes to see his lips twitching into a smile, as well.

"We're here."

He exits the highway and takes an unexpected turn onto a gravel road. I try to see—key word: try—but can't discern anything except for the vague shapes illuminated by the headlights of the car. A sign that reads "cul-de-sac" quickly passes on my left.

"Because that's not creepy at all."

His smile only grows wider.

Haze finally parks the car, pushes the gear into park, and kills the engine. He then turns off the headlights. We both get out of the vehicle, and what I see immediately takes my breath away.

We're on a beach. An enormous one. There's a complete absence of light, which reveals the most beautiful view I have ever seen. It's an endless sea of stars.

I can't remember the last time I saw so many.

"It's insane," I say quietly, almost to myself as he walks toward the back of the car to open the trunk.

"How'd you find out about this place?"

"Happy accident."

"You said you wanted to show me something that only happens tonight?"

"Yes, there's a meteor shower later. You're going to be glad I blackmailed you, you'll see." He teases.

My eyes widen tremendously as my lips part in shock. Is he serious? He gave up on annoying the living hell out of Kendrick for a meteor shower date on an empty beach?

He comes back to the front of the car, one of his hands full and the other checking the time on his phone.

"We have two hours to kill."

I look down at what he's holding. Blankets.

"How sweet. You got us blankets?" I tease. "Where's the picnic?"

He scoffs. "Oh no, these are for me. I only share my blankets with people who give me thank-you kisses."

I flush.

"You still haven't let that go, huh?"

"Nah."

He knew it was two hours away and that we'd have plenty of time together.

It doesn't take long for us to find the perfect spot to lie

down. The silence that follows is thick but comfortable. It's peaceful. Light. Haze is lying on his back with one of his arms under his head and the other alongside his body.

I do the same, tossing my hair to the front and wondering how I could live without these little wonders for so long. The artificial city lights take away the gifts Mother Nature gave us. They're always there. But the fake replaces the real.

Kind of like falling for someone. You might not see the feelings, but they're there. Always. Just because they're buried deep under denial and repression doesn't mean that they don't infiltrate your every thought and intoxicate every heartbeat. Just because something is bad for you doesn't mean you don't crave it with every fiber of your being.

That's what makes love the most dangerous feeling of all.

"Where were you?" I regret saying the words as soon as they come out.

"What do you mean?"

"You know what I mean."

He lets out a long breath. "I was around."

"Seriously? That's all I get?"

Irritation spreads across his face.

"What else do you want me to say, Winter? I don't owe you an explanation for everything I do. I'm not your boyfriend."

Harsh.

"Right." I sit up, staring at the ocean in the distance.

As soon as he says it, he seems to feel guilty. He sits up as well and mumbles incomprehensible words, blathering a confusing apology.

"No, it's fine. You're right. You're not my boyfriend. But I thought we were friends. My mistake."

He remains quiet, fighting a war within himself.

"I've been in and out of town," he finally whispers.

"Would it be too far to ask why?"

"I can't tell you anything else. You already know too much."

"I know too much? Are you serious? I know nothing about you except that you have a psycho brother and that you hate spiders."

He exhales. "I'm sorry."

I lower my head. "Me too."

Again, to push the irony even further, he has a hard time finding an answer good enough to give me.

"I'm hungry," he says.

"Seriously? Way to ruin a dramatic moment." I struggle to hold on to the anger that quickly spills out of me. I'm supposed to be mad at him.

"What? You're the one who mentioned a picnic."

"You should've thought about that before driving almost two hours out of town."

We laugh quietly.

"I wanted to say sorry," he concedes.

"For what?"

"The lies Bianca's been spreading about you."

So he did hear.

"It's fine. It's not your fault. She's... something, that one."

"Something doesn't even begin to cover it. You remember that time at the diner? Bianca sent Natasha to try and crash the date. Something about Natasha texting her that I was there with a girl. So, of course, as any sane person would do, Bianca took it upon herself to intervene."

It all makes sense now.

I thought it was quite strange that Natasha would do that to her friend when she knows Bianca has feelings for Haze. Turns out she actually is a good friend in her own weird way. Bianca, on the other hand, not so much. Asking one of your girls to try and seduce a guy you're interested in because you're afraid he might hook up with another girl? That's not okay.

"I kind of get it though," I breathe. "Having feelings for someone can make you do crazy things."

His gaze shifts to me. He doesn't speak for several seconds.

"Tell me about it."

I try to convince myself that it's just words. Letters put together to form sentences. That they don't mean anything. But the butterflies in my stomach say otherwise.

They mean everything.

I change the topic. "I didn't know you were such a romantic,

Adams. Beach date and all."

"I'm not."

"You're not what?"

"A romantic."

I hold back a laugh. "That's not what it looks like to me."

"Yeah, well, maybe you know a side of me no one else sees."

His words resonate in my brain. He's right.

He acts differently with me, and I can't decide if I should be happy, because it means that I bring the good out of him… or if I should be sad, because he's hiding the bad.

IT'S BEEN EXACTLY TWO HOURS SINCE we arrived to the beach. We've been talking about our beliefs, our dreams, the places we always wanted to visit, and the things we wish we'd never done.

No, I'm just kidding.

That would require Haze opening up.

We've been staring at the stars and trying to find constellations in the moonlit sky.

"This one looks like a purse."

"What? How is that a purse?" He cracks up, squinting.

"You don't see it? There, on the left." I point to the bundle of stars.

An alarm goes off on Haze's phone, interrupting my ridiculous attempt at giving him an astronomy class.

"It's almost time," he whispers.

We open our eyes widely, lying down on the blanket that now has sand scattered over it.

Then, we wait. For something, anything to happen.

When the distant and passing lights spread across the luminous sky, I realize that so many of us spend our entire lives collecting "beautiful things" when the really beautiful things are those we cannot possess.

Now that I'm watching something that's *literally* out of this world, the words Haze said to me on the rooftop haunt my thoughts. He's right. The house you live in, the car you drive, and the clothes you wear do not fill you with peace when you're lying in a hospital bed.

Little moments like this do.

I'm ripped away from my thoughts when I feel a warm hand on mine.

Haze's hand.

I know I should move away, tell him to stop, do something. But I can't. And I won't. I turn my head instinctively. He's staring at me. He rolls over to his side to face me. He should be looking at the meteor shower.

"You're missing the best part," I murmur.

He smiles, as well, and slowly leans in. My heart jolts against my rib cage. He's close. Too close.

His gaze lands on my lips, and just like it was in the bathroom a week ago, the tension in the air's so thick that I could cut it with a knife. Barely an inch separates us at this point.

"That's not the best part, Kingston."

He lays a hand on my cheek and slowly brushes my lower lip with his thumb. A million shivers scamper down my body as I close my eyes at the touch, my instincts taking over.

Then, he whispers something that makes my thoughts spiral out of control.

"This is."

Our lips collide and the oxygen runs away from my lungs. His kisses are gentle at first, like he's giving me a chance to reject him or push him away. But I don't. I can feel that he's holding back as he slowly caresses my lips with his. It's driving me insane, and before I know it, I'm kissing him back. Right away, I feel him smiling. He buries his fingers in my hair and deepens the kiss. I've never known anything like this. I've never known anything like *him*. It's like we both refuse to let go because if we do, we'll be brought back to reality. Back to this world where we know we don't stand a chance.

That's when the truth catches up to us.

His phone rings.

When he pulls away, the castle bursts into flames, the carriage turns back into a pumpkin, and the glass slipper breaks into a million pieces.

The fairy tale crashes, and my heart does, too.

He looks at me regretfully, curses under his breath, and picks up the phone. I sit up straight and stare at the sea with empty eyes. I just kissed my cousin's enemy. The ultimate player. Technically, he kissed me. But I kissed him back. It's obvious now that I've been lying to myself. There is no going back.

I like Haze Adams.

"YEAH, I GET THAT. I HEARD you the first time." Haze sighs, the irritation in his tone growing.

I'm not sure who he's talking to, but my guess is his brother. The argument only serves as an open door for numerous unpleasant memories to come rushing back into my mind. Might as well put up a sign that says "Room available for guilt, second thoughts, and doubts in Winter's head. Limited time only."

I kissed a guy whose brother violently attacked me.

"I said I got it. I'll see you tomorrow." He hangs up, letting his phone hit the ground. The bulging vein in his neck catches my eyes, making me wonder how he manages to look this good even when he's angry.

I don't know what to say. Or how to act. Do we just carry on like nothing happened? Or do we acknowledge that we just kissed?

A lot?

All I know is it can't happen again. No matter how much of a good kisser he is. I lower my gaze to his lips and ignore the desire bursting in a deep, unexplored place in my belly.

Winter, stop it.

"Sorry. Family drama."

I was right. He was talking to Tanner.

"Don't worry about it."

His eyes say it all. He's wondering how to act, too.

"It's getting late. We should get going," I say, getting up before he can get a word in.

I hear him sigh behind me.

"Sure."

I pick up the blanket and shake it to get rid of the sand clinging to it. We're halfway to the car when a drop of water hits my hand. I look up at the sky that's now fogged and cloudy. Great. Rain. Just what I need right now.

As we walk side by side, the weather goes from *let's annoy them* to *let's drown them* in a matter of seconds. The rain comes pouring down on us. We're already soaking wet by the time we reach the car and take cover inside. We have a two-hour ride ahead of us, and the rain is so bad, I'm afraid we won't have a choice but to wait it out.

"Shit," Haze mutters to himself. He's staring at his phone.

"What is it?"

"It's supposed to last all night."

"Damn it. What are we going to do?"

"The only thing we can do—be careful on the road. We can't

stay here forever, can we?" He turns the engine on.

I have no choice but to agree with him… and pray that we'll make it back home alive.

WHEN THE FOURTH KISSING-RELATED SONG in a row comes on the radio, the only thought consuming my mind is "*I sure hope you're enjoying this, Universe.*" We've been driving for an hour. There are only fifty minutes left before I can collapse onto my bed and forget this ever happened. The rain hasn't stopped. In fact, it's only gotten worse.

The song on the radio contains the lyrics "Kiss me before it's too late. Kiss me, that's all it takes."

Oh, the irony.

I look to my left and see Haze smirking.

Smirking.

As in, he thinks the unbearably heavy tension in the air is funny. Well, excuse me, bad boy, but I'm dying over here.

When we slow down and find ourselves stuck behind an endless line of cars, Haze frowns and stretches his neck to see what the reason is for the blocked road. Then, cars begin to turn around and cross to the opposite lane, going back to where they came from.

"What's going on?" I ask.

That's when we see the ambulance and flickering police lights from afar. It's quite clear that there's been an accident, and considering the terrible weather, I'm not surprised.

The access to the bridge is completely blocked. I hope everyone's okay. Next thing I know, a police officer comes knocking on the window, probably to tell us exactly what he's been telling everyone else. Haze rolls down the tinted glass.

"There's been an accident. Two cars went off the bridge into the lake. You have to find another way," the poor man struggles to say through the pouring rain

That's awful.

Haze thanks him and does a U-turn, watching the scene become more and more distant in the rearview mirror.

"Is there another way home?"

"Not that I know of. And even if there was, I'm not risking it." He points out to the windshield. "I saw a motel a few miles back."

His tone makes it clear he's not asking. Part of me is screaming because I have to share a room with him. But the other feels relieved because I won't have to face Kendrick's wrath just yet. He's been texting me all night, asking for an explanation that I can't bring myself to give him.

What could I say? Hey, Kendrick, I just wanted to let you know that I did exactly what you told me not to do and caught feelings for your enemy. What's for dinner?

We drive in silence. I don't dare say a word, afraid that I'll distract him. This kind of weather requires his undivided attention. When we see the motel in the distance and the numerous cars in the parking lot, we know that a lot of people had the same idea as we did.

We get out of the vehicle and run toward the entrance as fast as the wind and violent rain allow us to. The area around the front desk is crawling with people who are just as eager to escape the rain as we are. When our turn finally comes, Haze asks for a room with two beds. The employee tells him that they only have a room with one bed available due to the large number of unexpected arrivals.

Haze gives me a look that says, "Is that okay?" I shrug as an answer. What else can I do? Sleep in the car?

"It's fine," he tells the guy.

He completely ignores me when I try and pay for half of the room and hands the employee his card.

One night stuck in a motel room with Haze Adams?

Sure, why not?

WHEN HAZE STEPS INTO THE ROOM and drops clothes on the bed, I'm not sure if I should thank him or be upset. As soon as we settled into the room—not that we really needed settling because we have no luggage—Haze said that he had some dry clothes for me in the car. Something about always bringing some of his clothes in his trunk to be prepared.

And by prepared he probably means for when he needs to

change after sneaking out of his one-night stand's bed.

The thought stings although I'll never admit it.

"I'm going to take a shower," I say, and when he smirks, I know the awkward moment has passed and the Haze I know is back.

"A shower, huh?"

"Don't even think about it, Adams." I push the door open.

He grins. "I didn't say anything."

The last thing I see before entering the bathroom is Haze kicking off his shoes and throwing himself onto the bed. My shower is short and cold. When I step out of it, I happily put on Haze's dry sweatpants and hoodie. I'd hoped that they'd stop the shivers running down my spine, but they don't. I'm afraid I'm going to catch a cold. As soon as I exit the bathroom, he complains about the fact that the TV only has two channels: the news and a channel that merely plays old black-and-white movies. He rolls to his side, looking at me, and smiles. Silent, he carefully analyzes my clothes—or should I say *his clothes*.

"Why are you looking at me like that?"

He smiles. "Because you're adorable."

My cheeks heat up.

"Straight to the point, aren't we?"

"No time to beat around the bush anymore."

He's right. I've tried not to think about it, but I can't run from the truth any longer: the fight's the day after tomorrow, and I have to mentally and emotionally prepare myself for what I'm about to see. Haze and Kendrick fighting. Violently.

If Haze wins, I'll have to spend a month with him.

If he loses, I can never see or talk to him ever again.

And… I'm not sure which one is worse.

I lie down on the bed next to him and glance at the clock on the nightstand. 3:03 a.m.

I yawn. "I'm exhausted."

"Me too."

I slide under the covers as Haze turns off the TV. I shiver, tangled up in the cold sheets that haven't known human warmth in a while.

"Are you cold?" he asks, joining me.

"I'll be fine in a minute," I whisper.

He doesn't reply, sitting up straight in the bed and removing his shirt before throwing it across the room. I'd usually check him out, but all I can think about in that moment is the heat radiating off his bare chest. He's hot—in every way possible.

"Come here." His voice is low, demanding.

When he opens his arms, offering me a spot on his chest, I refuse to fight myself. I'm too exhausted. I rest my head on his torso and sigh in relief when his burning skin meets mine. This is the first real physical contact between Haze and me, but it isn't weird or stressful. It's surprisingly easy. *Natural.* He circles my waist with his arm and holds me tight. I listen to the sound of his heart beating, and, eventually, his breathing becomes regular.

I've never understood the people who say that home isn't a place. But now that I'm lying here with him, I know...

If home is a feeling, that's what it feels like.

FOURTEEN

Don't Let Me Go

"Hit me."

This isn't exactly what I expected him to say when I woke up at 8:00 a.m. after getting five hours of sleep. We woke up in the exact same position we fell asleep in, his eyes opening almost as soon as mine did. I thought he'd want to get breakfast.

I couldn't have been more wrong.

He doesn't want breakfast.

He wants me to punch him in the face.

Indeed, he's been asking me to attack him for the past fifteen minutes, but I can't bring myself to do it. Here I am, in a crappy motel room, in front of a very well-trained fighter, wondering if hitting him in the face would break my wrist.

When Haze said he wanted to show me something, I never would've thought that I'd end up here, fighting with him about *not* fighting him. Why did he suddenly decide to show me how to be a ninja? God only knows.

I'm assuming it has something to do with the clock and its incessantly rapid ticking. The fight's tomorrow.

Tomorrow.

Let that sink in, Winter.

"Seriously? You want me to hurt you?" I look up at him, and his eyes soften under my gaze.

"Nothing you do will hurt me as much as they'll hurt you if you don't learn basic self-defense, Winter." He blows out a breath. "Do you want to be some damsel in distress? No? Then prove it."

His challenging tone seems to be enough for my pride to take over. "Fine. But don't go crying when I kick your ass."

"No promises." He smirks. "Now, what are the weak points again?" The playful expression in his face dissipates as quickly as it appeared.

"Eyes. Nose. Neck…" I pause, trying to remember the last one. We've been at it for almost three hours. He's taught me so many moves I can't feel my arms anymore. I learned how to disarm someone pointing a gun at me, exactly how and where to kick a man—if you know what I mean—and how to get out of someone's grasp.

"Seriously?" he reprimands. "Knees. It's not that hard to remember."

I rub my eyes. "I'm sorry. I'm exhausted."

"Do you think they're going to care if you're exhausted? No, they won't think twice." He clenches his fists.

"Well, excuse me, but it's hard to be in fight mode when I've barely had five hours of sleep. You've taught me more moves than I can count. I think I'm good. Can't we just take a break?"

"No. You won't be able to take a break when they're trying to kill you. Can't you see how important this is? One wrong move, Winter. One, and you're dead."

Dragging my feet, I make my way to the door. I can't be around him when he's like this.

"Where do you think you're going?" he calls.

"Outside. I need some air."

"The fight's tomorrow. Who knows what could happen then? Are you trying to get yourself killed?" He seizes my arm, stepping in my way.

I scoff. "You want to ask questions? Fine. Here's one for you. Why the hell do you care so much?"

Only then do I realize my anger has made me step dangerously close to him. His gaze immediately drops to my lips.

Well, *shit*.

I move away, the heavy tension back to torture me. We all know what happened the last time we were too close. It's like the closer we get, the harder it is for me to think clearly.

"Because…"

He doesn't finish his sentence. Instead, he takes a step forward, bringing us back to the position we were in seconds ago. My mind screams to walk away. But my body is refusing. Locked in his breathtaking gaze, I find myself reliving the moment we shared on the beach. He doesn't speak, but he doesn't need to. His blue eyes say more than a thousand words ever could.

They say, "Push me away. Tell me to stop. Tell me it's wrong before I run out of self-control."

I don't say a word.

And silence is all he needed to hear.

My heart bursts out of my chest when he cups my face in his hands and crashes his lips on mine. I immediately give in to his eager and familiar lips, steadiness a foreign concept to my hammering heart. He kisses me with this fervent need that could drive any girl insane.

This time is different.

This time, he's not holding back.

He's hungry. No, he's *starving*. I said this could never happen again just a few hours ago. I should want him to stop. So why…

Why is it the last thing I want?

Our bodies collide as his hands travel from my hair, to my neck, to my waist, unable to stay in the same place for too long.

My brain isn't strong enough to go up against my desires. My hand tugs at his hair as he backs me up against the wall roughly. I can't stop a moan from escaping my mouth when he bites my lower lip, his fingers creating a trail from my arm to my collarbone. They stop on my tank top strap and slide the light fabric down my shoulder.

He leans forward, his mouth grazing my clavicle and sending a wave of shivers throughout my entire body. My fingers fall to his shirt. I can't want him. I can't want this. But I do.

I really, really do.

Just as I'm about to pull the fabric up...

Knock! Knock!

We jump and pull away like we've been caught committing a crime.

"Housekeeping!" a female voice says loudly.

We exchange the most awkward look possible. The "we just came back down to earth after a wild, breathtaking, and extremely hot make-out session and now it's weird" look. It's like falling from a cloud and hitting concrete.

Haze clears his throat and fixes his shirt. He is as overwhelmed as I am. I pull my tank top strap up, struggling to regulate my breathing. He answers the door, says something I can't hear to the maid, and comes back.

"Checkout's at 11:00. It's 10:45. That's their way of telling us to get the hell out."

I can't tell what he's thinking. I keep my head down and walk toward the bed to gather the few belongings I had on me last night.

What the hell is wrong with me? I can't believe I let it happen a second time. But most importantly, *I can't believe I want to do it again.*

"Yeah, we should go." I remember the text messages my cousin sent me last night. He's coming home at one, and he's literally going to kill me, then bring me back to life, then kill me again if I'm not there. "Kendrick's coming home in two hours. He's been training all morning."

Haze nods, reaching for his keys in his jacket pocket. "We've got a fifty-minute car ride ahead of us. Come on."

IS THERE ANYTHING MORE AWKWARD THAN spending fifty minutes in a car with a guy you were intensely making out with barely an hour ago and having to pretend it never happened? Probably. But right now, it doesn't feel like it.

Haze and I haven't said a single word to each other since we left the motel. He's cold. Distant. Exactly the opposite of how I'd expect a guy to be after a kiss like that.

"Shouldn't you be training, too?" I break the silence, unsure if I want to know the answer. The fight is tomorrow. I have no idea why he's here with me.

"I didn't exactly have time."

"Yeah but you could've left early to train. Why didn't you?"

I'm dying to know what's going on in his head. Why did he kiss me? What does any of this mean?

"I had other things on my mind." I know what he's talking about right away and wiggle uncomfortably in my seat.

"Not at all worried about the fight, are we?"

"Nope."

The coldness in his voice makes my blood boil. What's his

problem? I look ahead of me and see my house from afar. Maria's at work. Only Kassidy's car's in the driveway. No sign of Kendrick anywhere. Thank God.

Haze kills the engine. He doesn't move. I don't either.

"You wouldn't actually…" I pause. "Kill him, would you?"

He doesn't bother looking at me. "Not unless I have to."

Of course he couldn't be a decent guy and say, "No, of course not. I care about you and so I won't kill your cousin if it ever comes to that. *Peace out.*"

"What do you mean? We're talking about my cousin's life, and you're telling me that you might kill—"

He cuts me off. "What the hell do you want me to say, Winter, huh? That I'll cancel the fight? That I'll go gentle on him for you? Why? Because we made out a couple times? I don't owe you anything. He's nothing to me. He's an enemy. That's all. I don't know who you think I am. But I'm not that guy who goes soft for some chick he just met. I'll never be that guy."

His words feel like razor blades tearing through my flesh. His sudden change of tone and the anger radiating out of him renders me speechless. I clench my fists, a burning pain spreading in my chest.

"Is that why you went out of your way to get my trust? Why you kept showing up at my house and texting me for the past month? Because you're not that guy?" I shout. "Or maybe that's why you kissed me? Because you don't care?"

"I don't. I don't care, Winter. I don't care about you or Kendrick, or anyone else," he barks. "It was supposed to be fun. Nothing else. You weren't supposed to…" He doesn't finish his sentence, rage flowing out of him profusely. "I don't need you to guilt-trip me, okay? You knew what you were getting yourself into."

I'm confident that my eyes are bloodshot by the time he finishes his sentence. My emotions are at war. Anger, hatred, sadness… I can't seem to decide which one's going to win.

When I look at him and he denies me eye contact, Bianca's bitter words creep into my head: "You think you're so special, don't you? That you'll somehow be that one girl who makes him fall in love? News flash: you're not. And in the end, he'll get sick of you. Because guess what? You're not different. Or special. *No one is.*"

She was right. Kendrick was, too. All along.

"So, it's true, huh?" My words catch him off guard.

"What?"

"I'm a game."

He doesn't answer, looking down.

"I'm a way to hurt Kendrick."

No response.

"Say it." I raise my voice, holding back the tears to the point of pain.

"Winter, you're only hurting yourself even m—"

"Say it," I scream as loud as I can.

"Fine," he snaps. "It was a game. All of it. I wanted to piss Kendrick off and make you fall for me so that I could see the look on his face when I told him that I fucked his precious cousin. Is that what you wanted to hear?"

My heart splinters into a million pieces.

If the maid hadn't stopped us, I don't know what would've happened. If no one had knocked on the door, I might've removed his shirt and…

I don't even want to think about it.

God, I'm such a fucking idiot.

"You say your biggest fear is to end up alone," I say, my voice trembling. "Well, you sure are good at pushing everyone away."

I shake my head and rush out of the vehicle, slamming the door loudly. He didn't say anything. He didn't try to stop me. But at the same time, he said everything.

His silence did.

Silence is not just the absence of noise. It's the absence of possibilities. Possibilities of second chances and forgiveness. In the end, what hurts the most is not what people say. It's what they don't.

Silence puts an end to the endless cycle we put ourselves through. To this never-ending torment that they call "hope." Hope that it will get better. Hope that you'll find your way back. Hope that you'll get a happy ending.

Because you can't forgive someone...

Who's not sorry.

Haze's black car takes off in a roar almost as soon as I step out of it. I keep walking, refusing to watch him disappear although every fiber of my being is begging me to.

I step onto my porch and insert the key into the hole. Just as I'm about to unlock the door, someone beats me to it, opening it from the inside. I come face-to-face with the last person I expected to see.

"Will?" I try to find a reason for his presence at my house this early. "What are you doing here? Kendrick's at Alex's?"

Shock occupies his eyes. He seems nervous, stressed. One thing is certain: he was *not* expecting me.

"Winter, hey." He speaks rapidly. "I forgot something here. I had to pick it up before training."

"Oh. Okay." I force a smile, trying to ignore the painful pit in my throat and the tears begging me to let them out.

"See you later," he says, walking around me and making his way to his car that's parked on the other side of the street.

Well, that wasn't weird at all.

As soon as I'm alone, I collapse on a chair and let the tears roll down my cheeks as I bury my face in my hands like a pathetic mess.

You're such a dumbass, Winter. You did this to yourself.

I have no idea what I expected. That he actually cared about me? That he was texting me every day and showing up at my house because he liked me? It all started with a deal.

"Are you okay?"

I jump and look up. Kassidy is standing in the kitchen. I completely forgot she was home. She gives me a look I know so well.

Pity.

I wipe my eyes. "I'm fine."

She arches an eyebrow and sits down next to me.

"You're not fine," she whispers. "What did he do?"

I'm a bit surprised by her tone. She's not judging. Neither is she criticizing. That's new. I would've expected her to be super hard on me after what happened at the dinner. I hesitate, mentally battling myself on whether or not I'm ready to share the story with her. Or anyone.

"Winter, please. Let me be there for you."

Then I can't hold back anymore. The story spills out of me like a never-ending waterfall. Kass doesn't comment. I tell her everything. I tell her about the rooftop, the pool, the beach. All of it. She nods and chuckles at the funny parts throughout the story. I tell her about all the things that got me to where I am today. To being one more pawn on Haze Adams's chessboard.

To being a game.

"He didn't mean it," she says. "He's afraid, Winter. Typical boy."

"Afraid of what? That I caught feelings and he didn't?" I scoff. I refuse to let her get my hopes up.

"No, dummy." She pauses and sighs like she's wondering why she has to be surrounded by idiots. "He's not afraid because you caught feelings. He's afraid because he's feeling it, too."

To say this simple little sentence didn't amplify my suffering by a thousand would be a big fat lie. The last thing I want to hear right now is that he didn't mean it. I want her to tell me he sucks. I want her to tell me I'll be okay. That I'll get over him and his stupid blue eyes.

"Oh shoot. I'm late for my shift. I have to go. But please, call me if you need anything, okay?" she asks, giving me a quick hug. "Oh, and don't text him. Let him be alone with his lies for a while. Might be exactly what he needs."

I watch her walk out of the house in a hurry and enter the bathroom. I step in the shower, standing completely still under the hot water for a couple of minutes. The last words she said before closing the door echo in the back of my mind. *"Never underestimate a man's capacity to run away from something he's afraid to want."*

I feel it infiltrate my thoughts. It's small and faint, but it's enough to tear me apart like it never left. I bury my face in my hands, my wounds opening all over again. It's back. The cruelest part of it all.

The hope.

FIFTEEN

The Fight

Empty is the only word I can think of to describe how I feel right now. As I lie in bed and listen to the silence floating around the house, I can't escape the downward spiral. I went to bed at around 3:00 a.m. last night. To my great surprise, Kendrick never came home to lecture me about Haze. He texted me that we'd talk later and that he knows it wasn't my fault.

He doesn't suspect that anything happened between Haze and me, and he sees me as an innocent victim.

But I know I'm just as guilty as he is.

Speaking of Mr. Heartbreaker, I haven't checked my phone since yesterday. I turned it off almost as soon as Haze left because I don't want to know if he texted me.

But mostly… *I don't want to know if he didn't.*

After several minutes of my brain trying to convince my body to move, I get up from my bed, exit my room, and drag my feet down the stairs.

The fight is today.

The information's not registering.

I turn on my phone, walk into the kitchen, and yawn. I need coffee. As soon as the screen lights up, notifications come rushing in one after the other, and confusing feelings consume me. I hope that he texted me.

Just so I can tell him to never text me again.

I know, I don't make sense.

Seven messages await me.

At the exact same time, I receive an incoming call from Alex. They've probably been trying to call me for hours. I brush off the guilt weighing on me and pick up.

"Hello?"

"Well, hello, Miss I-Sleep-Until-It's-Four-P.m. We've been trying to reach you." I recognize Will's voice.

I gasp and my gaze jumps to the clock on the wall. "It's not even eleven yet. Stop exaggerating. I'm sorry for not taking your calls. I was exhausted."

"I assume Haze kept you up all night? You weren't too loud I hope." I can literally picture him wiggling his eyebrows like the perverted idiot he is.

I curse. Of course they would know about Haze by now. I'm not surprised that Kendrick told them all about his stunt. The crazy part is, Haze did keep me up all night. But not the way he thinks.

"Give me that," Alex says in the background.

Muffled voices and shuffling comes down the line. I can't restrain a smirk from remolding my lips, listening to them fighting over the phone.

These guys.

"Hello, Winter? Sorry about that." Alex's voice indicates that he won the war. "Will—" He moves the phone away from his mouth. "Don't eat that. It's for my sister's school."

"Just a little bit," Will's distant voice replies.

I snigger. "What's going on?"

"Damn it, Blake, can you take that cake away from him, please?"

I laugh.

"You guys are actual kids."

"Tell me about it." Alex exhales. "We'll be there to pick you up in fifteen minutes. Be ready."

"Wait, what?"

The line goes dead.

I can honestly say I've never gone up the stairs faster in my life. I throw on a sweater and a pair of black leggings, pulling my hair up into a messy bun. That's the best I can do today. I make sure to apply a little bit of makeup so that the numerous hours of sleep I didn't get last night aren't the first thing you see when you look at me.

While I wait, I select the other unread text messages I didn't have time to check yet.

I have one message from my best friend, Allie.

And zero from Haze.

But that's not what surprises me the most.

What I can't believe is the messages from the unknown number I completely forgot about until now. They didn't text me again after I left the hotel. I thought it was merely the result of someone messing with me. Obviously, I was wrong.

The messages were sent yesterday—more precisely right after Haze dropped me off.

> How ironic that you would push away the only person who cares.

I'm paralyzed, my breathing shallow.

> Enjoy the time you have left and watch out for the scars.

The scars? What the heck is that supposed to mean? What scars?

I read the messages over and over again, hoping to remember something, anything, about yesterday. Maybe it was a suspicious car parked on the street. Maybe it was someone walking on the sidewalk. It could be anyone, anywhere. All I know is the person behind the unknown number saw it all. They saw Haze and I get into a fight; they saw me bolt out of the car and cry my eyes out like a pathetic mess.

My stalker was here yesterday.

And he might be here *right now*.

I run to the window and shove the curtains open with one hand. No one except the neighbor. The nice granny who lives on the other side of the street waves at me while she waters her flowers. I wave back. For all I know, she could be the unknown number.

I'm completely paranoid.

When Blake's car pulls up in the driveway, the inevitable question comes to me. Should I tell the boys about the messages?

They would put the pieces together, understand that something happened between me and Haze, and make my life a living hell... but they might also be the only ones who know what "watch out for the scars" means.

Blake gets out of the car, probably to knock on the door, but I decide to save him the trouble and step outside.

"Come on, we have to go," he hisses when he sees me.

Immediately, I'm under the impression that Blake is either very angry at me or having an awful day.

"What's the rush?"

"We have to get you ready for the fight. That's the rush."

"What do you mean? I'm not the one fighting."

"Still, you need to be prepared for all the things you might see tonight."

"You think I've never seen two guys fight?" I arch an

eyebrow.

"You haven't. Not like this, trust me." He grows impatient. "Are you waiting for the grass to grow?"

Okay, *rude.*

We walk toward the car side by side, and I frown.

That's very out of character for Blake. I've never seen him in such a bad mood. I get into the passenger seat and buckle up, wondering what his problem is. I watch the vein in his neck throb in anger as he pulls out of the driveway recklessly.

And I thought Haze drove like an idiot.

I mentally slap myself when his name creeps its way into my brain again. It's only been a day since I fought with him and I can't stop thinking about him.

Feelings suck.

"Are you okay?" I ask.

"I'm sure I'm doing better than you."

I furrow my eyebrows. "What's that supposed to mean?"

"I'm guessing getting your heart broken by the town's bad boy isn't exactly pleasant."

He knows.

But how? Kendrick might've told him about Haze's stunt at the dinner, but that doesn't justify Blake's knowledge of... everything.

"I showed up at your house yesterday morning. After Kendrick told us about Haze's surprise visit, I thought I'd come and get it straight from you. I couldn't believe it. That you'd agree to go with him after everything he did, and well…" He pauses. "I saw him drop you off."

"I…" I begin, but he interrupts me.

"No need to explain yourself. The sight of you two fighting like a married couple told me everything I needed to know." His eyes become hard. "You've fallen for him. Like they all do."

I lower my head to my feet. I always knew they'd react this way. That's why I didn't want to tell them. Because I knew they'd be the ones to tell me the truth I so desperately feared.

"It was the only way Haze wouldn't ruin Kendrick's dinner. I had to go out with him. We made a deal—that's all it was." I can't believe I'm still trying to justify my actions.

"Let me guess, the part when you're bawling your eyes out in Kass's arms was also part of the deal?"

"Oh for God's sake, you saw that, too?"

"I saw enough."

How long did Blake sit outside the house? He might've seen the person behind the unknown number. I battle the urge to ask him if he saw someone suspicious, well aware that now is not the time.

Images of Will walking out of the house in a hurry burn within me. I still have no idea what he forgot that what was so important he had to come and get it at my house when Kendrick wasn't home. But most of all, who let him in? Maria was already at work, and Kass was still in bed.

"Did you tell them?"

"I didn't, believe it or not."

"You didn't?"

"Nope, because you will. You're gonna be the one to look your cousin in the eyes and tell him you're in love with the enemy, the guy whose brother almost killed him. That's not my mess to clean up."

He's right. The hatred settling in his tone feels like a never-ending punch in the chest. I wouldn't say I'm in love with Haze. I can't be in love with him. I can't love someone whose only goal was to use me.

I'm not that stupid, am I?

"I'm not in love with him," I blurt.

"Oh really? Because your tears told me otherwise, and that fight—"

"That was the last time, I promise. I won't go anywhere near him ever again. You don't have to believe everything I say, but you have got to believe that."

"Yeah, well, you see, even if I wanted to believe you, I couldn't. No girl is ever truly over Haze Adams. Trust me, I know."

I refrain from asking him to elaborate. Whatever ulterior motive Blake has for hating Haze's player ways so much, I don't want to know. I've had enough for the day.

"God, I can't believe you did that," he lashes out. "Have a thing for the guy whose brother once strangled you, the guy who, may I remind you, put a target on your back by making a deal that was meant to hurt Kendrick. The ultimate player, Winter."

He was never that guy with me.

But then again, he was trying to seduce me, so I guess I never really knew the real him.

In that moment, I wish I could deny what he's saying. I wish I could magically come up with an explanation for all the times I agreed to follow him. For the times I laughed with him to the point of tears and the constant text messages. I'd like to find the words to justify feeling the way I did when he kissed me in that motel room. I wish I could take our moments back, but I can't.

They happened.

And they were wonderful.

Even if they weren't *real*.

"I thought you were smarter than this," he says quietly.

I can't bring myself to apologize, wondering what I could possibly say that I haven't already.

Instead, I whisper the three words that sum up the way I feel better than an entire novel ever could.

"So do I."

"IT'S ABOUT DAMN TIME," I HEAR Will say when we

walk inside the house. I follow Blake into the living room where all the guys are. Except for one.

"Where's Kendrick?" I ask.

"He's upstairs, training. He'll call us when he's ready," Alex says.

I immediately notice Will has a cut on his lower lip. It's fresh, recent.

"Will, are you okay?"

"Do I look like I'm not?" He chuckles.

"Why is your lip bleeding?"

"Kendrick's been training, we told you."

They can't be serious.

"What the hell? You guys train on each other?"

"Usually not, but Kendrick stopped training during his recovery, so he's scared that he lost it." Will shrugs, changing the channels with the remote.

My wandering gaze shifts to Alex and Blake. They seem unbothered by Will's statement. Like it's a normal thing for them to beat each other up.

"So basically Kendrick punched you in the face and you're okay with it?"

"Of course I am. I'm the one who volunteered."

And this, ladies and gentlemen, is why I'll never understand men.

I scoff, sit down on the couch and watch Will change the

channels continuously. Alex quickly gets sick of it and decides he's going to take the remote away from him. Will wants to keep it, which results in Alex quite literally lying on top of him to steal it. I'm laughing at their imbecility when their bickering is interrupted by a knock on the door.

"I got it," Will says, bringing the remote with him to annoy Alex, who rolls his eyes. As soon as he opens it, someone pushes past him. We're all equally astounded to see her.

"Where is he?" she shouts.

"Nicole, what are you doing here?" Will asks.

"His car's outside. I know he's here." She opens every door frantically.

Alex gives in, probably terrified that she'll break something in his parents' flawless home. "He's upstairs."

When she thumps up the stairs loudly, I assume she's been here before, probably back when they were still together.

"Kendrick Kingston!" she shouts at the top of her lungs. The guys and I share a look. We don't need to talk. We're thinking the same thing. We quickly gather at the bottom of the stairs to listen.

"Nicole, w-what are you doing here?" Kendrick babbles.

"Don't you dare pretend that you don't know. How could you do this to me?"

"I really had to go. I'm sorry…"

"I give you my body, my soul, just like old times, and you

sneak out."

The guys' mouths part as mocking smiles take residency on their faces. We don't hear an answer from Kendrick, but what we do hear… is a very loud clap.

She just slapped him.

Well, I assume?

Unless she clapped her hands?

Why would she clap her hands?

Winter, back to the point.

Kendrick and Nicole slept together? And here I thought I was the only one making terrible choices.

"You leave without saying goodbye. You're an asshole, a dirtbag, a waste of space," she screams, obviously unaware that we can hear everything loud and clear.

That's when it hits me. I thought it was incredibly weird that Kendrick didn't come home yesterday to lecture me about Haze. He was busy with Nicole.

I bet the guys think she's a little crazy to show up for the sole purpose of making a scene, but I actually feel bad for her. I can relate; nobody likes feeling used.

"Nicole, calm down," Kendrick says.

"I was such an idiot. How could I think that you cared? How could I be so stupid to fall for you again?" Her screams turn to muffled sobs.

I feel like I'm watching a TV show.

"Wait… You love me?"

"Of course I do. I never stopped."

Oh for God's sake, Nicholas Sparks, get out of here.

"I love you, too."

"You do?" Nicole sniffles.

Silence.

Then, a smooch.

Oh, they're making out.

After what I assume to be a hardcore kissing session, they pull away for air. When we hear footsteps, we all rush to the couch, shoving each other.

"Guess who's back together?" Nicole announces, an enormous smile on her lips.

What? That girl can smile? When? How?

"No way?" Will musters the best surprised expression he possibly can, but the truth is written all over his face.

"That's great, guys," I say.

"We really didn't see it coming," Blake adds.

Kendrick frowns.

"You heard everything, didn't you?"

"Yep," we all say at the same time.

Our laughter intertwines. The East Side may be dysfunctional, but they're like family. And in the end, family's the most important thing.

It pains me to think that Haze doesn't really have any.

But I also find a hint of irony in the story of the boy who's terrified to end up alone but still refuses to let anyone in.

After the "we're back together" moment, Kendrick goes back to his endless training, and Nicole joins us in the living room. Truth is, the girl can be nice when she wants to.

Notice the words *when she wants to*.

"So… Winter," Blake says during a commercial. "Is there something you would like to tell us?"

Son of a…

He's going to do this now?

"No, nothing in particular."

"Are you sure?"

Can this possibly get any more awkward?

"Positive." I nod.

My answer irritates him.

Will and Alex give us a weird look and draw their attention away from us and back to the TV. I want to thank the Lord that they're not girls. Girls wouldn't have just ignored that. I swear, we're better than the FBI at finding out the truth sometimes. I lock eyes with Nicole, whose gaze is loaded with suspicion. I don't know why Blake wants me to tell them.

It doesn't matter what happened.

It's over. Done.

Why tell a story that never really began?

MY IDEA OF A GOOD TIME has always been to go see a movie, to go get ice cream on a sunny day, or to spend time with friends. They say you learn something new every day. Well, today taught me that watching Kendrick and Will take swings at each other for thirty minutes is not a hobby I'll be pursuing in the future.

The violence and recklessness of their actions quickly rendered me terrified. Blake was right. If I thought I'd seen two guys fight before, I'd clearly never seen two *trained fighters* fight. Every fist Kendrick put up, Will avoided. Every punch that Will threw, Kendrick threw back. And to make it even worse, Alex said that Haze is a far more advanced fighter than Will as he started years prior to him. If Kendrick can't beat Will, he won't be able to beat Haze.

Kendrick's incredible considering he's only been in the game for two years. But Haze has been around for four.

Needless to say that's not helping our odds.

My cousin tried to show me a couple of moves to defend myself in between breaks. Having to pretend I had no idea what he was talking about slowly but surely drove me insane. Haze and I already spent hours training so that I'd master the basics. It seemed so important to him to teach me how to defend myself. One more check on his "let's convince Winter that I care" list, I guess.

As we drive toward the moment I've so desperately been

trying to avoid, I feel myself trembling. My breathing is sharp, irregular. I can't deal with the burden of reality right now. I nervously fidget with my fingers, watching the neighborhood fall asleep as the lights gradually go out along the way. Kendrick's been sparing me the details until now. But he'll have to tell me everything when we get there.

"You need to chill, Winter. I can feel your stress." Will nudges me with his elbow.

"I can't help it."

"What are you so worried about? We've been training super hard for this. Kendrick will beat Haze."

"And if he doesn't?"

"He has to," Blake glances at me. "He will."

Gee, thanks. That helps.

"We're here," Kendrick says. "That's the farthest we go." The area is empty, deserted. He pulls up next to the creepiest tunnel I've ever seen. The darkness on the opposite end makes it hard to believe that anyone ever found the courage to cross it.

"Can't I just stay here? Do I absolutely have to witness this act of violence?"

Alex shakes his head. "The prize has to be present during the fight. I'm sorry. That's the rule."

"Who made up that rule? Is it written in stone? I'd like to see it stated somewhere, or I'm not going."

Will grins, getting out of the car.

"Call it an unwritten rule."

I try to swallow the lump in my throat and fail. When I finally gather the courage to get out of the car, I'm welcomed by utter and complete darkness. The tunnel hovers in front of us, reminding me of every horror movie where the girl dies *ever*.

They want *me* to go in *there*?

If I wasn't surrounded by extremely well-trained fighters right now, I'd have peed my pants already.

"So where is the fight happening? Are we the first ones here?"

Will scoffs. "Cute. You think because we're called street fighters that we actually fight in the street?" His gaze shift to the boys. "The Downside, huh? I thought we'd moved on from that."

Blake shrugs. "The fighter responsible for the deal gets to pick, you know that."

I assume it means whoever challenged the enemy into the fight gets to choose the place and time. Well, I guess I have Haze to thank for giving me nightmares for the rest of my life.

Blake speaks again. "Plus, it's the safest place right now. They'll never find us here."

I know that by *they* he means the authorities. Kendrick said that they heard about the fights from whispers on the street and rumors running around town. But it's like a unicorn. Hearing of it and actually finding one are two different things.

The fights constantly changing location make it near impossible to track the "show." That's what they call it. You need to be in the inner circle to know when or where they happen, and from what I've heard, that's not an easy circle to get into. That makes me wonder how Blake, who was the first one to get into it, did it.

"Okay." Kendrick steps in my way and looks deeply into my eyes. "We need to go over the basics before we go down there. One wrong move and everything could turn to shit. First, don't interfere with the fight—never. Even if Haze is beating the shit out of me, you don't say anything. Whatever happens, he won't kill me. He can't. Not if I surrender. Do you understand?"

I nod halfheartedly.

"Second, you have to be willing to surrender. Ten seconds on the floor marks the end of the fight. If you don't accept defeat when you can barely stand, your opponent will not be held responsible if the last punch kills you, whether it's voluntary or not."

In other words, he has the right to kill you.

Goose bumps creep onto my skin.

"Just like when betting on anything such as horses, car races, you only have one chance to bet and there are no refunds. You're responsible for losing your money. So in conclusion, keep your head down, don't draw attention to yourself, and everything should be fine, okay?"

Only then do I realize my eyes are flooded. Kendrick stares at me in shock. I can't handle the guilt. He's in this mess because of me. If I hadn't followed him, I wouldn't have to look over my shoulder every step I take. If I'd just stayed home, he wouldn't have to worry about what's going to happen to me if he loses.

When a tear rolls down my face, the coldhearted fighter standing in front of me comes apart and turns back into the little boy I grew up with, the boy who stood up to my bullies when we were six, the Kendrick I ate entire boxes of cookies with in secret.

"I'm so sorry you got dragged into this, cousin." He pulls me into a hug. "It's going to be fine, I promise. It'll all be over soon."

I should feel better, but I don't. It'll all be over soon, he says.

But for who?

As we get closer to the tunnel, I try and assemble the million pieces scattered in my mind. What's the Downside? And how the hell do we get there? Kendrick leads the way toward the unknown. When he activates the flashlight on his phone, the cement walls hovering over and around us reveal graffiti of all sorts. One graffiti tag in particular catches my eyes.

WS.

"We're in West Side territory," Alex explains when he notices the way I peer at the bold letters.

Of course we are.

That's not helping our odds *part two*.

The flashlight stops on something I'd say is rather confusing—although it does remind me that I shouldn't even be surprised at this point. A sewer grate. Again, the light refuses to pay us a visit, leaving me to fend for myself as I desperately try to see what's under it. The only visible thing in the man-sized hole is a rusty metal ladder embedded into the wall.

A sewer? Really?

Is this Haze's way of telling me I'm full of shit?

"What are we doing? Hanging out with the rats?" I ask when Kendrick easily pulls the grate up and uncovers the way to hell.

"You'll see" is all he says.

He begins to go down the ladder. Then comes Blake's turn, followed by Alex's, and finally, mine. As soon as my feet connect with the ground, I'm overwhelmed by an atrocious smell, my dinner threatening to make an appearance. On the bright side— there is no sign of water anywhere, which is good. Haze ruined my idea of love. I don't need him to ruin my shoes, too.

When Will puts the grate back into place and goes down the ladder, as well, I catch myself wondering what would happen if someone were to drop a block of cement over the grate. Would we be stuck here forever?

"Come on." Kendrick motions and walks ahead.

I follow them unwillingly. We take numerous turns,

venturing deeper and deeper into the tunnels. I try to keep up, but I know I wouldn't find my way back if I had to. When I make out a massive concrete door in the distance, I understand that I got it all wrong. This isn't a sewer.

It never was.

"Welcome to the Downside," Will says as Kendrick pulls on the door with a groan that indicates how heavy it is.

It squeaks open, revealing what seems to be a completely different universe.

People.

A lot of people.

I have no idea what that door is made of, but it sure is soundproof, considering that I never, and I mean never, heard any of the numerous voices on the other side. Everywhere I look, all I can think is *Cesspool of Unsavory Characters*.

A buzzing sound emanates from the white neon lights illuminating the room. Spread across the metallic ceiling, they flicker repeatedly, increasing the creepy vibe by a million. There are so many questions I want to ask, but I can't.

I want to know who built this place. Is it only used for the street fights? How did they manage to keep it undercover for so long? One look around the secret lair is all it takes for some of my questions to answer themselves.

Drug dealers, pimp, junkies, muscle heads.

The Downside isn't just for fighting.

As we make our way through the crowd, heads start to turn one by one.

Kendrick whispers, "Don't let them see your fear."

I do my best to ignore the intense anger and hatred pointed at us, keeping my eyes glued to the ground.

In the distance, a dense crowd is gathered in a circle, waiting for something. And that something is the fight. Soon, people begin to part, stepping out of our way to let us through, all the while making sure to stare at us in the most hateful way a human possibly can.

A couple of meters stand between us and the center of the circle.

"What's the North Side doing here?" Blake says through gritted teeth.

My gaze travels upward to the large flock of unknown and diverse faces. Kendrick wasn't lying when he said people came from everywhere to see the show.

When I see Ian, leader of the North Side and Haze's ally, I can't stop the thumping in my chest. Our eyes meet and he smirks, probably thinking of all the different ways he could murder me.

I peel my eyes away, fighting the burning need to look for Haze's face in the crowd. The person I see instead is Tanner. My breathing increases as I deny him eye contact. I can feel his gaze stinging in my skull. Then, after what seems to be an eternity,

Kendrick puts an end to my misery and comes to an abrupt stop. Blake, Alex, and Will do the same.

"Finally."

I recognize the voice who's been haunting my every waking moment. I can't bear to look at him, hiding behind Kendrick and the guys like a terrified puppy.

"We're here, Haze. Let's get this over with," Kendrick fumes.

"I'd like nothing more, but first… show me the prize."

My heart sinks.

I can't believe these words just came out of his mouth.

Out of obligation, Will, Alex, and Blake step aside, but Kendrick doesn't. He stays in position, clenching his fists as if to say, "Anyone who wants to touch her will have to go through me first."

Haze scoffs. "What are you afraid of? I'm not going to look at her to death."

The crowd cackles.

Kendrick sighs and moves barely enough for Haze to get a clear shot of me. That's when the last trace of will I have leaves my body, and I look up.

Our gazes lock.

There he is, across the circle, wearing his ripped leather jacket and his oh-so-usual arrogant and yet unbearably charming smile. Dark bags rim his piercing blue eyes, making it obvious that he hasn't gotten much sleep lately.

The blood coursing through my veins turns cold at the complete absence of kindness in his features.

Whoever this guy is, it's not Haze.

He looks like him. He sounds like him. But he's a stranger.

I never thought looking at a stranger could hurt this much.

"Ladies and gentlemen," Haze begins as cheers rise all around us. "Thank you for joining us tonight."

He steps into the circle. "As some of you may have heard, Kendrick here has been a very good fighter recently. Too good. He's actually been doing so well that some of you started to think he might be better than me." He pauses, mockery lingering in his tone. "So, of course, I have no choice but to put that to the test."

Great. All of this for an ego problem.

"But I thought we'd spice it up a little bit. Why not get something else out of it? You see, the East Side and I made a deal. If I win, I get to have this pretty little thing to myself for a month."

Everybody turns to look at me.

I think I'm going to be sick.

"But if I lose, Kendrick and his... *friend* here are free to leave unscathed. You know the rules. You know the game. No refunds, no second chances, no killing, and no interference. You've all placed your bets." Haze raises his voices. "Now, are you ready?"

The shouts grow in volume.

Kendrick and Haze both remove their shirts and throw them on the floor. Too much testosterone in here.

It's well-known that wearing clothes during a fight isn't recommended as the fabric can be pulled and used against you. Although they're not doing it to impress the ladies, I can tell from the looks on the faces of the girls witnessing the scene that they find the boys to be a sight for sore eyes. As for me, I can't even begin to think about that right now.

"No, Kendrick." I reach for his arm.

"I'm going to be okay. I promise." I can see the fear burning in the back of his eyes. "Remember, you can't interfere. Promise me."

"I—"

He insists. "Promise me, Winter."

I almost choke on the words. "I promise."

I clench my jaw as the tears come pouring down my cheeks, my poor eyes obviously unable to contain them anymore.

This is happening... and it's my fault. Haze and Kendrick stare at each other in silence, ready to attack. I hold my breath, waiting for the first move.

Then, the inevitable happens.

Haze takes the first punch.

Kendrick easily dodges it, but when Haze lands a bigger, harder one seconds later, he's not so lucky. Kendrick groans and steps back, struggling to maintain his balance. A single punch like this would be enough to kill me. His eyebrow's already bleeding.

Kendrick's fists then turn into white-knuckled weapons that send Haze flying to the ground. Two seconds later, he's back on his feet, rushing toward Kendrick and tackling him. Before Haze has the chance to attack, Kendrick knees him in the stomach and elbows him in the face.

I've never seen anything so horrible. The crowd clearly doesn't agree with me, cheering in satisfaction at this display of horrific violence. It's all happening so fast, it's hard to keep up.

One more punch, one more kick.

It feels like it'll never end.

Next thing I know, the tables have turned and Kendrick's under Haze. Both their lips are cut open. Haze's nose is bleeding, and Kendrick's eyebrow isn't doing much better.

Straddling him, Haze repeatedly punches him in the face, over and over again. Kendrick tries to dodge his punches but fails miserably, his arm dropping to his side in defeat.

He's not strong enough.

If Haze keeps this up, he's going to kill him.

I can't stop a loud scream mixed with sobs from escaping my lips at the thought. I don't care what happens to me. Kendrick doesn't deserve this. As if my intentions are written in the sky, strong arms surround me from behind before I can step into the circle and put an end to this madness.

"Winter, don't!" Will shouts, struggling to hold me back.

"No. Stop. Let me go," I beg, the hysterical tears stealing my sight away from me. I've never fought harder.

I scream again, but this time, it cuts through the piercing shouting of the crowd and echoes among its roar.

Haze hears it.

And he looks up.

It feels like time stops when our eyes connect. He's staring at me. I'm bawling my eyes out and fighting Will like my life depends on it. In that moment, when he sees me cry in despair, color drains from his face. For a short instant… for just a second…

I recognize him.

The Haze who protected me from Ian when he had no reason to. The guy who took me to the end of the world just so I could look at the stars. The guy who once admitted to me that he was afraid of spiders on a dusty school rooftop and helped me get out of a motorcycle helmet that was stuck on my head.

He's still in there.

It seems to happen in slow motion. He looks at me and says a million things without opening his mouth. *He nods.*

It only lasts a second. It's almost nothing.

But I see it.

It's like he said, "It's okay, I got this."

We're brought back to reality when Kendrick takes advantage of Haze's distraction and takes one hell of a swing at him. I feel relieved and guilty at the same time, which is something I never knew was possible. I distracted him and stopped him from hurting Kendrick, but now he's the one getting beat up. Kendrick's on top of him, hounding him with punches. Haze doesn't fight back.

Why isn't he fighting back?

He doesn't get up, covering his face with his hands in an attempt to protect himself. He's not on the offensive anymore. He's defensive. Kendrick gets up, kicking Haze in the stomach recklessly. Both of them are bloody messes at this point.

"Ten."

The crowd begins the countdown.

"Nine."

Haze rolls over to his side, holding on to his stomach in agony.

"Eight."

I'm praying that he'll stay on the ground.

"Seven."

Praying for all of this to be over soon.

"Six."

Please, Haze…

"Five."

Don't get up.

"Four."

The sobs are suffocating me.

"Three."

Ian and his fighters scream for him to get back up. I frown, narrowing my eyes. There's something about them. Something I didn't notice that night in front of the school.

"Two."

Ian turns his head, and our eyes meet. He smiles.

"One."

The oxygen abandons me. I blink in disbelief.

"Zero."

It's over. Kendrick won.

But the sound that cuts through the thick air right after tells me that I couldn't have been more wrong.

It's not over at all.

The gunshot echoes through the screams of despair. The lights go out in a piercing and vibrant noise. People start running in panic, shoving each other, all with one goal and one goal only: to survive.

I hear Haze calling my name. I hear his voice in the chaos.

But he doesn't hear me.

He doesn't hear me when somebody violently yanks me from behind and twists my hair around their fingers.

He doesn't hear me when the soaked cloth is pressed against my mouth and my senses spill out of me.

I know he'll never hear me when my knees surrender and I feel myself falling. As I slowly slip out consciousness, I wish I could go back and tell them the truth. All of it. And the last thing I see before all turns black… is the memory of Ian and his fighters staring at me across the room.

They all have scars.

SIXTEEN

Save Me

The room was silent.

No one was brave enough to speak or move a muscle, the tension in the atmosphere unbearably heavy. Like the numerous fighters in the room feared even breathing too loud would be enough to send the East Side leader into a spiral of uncontrollable anger, they stood there, helpless.

He had been sitting in silence with his face hidden by both his hands for the last twenty minutes. His friends, who usually cheered him up, couldn't seem to find the words to ease his pain.

The room was wrecked.

Glass and furniture were scattered across the kitchen floor.

The Kingston house had never been such a mess, and Kendrick was to blame for its destruction. Exhaling, he remembered the dread he felt when the lights came back on and he looked around to see that she was gone. Winter was gone.

That's when the silence was ripped away by a knock on the front door.

"Tell me it's not your mother who forgot her keys again," Alexander said, his gaze nervously wandering around.

"Can't be. She's working a night shift," Kendrick whispered.

"And Kass?" Will asked, something shifting in his eyes.

"She's at Morgan's."

Will gave Kendrick a faint nod. Alexander sighed and got up to open the door that would reveal the last person on earth they wanted and expected to see.

Hatred. Rage. It was all Kendrick could feel when he grabbed him by the collar of his branded clothes and punched him.

"You. You fucking did this," he yelled, infuriated.

The blue-eyed boy took the hit. Seconds later, he had been pushed against the wall violently, the foundations of the old house creaking under the sudden duress. Avoiding a second punch, he pushed Kendrick to the ground.

"How is it my fault? I'm not the one who took her," Haze spat, as angry as could be.

"If you hadn't made that stupid deal in the first place, none of this would've happened." Alexander and Will held their friend back before he trashed the house any more than he already had. It wouldn't be easy to clean up, and they didn't need more problems.

"Well, maybe if you hadn't been so careless to let her follow you to our meeting, she'd still be here right now."

Kendrick barely held it together. "How dare you show your face here? You never cared about Winter. Get out."

Haze looked down, an unreadable expression crawling in his eyes. He didn't move, persistent.

"I'm not going anywhere. I want to help."

"You want to help? Are you serious? You're the reason she might be suffering right now."

Haze's face twitched in discomfort at the thought.

"What would you get out of it?"

"I have my reasons" was all Haze could say.

"You have your reasons. I'm supposed to believe that my enemy wants to help because he has his 'reasons'?" He used his fingers to create air quotes. "You're going to have to do better than that, Adams."

The West Side leader didn't answer.

"Oh for fuck's sake. Isn't it obvious?" Blake hissed.

Heads turned in his direction.

"They have a thing, you idiots." He rolled his eyes. "They've been doing…" He paused. "…whatever the hell it is they've been doing for a while now."

Kendrick's lips parted as his hand turned back into a position it knew so well: a fist.

"You slept with my cousin?" he raged, stepping dangerously close to Haze.

"No, of course not. We're… friends."

Blake scoffed. "Friends, my ass."

Haze sighed. "That's not what I came here to talk to you about. Do you want to bring her back home or not?"

"Don't you dare pretend like you care about anyone but

yourself," Kendrick said, bitter. "How do I know you're not the one who took her in the first place?"

"I'm not. Would I be here right now offering to help if I was behind her kidnapping?"

Kendrick growled. "Your reputation says yes."

"You don't have to believe me. But trust me, you're going to want to hear what I have to say."

Kendrick didn't answer. Nor did he try and break Haze's nose, which was a start.

"I found this at the Downside."

Haze slid his hand into his pocket and dropped something on the kitchen table. It only took a second for the boys to recognize the crappy cell phone Winter constantly complained about. The screen was cracked and shattered in multiple spots, but, thanks to some unknown miracle, it still worked.

"Someone's been texting her with an unknown number."

The boys frowned and shook their heads in disbelief. He was lying. He had to be. Winter was an open book. She would've told them about it, right?

Right?

"It started days ago." Haze pointed to the phone.

Kendrick, Alexander, Blake, and William stared at it with uncertainty. A hush descended over them.

"Go ahead, take a look."

Kendrick was the first one to give in to the curiosity. Quickly, text messages flew past his eyes. When he read the word "scars," he knew instantly. He looked up at Haze. His nemesis had just saved him an considerable amount of time. Not to mention, he was the only one with a connection to the North Side. The corner of Haze's mouth lifted into a faint smile. They needed him, whether they liked it or not.

He arched an eyebrow. "Do you want my help now?"

EMPTINESS HAD NEVER SAT WELL WITH Haze Adams. He always thought that having someone tell you they hate you was better than having that someone not talk to you at all. That's what his parents had raised him to think anyway.

As a kid, he would've chosen hearing his mother tell him that he did something wrong over being ignored by her for weeks any day. It'd started when he was fourteen years old. And it'd stuck with him ever since.

He'd known a lot of emptiness in his life.

But the emptiness that Winter had left was probably the worst.

Haze wouldn't mind Winter hating him if it meant she'd be alive to do it.

If there was one thing he didn't expect when he first met her, it was that he'd end up in the same car as the East Side, driving toward the North Side's lair to find her. They'd have forever to hate each other. But right now, working together was their only chance to get her back.

When he decided to show up to Winter's house, he didn't know how much Kendrick knew about them, but now, it was clear that the answer to that question was *nothing*. He couldn't believe that he was coming to them instead of working alone, but he knew he needed backup and couldn't exactly turn to the West Side. They were already suspicious that he'd lost the fight on purpose.

"Let's make this clear. As soon as we find her, you're out of her life for good. You know that, right?" Kendrick spat, his eyes on the road.

"Assuming she's still alive when we find her, then yes, I'll hold up my end of the deal," Haze said as an impenetrable silence filled the car.

He was right, and they knew it. She could be anywhere, suffering, agonizing. She could be dead by now.

Every cell in Haze Adams's body told him to break something, but he held on by a thread.

"Don't you dare say that. She's still alive. She has to be," Kendrick muttered.

He wished that Kendrick was right.

"I hope for your sake that you know what you're doing," Will huffed when they parked the car a couple houses away from the apartment complex Ian and his fighters hung out at.

Haze led the way, stepping out of the car with the unshakable thought that it was too easy. It didn't feel right.

"Alex, you stay in the car in case we have to get out of there in a hurry. The rest of you, go look in the other apartments. I've got this. Text me if you find anything, and I'll reach you if things get heated. Remember, at the first sign of complication, you jump in with the smoke bombs." They nodded in agreement.

They quietly sneaked in through the back door of the old apartment complex Ian had claimed as the North Side's spot and parted ways, leaving Haze to fend for himself. He took a sharp breath, knocking on the old apartment door loudly. The room immediately became quiet on the other side.

Footsteps. Then nothing.

"Who's this?"

"Seriously? A wooden door? I could kick the door in right now. I thought you were more careful than that."

"Yeah, well, few people know about this place. We're not worried." Ian unlocked the door and pushed it open, forcing a smile at the sight of Haze. "Come on in, partner."

He stepped aside as Haze walked into the three-bedroom apartment where the smell of cigarettes, alcohol, and weed greeted him. Everywhere around him, Ian's boys were drinking, smoking, or making out with escorts.

Some gangs were worse than others.

"Can I get you anything? A drink? A girl perhaps?"

Simultaneously, two girls wearing lingerie looked up.

"No, I'm good. I won't be long."

"You're the boss." He paused, motioning for Haze to sit at the poker table placed in the center of the room. "To what do I owe the pleasure?" Ian brought a joint to his lips, sinking into his seat.

"Just looking for a chat."

"About what, my friend?"

"I wanted to congratulate you on the East Side girl's kidnapping. Kendrick and his guys are a wreck right now."

"Oh, I'm flattered, man."

Haze dived his hand into his pocket, ready to press Send on the prewritten message. If Ian was responsible, the East Side would be there in a couple of minutes.

"But I can't take credit for something I didn't do." Ian took a sip of his drink.

God damn it, Haze thought, removing his hand from his pocket.

"Well, if you didn't do it, who did?"

"I can't tell."

"You can't, or you won't?" Haze struggled to keep a stern face.

Ian leaned back in his seat, frowning.

"You know, Haze… if I didn't know you any better, I'd say that you seem to care a hell of a lot about that girl."

Haze stiffened. "I don't. Just wondering who I have to thank for destroying my enemies, that's all. I thought we had an alliance." He got up. "I'll go tell the others I was wrong."

He turned away, heading for the door.

Three.

Two.

One.

"Wait," Ian called.

Haze smirked. *Predictable*. Having the West Side as an enemy was something no one wanted.

"Haze, man, chill, no need to get angry," Ian faltered.

"I came here looking for answers that you refuse to give me. I'm afraid that's not what an ally would do."

"I'll tell you everything I know."

"Don't bother. I think I'll go ask Vicky. Maybe she knows more than you do."

The second Vicky's name was announced, the conversations going on around them ended abruptly. Ian clenched his fists, his fighters glaring at Haze hatefully. It was well known in the street fight world that falling in love made you weak, but it didn't stop the fighters from wanting someone to come home to.

It was human nature at its best.

"She's got nothing to do with this. Leave her out of this."

"Neither did Winter, and she still got taken. Looks like there's no such thing as justice, you see?"

"The girl's probably already dead. Do yourself a favor, man.

Move on."

Haze laughed. "Is that what you would do if it were Vicky?"

Ian went from annoyed to pissed.

"I've got backup—a lot of backup. You're going to tell me where you keep her, or I'm blowing this place up."

Ian reached for his pocket.

"I wouldn't do that if I were you. I see one of you pull out a gun and we're all dead."

Ian narrowed his eyes. "You're bluffing."

"Am I?"

"That would kill you, too."

Ian's words sneaked into Haze's thoughts.

The girl's probably already dead.

"How are you so sure I have something to live for?"

"I didn't take your damn girl, Haze. Why would I do that? We had an alliance."

"According to her phone, you did." Haze selected the conversation. "'Watch out for the scars,' really? You expect me to believe that's a coincidence?"

"I never sent her that. Think about it. Did it ever occur to you that I've been set up?"

Only a fool wouldn't have considered that option. But Haze refused to look further into it. Because if he was right, if Ian had been set up by the other person he had in mind, everything was going to change. Everything would collapse. One of Ian's guys got his gun out before Haze could retract himself. Out of all the directions the bullet could've taken, it decided to hit the wall, inches away from his head. The gunshot was the East Side's cue. They kicked the door in, throwing the homemade smoke bomb Haze had stolen from his brother's stash mere hours after Winter's disappearance. He still couldn't believe how many weapons and bombs his brother had locked up in their house. Making the most out of the North Side's momentary blindness, they dashed down the stairs and into the vehicle waiting for them out front. The car took off in a roar, screeching around the corner at full speed.

"How did you get him so scared?" Blake asked, panting.

"Threatened his girl. Always works."

"That's all?" Alexander added, glancing in the rearview mirror, the fear of being followed eating him alive.

"I may also have pretended that there was a bomb," Haze said. Distant smiles tugged at the corners of their lips. Enemy or not, the guy was good.

Kendrick glowered. "The entire building was empty. That's not where they're keeping her."

"I know. I think we got it all wrong."

"What? Why?" Will said.

"We've been set up. It wasn't Ian."

"You got someone else in mind?" Kendrick blew out a breath.

The veins in Haze's neck bulged in exasperation. Saying it would make it official. It would make it *real*... and Haze wasn't quite ready for that.

"Yes... And I hope I'm wrong."

SEVENTEEN

Lost

Winter

You know that moment when something you thought would never happen to you, happens to you?

That moment you realize that you're not going to wake up in your bed, that you take for granted because you've never actually had to find out what it's like to sleep on the floor, and sigh in relief because it was just a dream? That's what I've been going through ever since I woke up. Who knows how long I've been knocked out. Hours? Days maybe?

My head hurts so bad.

Scratch that, my entire body hurts so bad.

I'm lying on a cement floor. It's cold. Hard. This leads me to assume that I'm in a basement, which are only a thing in higher areas in Florida.

We're not anywhere near Maria's neighborhood.

That's the closest I can get to knowing where I am.

Tight ropes circle my legs and wrists as a blindfold presses against my eyes. The large piece of duct tape covering my mouth gives me no other choice but to use the only sense available to me: hearing.

I focus on the squeaking sounds and footsteps on what seems to be an old wooden floor above my head. Everything about this place says no one will ever find you here.

Fun.

They tossed my phone at the scene, which doesn't seem smart if, like I suspect, the North Side is responsible. Kendrick and the guys will find my phone—if it still works at all—and figure it out.

This can only mean one of two things: Ian is new to this whole kidnapping thing, or everything he does is for a reason and it's all part of a bigger picture.

All I know is, evil plan or not, the only thing keeping me going is the hope that Kendrick will find me. Too bad my luck has run dry too many times in the past for me to get my hopes up. I'm the girl who gets her head stuck in a damn helmet for God's sake. Where's the luck in that?

I haven't screamed since I woke up, terrified I'll do nothing but catch my kidnappers' attention and bring an even worse fate upon myself. But I know that if there's even half a chance that someone could hear me, I have to try.

So I do. I scream as loud as I can through the tape blocking my mouth. Over and over again. Just then, the footsteps stop.

"She's awake," I hear a deep voice mumble.

The only bright side is, I can hear everything they say. If I do get out of here, I might know exactly who took me. When the door creaks open and footsteps come down the stairs, I know that I was right. This is a basement. My first instinct is to close my eyes and pretend to be sleeping.

"I thought you said she was awake," a husky voice says.

"She is. I heard her."

"What do we do with her?"

"Now…" He pauses and says the one sentence that makes me wish they'd killed me at the Downside instead. "We have some fun."

"She's pretty cute, isn't she?" They sound older—multiple years older. I might not be able to see their faces, but my guess is they have the creepy looks to go with the voices.

"He said not to touch the girl," Man Number Two reprimands.

"He doesn't have to know."

"He'll find out. He knows everything." His voice quakes with fear.

I hear one of them take a step forward.

"What are you doing?"

"Nothing, man, relax."

Tears well in my eyes. A hand is laid on my shoulder, pressing onto my skin. It moves downward to my chest. I start to wiggle, desperate to get his hand off me. I thank the Lord when the second stranger takes care of that for me.

"Back off, Owen. I'm serious," he threatens.

Owen. I got a name.

"Damn it, don't you know what fun means?"

"I know what trouble means, and that's what we're going to get into if anything happens to that girl before he says so."

Before he says so? This means that Ian is only keeping me safe to make sure he can hurt me later at his convenience.

"What's so special about that girl anyway?" Owen spits.

"Haze Adams and the East Side would throw themselves in the fire to keep her from harm's way. That's what's special. Let's go. Girl might not see, but she still got ears."

They go back up the stairs, slamming the door and bolting multiple locks on the other side. I let out a breath, relieved that it's finally over... Or at least, *for now.*

EIGHTEEN
The Ugly Truth

"He's late." Kendrick hissed in impatience. The only sound occupying the Kingston kitchen was the tapping of his foot against the floor. The broad-shouldered fighter stood tall with his arms crossed against his chest.

"He'll be there soon. Relax," Haze replied.

"Can we trust him?" Blake asked.

"Devon's never let me down before."

"You're not answering my question, jackass."

"Listen, trustworthy or not, Devon's our best option right now, so shut up and deal with it."

It was the morning of day two. It had been more than twenty-four hours since she had been taken God knew where by God knew who. Day two was usually the day the kidnapper called to either ask for money or something along those lines. But nothing. Just dreadful silence. It was like whoever took Winter only wanted her gone.

A loud thump on the door interrupted the horrible scenarios spinning in Kendrick's head.

"Finally." He opened the door.

The fighter took a sudden step back when the weary-looking

guy standing on his porch pushed past him and walked inside the house. He looked around twenty-three years old, wore full-rimmed glasses, torn jeans, and a gray T-shirt with nonidentifiable stains on it. Kendrick's first impression was that he looked like the definition of the video-game addict who spent the majority of his time in his parents' basement.

"Thanks for coming." Haze motioned to sit down at the table.

Devon nodded, glancing around the room in an unbothered yet strangely judgmental way.

"Is this your first time doing this?" Kendrick asked.

Devon didn't reply and looked straight into Kendrick's eyes as a reply. He then dropped his backpack on the kitchen tiles and unzipped it.

Will mocked, "Okay? That's not creepy at all."

"Devon's a man of little words," Haze replied.

Kendrick repeated, "Has he ever done this before?"

"Yes. Now, stop talking and let him do his job."

Devon sat down at the kitchen table and got a computer out of his backpack. Ten minutes later everything was set up, and although Will, Kendrick, Alex, and Blake had no clue what was happening, they tried their best to pretend they did.

One look from Devon was all it took for Haze to understand.

"It's ready," Haze said.

Static.

A couple of rings.

Then a voice.

"Hey, it's me. I'm naked on my bed waiting for you."

The East Side chuckled immaturely, trading glances.

"Not tonight, Rose. I'm busy."

"With what?"

"I've got this thing. Sorry."

"Is it another girl? It's Chloe, isn't it?"

"No, Rose, just drop it."

"It's another fight?"

"Yeah."

"Tell me it's not what I think it is."

There was no response.

"Yeah, okay, got it. Don't call me ever again."

"Rose, wait—"

The line went dead.

"Really? A booty call? That's all we get? I thought tapping the phone was supposed to be the answer," Kendrick critiqued.

"It is." Haze paused. "The number who sent Winter those text messages will lead us right to the person responsible. It's the fastest way to track them. All we need is a little clue."

"Then what?" Will asked.

"We wait. Even if we do find out who's responsible, we can't just attack without preparation. We don't know where they're keeping her. Or how many of them there are."

Devon looked at Haze and motioned to get closer to the table, pointing at his computer screen.

"The booty call happened an hour before the fight and Winter's kidnapping," Haze read out loud.

Haze locked eyes with Devon, and he didn't need to speak for him to understand.

"We got another call."

Crackling noises.

A couple of rings.

Then a voice.

"Hey, man. I just wanted to call and let you know that… well… rumors are spreading."

"About what?"

"You know what. The girl's really starting to be a problem."

A long silence followed.

"I'll handle it."

"Thanks, Tanner."

The line disconnected.

"I—" Haze opened his mouth to speak but ended up closing it.

He immediately pulled himself together like he'd realized that this was not the time to have a "damn it, my brother's evil" moment.

"How could you not recognize your brother's number?" Kendrick finally asked.

"I don't have this one registered in my phone. He's got two different lines apparently."

"What do we do now?" Will asked hesitantly.

Kendrick could sense his friends' fears and doubts from a mile away. He couldn't help but be afraid that Haze wouldn't be willing to do what it took now that it involved his own blood.

"The only thing we can do." Haze let out a heavy sigh. "We bust his ass and save the girl."

"NICE PLACE," WILLIAM SAID IN AWE of the Adams house. It'd been a while since Haze had stopped to look around and feel grateful for the life of luxury his parents had given him. He heard the admiration in Will's voice and couldn't help but find a hint of irony in the situation.

Crazy how one's curse can be somebody else's blessing, he thought.

Some had the loving parents.

Some had the big house and money.

Haze had yet to meet someone with both.

When he saw Tanner's cars parked in the driveway, he mentally battled himself on whether or not he was ready to face him.

"We need a cue. A word I'll say to let you know I need backup," Haze reminded them as he set up the microphone he planned to hide under his jacket. It was directly connected to the

East Side.

"Okay, huh… what about 'do you think my ass looks fat in these jeans'?" William cracked up.

"I'm not saying that."

"Fine, then just say…" Kendrick was interrupted by a Destiny's Child song on the radio. "Bootylicious. Fit the word 'bootylicious' in a sentence, any sentence, and we'll come to the rescue."

"Really?" Haze fought the urge to face-palm himself.

"Really." Kendrick smirked.

Haze made a face and got out of the car, walking toward the house he used to call home. He felt his heart tightening in his chest. The lame humor really was a family thing. That's something Winter would've said.

He walked through the front door, feeling like a pure stranger in this place he knew so well, and fixed the microphone under his leather jacket one last time.

"Tanner, you home?" he shouted.

"In here," Tanner called from the living room. "Hey," he said at the sight of his younger brother walking in and sunk deeper into the couch.

"It's been a while." Haze forced a smile.

"Yeah, well, it's not my fault you're constantly running around with the East Side chick," Tanner said, getting a cigarette out of a pack.

"I won't be doing that again anytime soon. Haven't you heard? She's been taken."

Tanner shrugged. "Really? Good news."

"You wouldn't happen to know anything about that, would you?" Haze tried to repress the burning anger building up inside of him.

"Nah."

He quickly knew he was going to have to do this the hard way.

"You know, I didn't expect you to understand. You never truly cared about anyone."

Tanner frowned.

"I mean, until Rose."

The reaction was immediate.

He got up, his jaw clenched. "How the hell do you know about Rose?"

"The same way I know you took Winter."

Tanner put up a fist, which Haze easily dodged. He took a swing at him, and Tanner crashed against the wall, his mouth bleeding. Tanner could never get used to his little brother surpassing him over the years.

"So you know, since you've taken my girl—which isn't really nice, by the way—I've thought about it and… it's only fair that I take yours. What do you think?"

Holding his brother up by the grasp he had on his clothes,

Haze found himself wondering why he'd been so unlucky in the sibling department.

"I'm going to make a deal with you. Return Winter to me and I'll leave Rose alone, how about that?"

"You wouldn't dare touch her. You're the nice one, brother." Tanner said, revealing his bloodstained teeth.

"Am I? Because I have people in front of her place right now waiting for my orders."

Tanner smiled as an answer. Haze groaned, his remaining self-control rapidly leaving him.

"Rose and I are done. I don't care anymore."

Haze grunted. "Why the hell are you doing this, Tanner? What do you expect to get out of this?"

"I want my brother back. Not some mushy, whipped, weak version of him."

"You want your brother back? If you touch as much as a hair on her head, you'll lose him forever, you hear me? Just return her to me safe and unharmed."

"Unharmed, huh? I'm afraid it's a little too late for that."

Haze's breath caught in his throat.

"What did you do?"

"Well, she was a problem. And you know what I do with problems…"

He paused.

"I get rid of them."

The punches Haze had taken at his brother in the past while training had always been somehow restrained. It wasn't the real thing. But now, as he punched the heartless monster he had the misfortune of calling family, he wasn't holding back. Not anymore.

The only thing they had in common was blood.

Tanner had made that clear.

"She's not dead. You're lying," he shouted, bombarding Tanner's face with strikes. "Where is she?"

"I told you, she's dead. Not before I had something from her of course. She was a piece of work, but the sex was worth it." Tanner smirked. "You should've heard her scream. She just wouldn't stop, and it turned me on even more."

Haze felt sick to his stomach. The East Side could hear every hateful word escaping his brother's mouth.

"I can't believe I'm going to say this," Haze muttered under his breath. "Bootylicious!" he screamed at the top of his lungs.

The East Side would probably kick the door in at any moment. They'd help him restrain Tanner and force him into revealing Winter's whereabouts. It couldn't possibly get any worse.

"You fucking psycho." Haze rammed his fist into Tanner's jaw one last time.

When the door was kicked in, a feeling of relief settled over Haze. Will, Kendrick, Blake, and Alex were coming to help him handle Tanner.

"I'm sorry. I can't let you do this," a familiar voice said from behind him. Before Haze could turn around to identify the person who'd come bursting through the door, he collapsed heavily onto the hardwood floor with a thunk.

He thought it was the end.

But the needle entering his skin told him otherwise.

There was no blood, no pain.

Just darkness.

NINETEEN

Found

Winter

I've always wondered what it would be like to freeze to death. Some say it's like falling asleep or slowly slipping out of consciousness. Now that I'm cradling my knees against my chest and rocking back and forth in a pathetic attempt to warm myself up, I'm afraid I won't have to wonder for much longer.

In a way, this might be God doing me a favor. Taking me away before Ian decides what he wants to do to me.

I've been crying in silence for the past five minutes, my stomach grumbling painfully. All hope is gone.

Dead.

Just like I will be… *sooner or later.*

Slightly less awful kidnapper aka Man Number Two came back down alone shortly after Owen laid his disgusting hands on me. He removed my blindfold and disappeared back up the stairs in a hurry. I don't know why he did it.

My money is on *guilt.*

I'm not even anywhere near figuring out where I am, the only source of light in the gloom of the basement coming from the small gap under the door at the top of the wooden staircase.

One door.

That's the only thing standing between me and my freedom.

"Drop him here," a voice I believe belongs to the monster named Owen screeches.

They're back. I haven't heard them talk or walk for the past thirty minutes. Where did they go?

"What do we do with him?"

"Tie him up before he wakes up. You have a couple minutes," a slightly deeper voice replies.

That's a new one. There are three of them now. That voice... I've heard it before. But where?

"What about the plan?" Owen asks.

"We stick to it. He wasn't supposed to figure it out this fast, but it'll have to do. Make sure he stays quiet. We don't need to draw attention to ourselves. I have to go. Don't mess this up," he threatens. "Oh, and one last thing, no blindfold. I want him to see everything."

Not long after, I hear a door closing.

"'Make sure he stays quiet.' Like it's that easy," Owen says.

Minutes pass.

Man Number Two sighs. "There, he's tied up."

"It doesn't matter. He's going to wake up and lose his mind. I don't want to deal with this shit."

"What else are we supposed to do?" Man Number Two

replies.

"We throw his ass downstairs with her."

"But he said—"

"Who cares? We'll bring him back up before he returns. We both know he could've beaten the living hell out of that East Side kid if he wanted to. He's going to find a way to escape. I say we play it safe and lock him up just to be sure."

"But—"

"That's freaking Haze Adams. Do you really want to deal with him?"

My heart stops.

Haze…

Haze is here.

I think I've never been more happy to hear this boy's name in my entire life. Why did they take him? So many questions prowl back in forth in my mind.

"Fine. But we bring him up before he comes back, and if we get in trouble, I'll say it was your idea in a heartbeat, got it?"

"Whatever."

They unlock the numerous latches, and the door swings open. I don't move a muscle, my back facing them as the ropes continue to dig deeper into my skin. They throw his body down the stairs—not without complaining about how heavy he is first—and chuckle evilly.

"There, go be with your girlfriend," Owen says, mockery

thick in his voice.

I hear Haze groan in pain as soon as they go back to where they came from. I'm guessing getting thrown down the stairs was enough to release him from whatever sleeping drug is running through his veins. My heart pummels in my chest.

"Fucking shit," he mutters under his breath, wincing at what I'm pretty sure is a killer headache.

I try and call out his name, but it comes out in a muffled sound, thanks to the tape covering my mouth.

That's when he sees me.

"Winter?" He squints his eyes. "Oh my God."

He looks down at his hand and feet that are heavily tied up with zip ties. I'm guessing they ran out of ropes.

"Hold on. I'm coming." He tries to untie himself.

I want to tell him that it's no use, that he's wasting his time, but when he pulls his hands up and bring them back down in a fast movement, snapping his hands against his legs, the zip ties break instantly.

I can't believe my eyes when he gets up from the ground and frees himself entirely. Did he just untie himself in less than five minutes when I've been struggling for hours?

One more piece of evidence that he's not human. He runs to me, kneeling down to my side. He unties me, we beat the kidnappers, and we escape.

Just kidding, I'm still tied on the ground like a sausage.

"Ouch." I hear him run into something.

The wall.

"I can't see shit in here."

Allow me to revise myself. Haze Adams is not human except when it comes to walking in the dark.

He kneels down by my side. "It's going to hurt."

I wince when he removes the tape from my mouth briskly. Tears come up to my eyes, but for the first time, they're not only caused by pain. They're happy tears. No matter what happens from this moment on, I know that it'll be slightly less horrible. I know it'll be okay.

Because Haze is with me.

"How did you do that?" I ask, staring at his now free hands.

"I've been around a long time, Kingston."

He throws the ropes that used to hold me prisoner across the room and holds out his hand to me, which I accept. He helps me up. No matter how much I want to stand on my own two feet, my empty stomach and dehydrated body disagree. My knees give out, and I quickly feel myself falling backward. Instantly, he catches me, his strong arms circling my waist as he holds me against his chest.

"I got you," he whispers in a raspy voice, his breath fanning my lips. *"Always."*

When I manage to get a grip on my senses, my gaze connects with his and we're back to being two kids sharing our secrets and biggest fears on a rooftop. For one fleeting second, I dare forget that we're trapped in a basement, and the only thing I'm a prisoner of are Haze Adams's eyes.

I shake my head. "I'm fine."

"You're not fine. We need to get you out of here. Fast." He glances around the room the same way I did earlier.

"Don't bother. There's only one way out." I motion to the door. He turns his head, revealing bruises scattered under his left eye.

"You didn't get this from the fight. What happened to you?" I exhale, my fingers brushing over the marks on his skin. He softens at the touch, his shoulders relaxing. Then, like reality just came rushing back into his mind, he stiffens up again.

"No time to explain. We need to get out of here. Long story short, we tapped the cell phone that was sending you the messages and—"

"Wait, we?"

"I've been working with your boys."

"No way. You and the East Side?"

"What do you think we've been doing this whole time? Playing Uno? We've been looking for you."

For a guy who doesn't care… he sure went to hell and back to find me.

"Thank you," I say, emotional. It might be the exhaustion, the hunger, or the fear of dying I went through for the past two days, but I can't be mad at him anymore.

He went against everything he believes in and helped his enemy… for me.

"What? You didn't think I'd let my texting buddy die, did you?" He musters a small smile.

"I'll admit, the basement and ropes gave me doubts for a second." I find myself smiling, truly smiling, which I didn't think was possible in a situation like this.

"Did you find out who's behind this?"

"Yes." His jaw tightens. "My brother."

"But… the text said…"

"I know. Tanner set us up. We went over to Ian's lair, looking for you. It was always his plan to send us on the wrong track. But he still wanted us to find you. Just not too fast."

I remember the words I heard earlier.

"Tanner wanted you here, too. I heard him say it. He said he wanted you to see everything."

Haze clenches his fists. "I'm not even surprised. That's some sick twisted shit, just the way he likes it."

His eyes light up in realization.

"Wait. There's a reason he didn't do anything to you until now. They're keeping you safe for when he's ready. I have an idea to lure them in here. When they come, I'll knock them out and find my leather jacket. They took it to make sure I didn't have any weapons."

"Your jacket? Why?" I frown, praying he's not seriously worried about fashion in a moment like this.

"There's a mic hidden in it. It's connected to the East Side. All I have to do is let them know where we are."

I can tell from the way he purposefully avoids my eyes that he's not telling me everything.

"Haze, what is it?"

He sighs. "I don't know what happened to them. They were supposed to come and help me handle Tanner, but they never showed. Someone else did. The bastard got me from behind. I could've sworn..."

Fear crumples my heart.

"Sworn what?"

He seems hesitant. "Never mind. It's not important."

"Do you think they're okay?"

"Don't worry, these pricks can defend themselves. We wouldn't be in this mess in the first place if Kendrick was easy to get rid of." His eyes meet mine. "Now, are you ready to get out of here?"

I nod in determination. "I've never been more ready in my life."

"HELP. SHE'S DYING," HAZE CRIES FOR the second time in a row as I lie on the stone-cold floor with my eyes closed. "Don't pretend like you don't hear me. She's not moving. I think she fainted."

The wooden floor above our heads squeaks and distant voices reach our ears.

"Damn it, go check it out."

"You go check it out," Owen argues.

"What? Why me?"

"Because you're a scared little bitch who doesn't want to have to tell Tanner that the girl's dead. That's why."

"Fine," Man Number Two scolds. "But next time's on you."

Seconds before the door opens and lights invade the dark basement, Haze retreats to the darkest spot in the room and gets on the floor, bringing his fists and feet together. If we're lucky, he won't have time to notice the absence of zip ties on his skin. We're relieved when we don't hear Owen lock the door on the other side. They're obviously not worried.

Well, they should be.

Man Number Two glares at Haze, irritated. "What the hell is your problem?"

"She fainted and she's not waking up. I'm pretty sure you don't want her dying before my crazy pants of a brother says so."

With my back facing the opposite direction, I can't see how close Man Number Two is to me—and to getting his skull kicked in—but I can feel one thing: his fear.

"If you try anything, I'll kill you right here, right now. With my bare hands and without hesitation, am I clear?" he tells Haze but I know he doesn't mean it. He seems like the nice one to me. The guy who got swept in his friends' messes and can't back down anymore.

"Oh for God's sake, sure, whatever you say. Just help her."

The man hovers over me, leaning in to place a trembling hand on my shoulder. Just as he's about to shake me awake, Haze makes it his pleasure to catch him by surprise and introduce him to his fist. He puts up a fight but doesn't last long. Haze wasn't lying when he said he's been around a long time. He knew exactly where and how to hit him to silence him. The unprepared guy drops unconscious.

"It's now or never. Come on." Haze motions for me to follow him, leading the way toward the stairs.

Every step we take feels like the last one. Constantly looking over our shoulders at the inanimate body on the ground, we slowly go up the stairs until we reach the door. It's honestly a miracle Owen didn't hear the creaking of the staircase.

I peek through the keyhole, looking at what seems to be a reception room. It's big, spacious, but it looks dirty and neglected. No sign of Owen anywhere. Haze peeks, too.

"This is the abandoned hotel on Route 9," he says quietly.

I know exactly what he's talking about. This is where it all began. I remember the shadow passing through the window when Will locked me in his car days ago. I never would've thought that I'd end up here when my phone first chimed. Things would have been so different if I had just found the courage to tell the guys about the messages.

"You got about fifteen seconds to escape. You run to the door, and you never look back, do you understand me?"

"What? No," I whisper. "I'm not leaving you."

"If you get a chance to escape, you take it. I can take care of myself in here. You, not so much."

I can't bring myself to answer, and I know he doesn't find the reassurance he seeks in my eyes.

"Winter, no matter what happens once we open that door, you can't look back. Promise me. Even if he shoots me, even if I die, you run."

The painful pit in my throat grows harder to ignore. Raising an eyebrow in expectation, he stubbornly refuses to look away until I tell him what he wants to hear. I look down. This results in him delicately lifting my chin up with his finger and staring deeply into my eyes. His touch is like a drug. A simple yet unforgettable high that disconnects you from reality.

"Winter, please."

It takes everything I have to say it. "I promise."

He smiles sadly.

"On three."

That's when it hits me.

After all this—after all this guy and I have been through since the day I met him in the hallway—I never let myself like him.

Like *really* like him.

I never found peace in my feelings, incessantly scolding myself over the way he crept into my mind every time I closed my eyes, the way his touch lingered on my skin long after he'd left me.

I even beat myself up over the way he made me laugh. I shouldn't find him funny. It's wrong, I constantly told myself.

I shouldn't be thinking about that in a moment like this, but now that we aren't sure whether or not we'll live past this day, my priorities are different. I think about what's going to happen if Haze doesn't make it out and I do. I'll regret not telling him that I was wrong about him. It wasn't right before, but it is now.

Haze Adams is the right guy… and I have to tell him.

"Wait." I clasp my fingers around his arm before he begins the countdown.

His blue eyes lock with mine the way they did so many times before.

"I need to tell you—"

He cuts me off. "Don't." He tucks a strand of my hair behind my ear. "Whatever it is you have to say, it can wait until we're out of here."

"But—"

He interrupts me again. "Do you trust me?"

"I…" My eyes shift to his. "Yes."

"Then trust me on this. I am not done annoying you just yet, Kingston. Not even close."

He leans in slowly, and I see the hesitation in his face when his eyes land on my lips. He exhales and presses his lips to my cheeks instead. When he pulls away, we know...

It's time.

"Three."

I inhale.

"Two."

Haze and I share one last look.

"One."

The unnamed man screams from the basement. "You son of a bitch! Owen, don't let them get away!"

"Now!" Haze yells and swings the door open. The sound of footsteps running up the stairs is my cue. For the first time in a long time, I don't overthink, I don't hesitate, I just act.

I do what Haze told me to do: I run faster than I ever did in my entire life.

"Get the girl!" Owen screams at his partner. I hear punches left and right, and although every fiber of my being is imploring me to turn around and see if Haze is okay, I don't. I can't.

Like he heard my thoughts out loud, he shouts at the top of his lungs, "Don't stop!"

I see the door.

It's right there.

I can make it… Just a couple more steps…

I finally reach it, my fingers wrapping around the doorknob. I can get out. I can be free. But when I hear Haze screaming in agony, I lose all control of my body and do the one thing I promised him not to do. I look back.

There he is, on the ground, with two guns pressed to his forehead by Tanner's masked guys.

"What the hell are you waiting for? Go!"

Owen barks, "You're going to be a good girl and come back here with your hands in the air, or he dies right now."

"He's bluffing. My brother would never let me die. Go. Now!"

I have to trust him. I have to believe that he knows what he's doing. The adrenaline makes the choice easy. I turn the doorknob, slam the door open, and freeze in place.

Someone is waiting for me on the other side. At first, I'm relieved. I want to jump into his arms. But the look on his face is… different.

"Going somewhere?" He grins, taking my wrist prisoner and dragging me back inside against my will. In that moment, as I stare at him in shock, my world comes crashing down. Every belief I had, everything I thought I knew, all gone and destroyed… by the betrayal of this one person.

"Blake?"

TWENTY

Last Chance

"Why didn't you go, Winter? Why did you look back?"

These are the words I've been hearing on repeat for the past twenty minutes. I wish I had an answer to give him. But I don't. Hearing him scream in pain was all it took for me to break my promise.

And I'd do it again in a heartbeat if it meant he'd be okay.

"I couldn't leave. They were going to kill you, remember?" I try to think of all the possible scenarios. Each time, they end the same way: with Mr. Traitor shoving me back inside and tying me to a chair. "Plus, Blake was outside. He would've stopped me anyway."

Haze scoffs. "Maybe but you could've tried. That's all I asked."

They decided to move us out of the basement, which means they're either ready to kill us or... they're ready to kill us. That pretty much summarizes it.

We're now in the reception room, both tied to chairs with our hands behind our back. Of course, they made sure to place Haze's chair and mine in opposite directions so that we can't see each other's face or do anything that would allow us to find comfort in one another.

Finding out that Blake was a traitor felt like getting my heart ripped out of my chest at first, but then, the answers to every question I ever asked myself about him came to me. Things started to add up and make sense. Like the first time a gang tried to kill me at the party and Blake mysteriously disappeared without an explanation. He wanted me to die. Or the time he busted me for spending time with Haze and I just happened to receive a message from the unknown number at the exact same time. It was him all along. Working on both sides.

I guess I trusted him to the point of overlooking these gigantic red flags. Shame on me for believing in him.

Tanner's guys went out of the room several minutes ago to make some calls. Something about needing backup in case we pull a stunt like that again and actually succeed.

"Can you untie yourself like you did earlier?" I ask.

"I wish. They learned their lesson. I don't know how to get out of handcuffs."

I sigh, throwing my head back. "Awesome."

"We need to get to the microphone and turn it on."

I look to my left to see Haze's jacket on a table a couple of feet away. I can't even begin to imagine how many people trespass here. Must be why Tanner was so worried about the noise. The neighbors probably have 911 on speed dial.

"From there, all we have to do is hope the connection isn't broken and tell the East Side where we are."

"How'd you even know we were in the hotel, by the way?"

"I used to come here before it closed. It used to look good, believe it or not."

The ripped curtains, stained carpet, multiple cigarettes butts, and empty beer bottles scattered all over the floor make it near impossible to imagine. I'm sure it was marvelous once upon a time, but now… it's the definition of a dump.

"Bring your chair closer," he says.

I do as I'm told, desperately trying to move the piece of furniture without falling backward.

"I can reach you. Don't move." I feel his fingers grazing mine as he works his magic behind me.

A couple of seconds is all he needs.

"It's done. Go!"

The searing pain of the ropes on my wrists fades away, and I know that if we ever get out of here, I'll have to ask him to show me how he does it. Realizing there's just one slight problem, I look down to my feet that are still tied together.

This is great.

Jumping like a rabbit it is.

I can hear Haze hold back a chuckle when I begin the most ridiculous "walk" of my life toward the jacket on the table.

"Turn it on."

"How?" I ask, examining the tiny microphone that fits in the palm of my hand carefully. It's no wonder that Tanner's guys didn't find it.

"The switch's on the side. It's easy."

When I see a gleaming green light blinking, any trace of shame I might've felt when I was leaping ridiculously vanishes.

It was worth it.

"We have no confirmation that the connection is strong enough. They might not hear us, but we have to try."

"Kendrick, it's me, Winter. I'm alive and with Haze in the abandoned hotel on Route 9. Tanner did it and he's got backup. A lot of backup. Including Blake—yes, he's a traitor. I wish I didn't have to tell you like this. Bring as many guys from the East Side as you can." I repeat the message as many times as possible in case they didn't catch it.

I turn back to look at Haze. "What do we do now?"

"Now... we wait and we hope that they heard us."

The look of defeat on his face tells a story of its own. He isn't used to feeling weak... helpless.

"So... they're either coming to get us, or our message disappeared into thin air and never reached them."

Haze's eyes divert to the floor. "Pretty much."

Footsteps come tumbling down the hall the next second.

Panic takes over him. "Come back. Fast."

I drop the jacket where it belongs and jump back to the chair I just escaped from. Sliding into the same position I was previously in, I hold my hands behind my back in an attempt to fool them into thinking I'm still tied up. I'm barely back into position when Tanner's right-hand men enter the room and glare at us angrily.

"Tanner and his guys are on their way. Don't even think about trying to escape again," Owen spits.

He's still wearing his coward mask.

Then enters the one person I still can't get used to seeing in the bad guy's team: Blake.

"Look who we've got here—Mr. Bad Boy and the East Side girl."

I can't stop myself. "Don't forget Mr. Traitor."

He raises an eyebrow. "Can you believe it? She's tied to a chair and she still tries to play smart."

"How could you?" The words burst out of my mouth.

"Well, you see, I've become familiar with something called staying on the winning side."

"We trusted you. Kendrick called you his brother."

"I do hope he can forgive me one day and understand I had no choice. As soon as you showed up, I knew the East Side would go to shit. And guess what? It did. There was no way I was staying on this sinking ship."

"No choice? You could've stuck by your friends—that's a choice. But you know, whatever helps you sleep at night."

"You talk a lot for a girl whose life is literally in my hands." He leans forward, his fingers trailing down my cheek. I pull away in disgust.

"Where's the East Side now?" I ask.

"They think I'm off meeting a source who has info about the kidnapping, those dumbasses. They're so desperate to find you they would've believed anything. You should've seen their faces when they woke up in the car in front of Haze's house. They couldn't understand why they'd just passed out when you needed them. I bet they still think one of their enemy planted the sleeping drug into the car."

It feels like the weight of the world has been lifted off my shoulders. They're okay. They're alive.

"You know what's funny?" Blake plays with a strand of my hair before letting it fall back on my shoulder. "I used to think you were cute. Until you followed us to the meeting, that is. It took me a while before I actually changed sides. But Tanner just had so much more to offer... I couldn't say no. I knew I had to get rid of you."

I cry. "What did I ever do to you? Why do you hate me so much?"

"Oh, but you see, I don't. I don't hate you at all, Winter. I don't care much for you, to be honest, but you know who does? Haze." He smirks, "And the worst part is you actually think he wants more than to jump your bones."

Haze doesn't answer nor deny it.

"Do you really think he would've laid eyes on you if you

331

weren't the East Side girl? He may care about you now, but if you hadn't been Kendrick's cousin, you'd be another one of his conquests that he'd laugh about with his friends."

He's lying. That's not the Haze I know.

"Stop," Haze huffs.

"Why would I do that? The girl deserves to know the truth. She's a temporary girl. Just like they all are. Just like Riley."

My lips part. Riley?

"But he didn't tell you about her, did he?"

I wait for Haze to explain himself. Wait is the key word here.

"How the hell do you know about that?"

"Of course he didn't tell you. Why would he tell you he got a girl pregnant?"

My lungs collapse.

Haze is a father?

"Don't you dare talk about things you don't understand."

"Oh, but I do understand. She was sixteen when you got her pregnant, wasn't she? Then you left her to rot. Because even though you said that you cared, in the end you were still this heartless piece of shit, and she was still a temporary girl."

"Enough," Haze barks.

"You'd like that, wouldn't you? For me to stop divulging your darkest secrets? You don't want Winter to know you're a father? You don't want me to scare her away? Well, don't worry, she's too stupid to be afraid of you. If she was even a little bit smart, she would've run away from you a long time ago."

"I'm not a father. She said she'd get an abortion."

"And you never cared to check?" Blake spits.

Haze's words seem to have left him at first.

"How the hell do you even know about Riley? I haven't heard from her in years."

"Oh, that's funny. Neither have I. She never wrote. Never called. All because of you. You knew her parents would kick her out, and they did. Well, I lost my sister that day, my only real family—and now you're going to pay."

Haze sighs in realization. "You're her brother. The one they sent away."

"Ding, ding, ding! We have a winner." Blake begins to walk around us in circle. "You can't even imagine my surprise when I heard that she'd run away. My parents were never the same. My mother would've done everything to get her back home, but my father couldn't stomach the thought that his daughter was the trashy girl who'd gotten pregnant at sixteen. They divorced five months after. You destroyed my family. You're the reason I might never see my sister ever again." He punches Haze in the face as hard as he can.

I wince in helplessness. I don't want to judge him, but what does that say about him? He let her down and alone with a baby at sixteen.

"If I wasn't tied to a chair right now…"

"Keep making threats, Adams."

"Is that why you're working with my brother? Because you want to kill me?"

Blake snorts. "Kill you? Please. Your brother would never allow that. He still believes that you can be saved. But we have something in common, him and I. We both want her gone." He turns to me.

Haze raises his voice. "What does she have to do with any of this?"

"I don't know about your brother. He says he wants to set you back on the right path. As for me, I'm just doing to you the same thing you did to me."

He pauses for a dreadfully long moment.

"Taking someone you care about away from you."

He tilts his head to the side as he analyzes me thoroughly. Then he says the three most terrifying words I've ever heard in my life.

"Hold her still."

Tanner's guys don't flinch. One of them leaves the room and comes back with a baseball bat. I see it, and in this moment, I know... miracles don't exist.

The first man pins my body down with all his strength while the second holds the bat up in the air. I can't move my arms. All I can do is scream and wiggle. How ironic that even when my arms are free, they're not.

"Don't you fucking dare," Haze screams, fighting to get out of his chair. "I'll kill you. I swear to God."

"Enjoy the show" is the last thing I hear Blake say before his guy takes a powerful swing at my leg and I scream in the most excruciating pain I've ever felt.

I don't shed a tear. Somehow, I know my misery is what they want and I'll be dead before I give it to them.

In that moment, as I hear Haze shouting at the top of his lungs to get them to stop, I wonder if my life has been what I wanted it to be. I see myself growing up in Canada without a father and wonder if he'll show up to my funeral. I remember every little moment I wasted being sad. I think of every single person who told me to stay away from Haze, and I wonder how different things would be... *if I had just listened.*

"That's enough," Blake says.

"You're dead. Dead, you got it?" Haze shouts.

Through the tears I hold back, I look at the traitor standing tall in front of me. He's smiling.

"I hate to cut this short, but Tanner's going to want to see results, and well... I'm getting bored."

He gets something out of his pocket.

A gun.

This is it Winter, you're going to die.

He points it at me. "Any last words?"

My eyes darken. Unbidden, a voice plays in my head on a

loop. And that voice… is Haze's. "Do you want to be a damsel in distress? No? Then prove it."

I'm not dying today.

"Yes."

I pause.

"You were right, Haze. One move makes all the difference."

Blake frowns, "What?"

From there, the events unravel so quickly the traitor can barely keep up. He doesn't expect my hands to be free, which gives me the advantage. I use the technique Haze taught me to disarm someone by chopping at his wrist with one hand and pushing the barrel of the gun in the opposite direction with the other. Blake's face drops as his gun crashes to the ground several feet away from him.

He's trying to pick it up when another gun goes off in a deafening noise. At first, I think that one of Tanner's guy fired at me, but I'm still here when, clearly, I should be dead and bleeding out on the floor.

The shriek of pain that follows explains everything.

Blake's lying on the ground, his leg covered in blood as he bawls his eyes out.

"Here comes the rescue squad," a voice screams as people rush inside the building from every possible entrance.

But it's not just anyone.

That voice belongs to Will.

The East Side is here.

"Winter!" Kendrick's voice rings in my ear, and I'm overwhelmed by a thousand emotions. The numerous fighters Kendrick brought easily manage to get Owen and Man Number Two under control. Too bad Tanner's not around to witness his evil plan fail. Will unties me and sets Haze free after he steals the key to the handcuffs from a knocked out Owen.

"Get them out of here," Kendrick calls to his friend. "I'll take care of the traitor." He then gets on top of Blake, pulling him up by the grasp he has of his collar.

"Kendrick, I—"

"No, you don't get to speak. You are dead to me from now on. You are nothing. If you ever try to hurt my family again, I'll kill you and make it so painful you're going to wish you were never born, you hear me?" Kendrick circles Blake's throat with both his hands.

"I'm sorry. I had to survive," he chokes out.

Kendrick spits in Blake's face as a response. "Yeah, well, what's the point of surviving if it's to spend the rest of your life alone?"

The punch he gives him when he finishes his sentence renders Blake unconscious.

"Come on, we have to go. Now!"

Kendrick throws something into the room and a foggy cloud of thick gas quickly fills up the atmosphere as we rush out of the

337

building through the nearest entrance.

It's over. The nightmare is over.

My cousin's voice cuts through the uproar. "Run. Get to the car."

We see it—Kendrick's car in the distance. Alex is waiting inside. I bite my lower lip roughly, reliving the excruciating pain I've been through barely minutes ago every time I take a step forward. I'm supposed to be running when even putting pressure on my toe hurts me.

"Her leg. She's hurt," Haze screams through the chaos.

We're this close. This close to escaping.

But when we hear rattling gunshots, my first instinct is to run… and my leg can't take it.

I collapse to the ground, screaming in agony.

The asphalt doesn't hurt. What truly hurts is the big chunk of glass entering my flesh.

Cutting my leg open with what I assume to be a beer bottle and bleeding profusely feels nothing like I expected. The pain isn't even the worst part.

Watching my last chance to escape burst in flames is.

Haze bellows from afar, "No!"

I try to get up. I know Tanner's guys aren't far behind. I'm holding them back. They need to leave me.

I close my eyes, unable to see the red fluid gushing out of me any longer. I feel brawny arms pick me up from the ground. He's running, holding me up like I'm weightless.

"No, no, no. Fuck! Winter, stay with me." I recognize Haze's voice instantly. It sounds so close but yet so far. "Open your eyes."

"What the hell happened?" Kendrick's voice is followed by the sound of a car door being slammed open. Haze puts me in the back seat and scrambles inside, followed by Will. The vehicle takes off in a booming roar.

Every ounce of strength I ever had leaves me, my body no longer listening to my brain. I always had no tolerance for pain, not to mention a phobia of blood ever since I was a kid. I struggle with my time of the month. So watching liters of blood pour out of me? I don't think so.

"You're going to be okay. It's over," Haze says. "Open your eyes, Winter. Look at me."

Using the very last of my energy, I open my eyes, just enough to see the pain in his.

Even if I do survive this, Haze lost the fight. He has to hold up his end of the deal. We can never see each other again.

It's now or never. I have to tell him how I feel.

"Haze, I—"

He cuts me off, his voice trembling. "Don't speak. Save your strength." He tucks a piece of my hair behind my ear. I can feel and hear the car screeching down the silent roads. I think back to the multiple gunshots. There's no way nobody in the neighborhood heard it. The cops are probably already on their way.

I can feel myself slipping away… from life… from reality…

From him.

Haze whispers, "It's my turn to speak."

All my senses dissipate, and I can't bring myself to fight it anymore. The darkness takes over me.

"Keep her awake," Kendrick yells.

I can no longer speak or move a muscle.

But he makes it better.

Four words. Sixteen letters.

He said it. I bet he thought that I wouldn't hear.

But I did.

And I'll never forget it.

"I love you, Kingston."

ACKNOWLEDGEMENTS

To my boyfriend, thank you for sticking by my side when I doubted myself and encouraging me to chase my dream no matter what people said.

To Tigris Eden, thank you for taking the time to answer my questions. Your expertise and your precious advices made all of this possible and so much easier.

To Jen, thank you for introducing me to the website that changed my life. We might not talk anymore but I'll never forget what you did for me. You used to say that my stories were piling up and that I should just stick to one. Well, I finally listened to you.

To AJ and Nathalie, thank you for helping me get in touch with the right people and introducing me to self-publishing.

To Marie, the best sister there is. Thank you for being a reader as well as a best friend and being completely honest with me about the plot. But most of all, thank you for loving Haze's smirks and Winter's clumsy ways as much as I do.

To Sandra Depukat, thank you for being a great editor, answering all of my questions and showing Haze and Winter some love along the way.

Again, thanks to my father for taking me in while I wrote this book every night and day. You never made me feel like I was jobless or "lost" in life. You told me you'd rather see me try and fail a thousand times than settle for something that would make me unhappy. I'll never find the words to express how grateful I am that I got you as a father.

And last but not least, to the 30,000,000 people who gave Unwritten Rules (The Bad Boy's Rules) a chance online, thank you. You made this possible. Thank you for coming back to read every chapter, waiting for my updates, no matter how long they took, and lifting me up when I was down. I love you more than words can say and I'd be nothing without you. You Wazers brought Haze and Winter to life.

ALSO BY ELIAH GREENWOOD

Unspoken Rules (Book 2 in the Rules series)
AVAILABLE ON AMAZON AND ALL RETAILERS.

Unbroken Rules (Book 3 in the Rules series)
AVAILABLE ON AMAZON AND ALL RETAILERS.

Forgotten Rules *(Will & Kassidy's story*, Book 4 in The Rules series) **AVAILABLE EARLY 2020**

Forsaken Rules *(Will & Kassidy's story,* Book 5 in The Rules series) **AVAILABLE EARLY 2020**

Heartbreakers For Hire (Book 1 in the Heartbreakers series) **AVAILABLE LATE 2020**

ABOUT THE AUTHOR

Eliah Greenwood is a Canadian 21-year-old author who started writing books online when she was fifteen years old. When her story "The Bad Boy's Rules" reached 30,000,000 reads, she decided to give her loyal readers what they'd been asking for and self-publish.

Don't forget to leave a review for **Unwritten Rules** on Amazon!

CONNECT WITH ELIAH

www.eliahgreenwood.com

Sign up to Eliah's Newsletter for free books, updates on new releases and exclusive giveaways!

https://www.eliahgreenwood.com/subscribe

Follow Eliah on Instagram for previews of her next book and your Haze and Winter fix:

@EliahGreenwood

Made in the USA
Columbia, SC
01 July 2020